Red Jihad

Sami Ahmad Khan read Literature at Hindu College and Rajdhani College, University of Delhi. He then completed his master's in English Literature at Jawaharlal Nehru University. He is a PhD Scholar at JNU, where he is working on Science Fiction and Techno-culture Studies. Currently, Sami is on a Fulbright Fellowship at The University of Iowa, USA. He has engaged in film production, teaching, theatre and writing. His short stories, plays and articles have been published in magazines and academic journals. This is his first novel.

Sami can be contacted at sakhan1607@gmail.com

Red Jihad

Red Jihad

BATTLE FOR SOUTH ASIA

Sami Ahmad Khan

RUPA

First published in 2012 by
Rupa Publications India Pvt. Ltd.
7/16, Ansari Road, Daryaganj
New Delhi 110002

Sales centres:
Allahabad Bengaluru Chennai
Hyderabad Jaipur Kathmandu
Kolkata Mumbai

Copyright © Sami Ahmad Khan 2012

Second impression 2012

ISBN: 978-81-291-1987-2

10 9 8 7 6 5 4 3 2

Sami Ahmad Khan asserts the moral right to be identified
as the author of this work.

Disclaimer:
For authenticity, the author has used names of some real places,
people and institutions as they represent cultural icons of today
and aid storytelling. There is no intention to imply anything else.

Printed in India by
Replika Press Pvt Ltd
310-311 EPIP Kundli
Haryana 131028 India

Abbu and Mummy, this is for you

Prologue

Spin Boldak, Durand Line, Afghanistan

Local time: 1030 hours
Date: 21 February 2014

Rehan Stanikzai sneezed.

His hands flew to his nose and tried to cover it in an unsuccessful attempt to suppress the bang, a rather futile gesture as the sound was already away. The thunderclap bounced off the bare walls and came back even louder. Rehan realized a split-second later that it was the echo of the tube-shaped, paper-wrapped parcel he had impulsively dropped. He quickly bent to pick it up. It felt warm, almost alive, in his hands. He cautiously peered behind him and gently tiptoed out of the two-storeyed, red-brick house. With clammy hands, he shut the dilapidated, creaking door behind him.

Do not let her wake up, a voice at the back of his head screamed. He acknowledged it with a curt nod and then forced his mind to calculate the chances of his escape. She was asleep on the first floor. If she had been woken up by his sneezes and heard the creaking of the door, it would take her about ten seconds to get up, another ten to orient herself and realize what was happening, five to wear her chappals, and fifteen seconds to climb down to his current location. Forty seconds that separated freedom from captivity.

All of a sudden, his left cheek started to sting. Mathematical calculations evoked in him a sensation of his cheeks being hit so often, that it had made the linkage between the stimuli (mental calculation) and the response (pain) almost immediate by now. He muttered a short prayer for her not to have woken up. After all, mothers were the same all over the world, especially those who had a son with an examination the next day.

He forced the pain out of his head, wiped his nose with the sleeve of his kameez, and zealously jumped over the dog lolling on the steps of his house. He saw the head of the dog rise an inch above the ground. Its eyes followed Rehan curiously, trying to ascertain if he was a threat. Rehan landed on the other side and continued walking without breaking his step. The dog concluded it was in no danger of being kicked. Its ears curled up and it sunk back to sleep.

Rehan turned his head in the direction of the street. He immediately sensed something was wrong. The old Hollywood film poster was still in its rightful place but the poster of re-released *3 Idiots* directly opposite his house was half torn. A growl escaped his throat. Clearly, Adil had tried to take a part of it home the night before. Rehan muttered a curse under his breath and started walking down the street.

It was not very crowded. An old radio blared out sensuous Bollywood songs straight off the External Services Division of All India Radio. Four men sat at a nearby shop sipping cardamom tea. The skinny hairstylist, a recent hit in post-Taliban Afghanistan, lay on a cot playing carom with a CD shop-owner, another specimen of the diversification of occupational classes. A few boys, young enough to be allowed out of their homes unsupervised but not old enough to have their own full-fledged sports equipment, were half-heartedly trying to fly a torn kite. A few elders, with their hookahs dangling casually from their mouths, sat huddled together remembering old days of rebellion against the Soviets and the Taliban. A hand-driven cart was slowly doing rounds trying to sell household goods.

None of this was able to capture Rehan's attention for more than a second, his brain instantaneously moving on. There were better things to do, Rehan thought, than ponder over the fate of an insanely beautiful Bollywood heroine, even though she was so gorgeous only because she had Pashtun roots. Rehan felt light-headed all of a sudden, and his blood warmed up to yet pleasanter imaginings. However, his chain of thought was broken as he found what he was looking for.

A bunch of boys stood in a semicircle at the far end of the street, squinting at a deity in the middle with hope in their eyes and greed in their gait. The deity was nothing special—just a number of chipped bricks balanced delicately on top of each other, against which stood a tall boy holding a pitifully tiny bat, still managing to look intimidating.

Rehan started to run towards them, tearing off the paper wrapping of the parcel he was carrying. Soon he wielded his own brand new, full-sized BDM bat, a gift Abba got him from Kabul. Rehan clutched the bat firmly in his hands. He would score well. The better bat was *his* this time.

He jumped over a drain and started to wave his bat in the air to attract their attention. He was cut short by a sudden commotion. He heard someone scream. It was not a joyful scream of 'catch-it' or 'got-the-queen', nor a wail of despair following a dropped catch or the striker harmlessly rebounding without pocketing anything. Nor was it a housewife shouting at the cart vendor who had given her faulty goods, nor was it the lament of an old guard protesting against how things had changed — or had not.

A piercing noise cut through the lull of the street, infusing it with a sudden spurt of activity. It was as if, for a minute, the street became an advertisement for an energy drink. The men drinking tea suddenly stood up and started to run for cover. The elders, with agility far past their age, dived behind a wall and reached for their cell phones. A fat, dark man rushed up from behind and pushed Rehan out of his way, motioning at the sky with his smudgy fingers.

The screaming stopped as abruptly as it had begun. Rather, it was drowned by an even more deafening noise. A steady drone of engines — an attacking aircraft's engines — straining to get out of a bombing dive.

Two grey birds, roaring and growling, shot into view overhead. Even before Rehan could open his mouth to scream, they swooped down and flung their deadly cargo at him. In the blink of an eye, the birds vanished into the horizon, leaving a trail of smoke behind them in what appeared to Rehan, aesthetically pleasing designs. Something exploded in the distance.

Rehan knew that aircrafts meant something bad was about to happen. The Afghan DNA was allergic to birds by now. The checkered history of air raids had made the Afghans wary of anything that they could not reach and cut down with their Kalashnikovs. The noise that had receded by now, started to rise again. It seemed the aircrafts were coming back for another pass.

Five seconds later, they did.

The tea stall exploded. It seemed to jump two hundred feet in the air and pelted its remains on Rehan, mocking him. He coughed, his cold exacerbated by the smoke. He tried to stand up but felt the street erupt near him. He hit a wall and sank down, air knocked out of his lungs. Another explosion rocked the street. A stone hit him on the head. Rehan felt warm blood oozing out and dripping down his face. He passed out.

The world suddenly became more normal. Rehan dreamt that a swarm of angry bees wearing red bonnets was pursuing him, eating a newly launched ice cream and talking in a language he had heard before. His mind kicked in, urging him to wake up and find shelter before he was hurt further. He had, evidently, not reached the 'I-don't-care-just-let-me-die' stage. His mind forced him to come around a short minute later, with stinging eyes, ringing ears, and a splitting head. He instinctively raised his head and looked around.

His house was no longer standing. There was only the rubble of collapsed buildings all around. A funny feeling struck at his stomach. Before he had a chance to think any further, he heard a foreboding din fill the narrow alley and a deafening whoosh, followed by a loud boom. The ground shook as he hugged the electricity pole tightly to prevent himself from falling down. Thankfully, the first blast had cut off power to the pole.

He tried getting up and rolled behind a heap of rubble. He saw a wisp of smoke emanate from one of the birds as it flew dangerously close to the newly installed cell phone tower on his street. The tower swayed for a bit, as if drunk, and then fell over their cricket pitch, covering it with rubble and molten steel and rendering it unplayable, thereby destroying in a blink what the boys had worked so hard to perfect for months.

Months! Rehan felt a wave of anger overwhelm him.

He jerked his head up, screamed, and thrashed around in frustration. Without thinking, he picked up the largest stone he could find and flung it with all his might at the incoming bird. The stone fell at a puny distance. At the exact moment, he felt another explosion blast away dirt in close vicinity. Rehan pressed his back to the last standing wall of the locality and prayed to God that the damage to the pitch was repairable.

◆

Lieutenant Commander Robbie 'Bozo' Frazer whistled softly as his F/A-18E Super Hornet, swerving for another pass at the target, glinted in the sun. The aircraft was a 4.75-generation upgrade belonging to Strike Fighter Squadron 81, The Moonliners, and was operating from the USS *Karl Winston*.

Frazer was on a tactical bombing mission and chose to fly dangerously close to the ground. First, it provided him with even greater accuracy, even though the accuracy of the precision-guided JDAMs and Paveway series of laser-guided bombs he carried was very high even when dropped from heights. Low-flying meant he could also use the air-to-ground missiles and the internal 20mm aircraft-gun more efficiently in such a mission, especially when the ground-to-air resistance had almost been neutralized. The nose mounted M61 Vulcan Gatling gun with its 578 rounds is too handy a weapon not to be used, he thought.

Two, flying low gave him greater control over the target, apart from the psychological edge. It struck fear in the heart of the enemy. In addition, he could easily collect intelligence and positively verify the completion of the task.

Third, it minimized collateral damage. Even precision attacks in a populated area were not easy to carry out. Low-flying attacks solved much of the problem. Moreover, even if there was no need to escape radar detection, he thought, staying close to the ground gave him more...spunk. He actually smiled, wiped a drop of sweat off his forehead and adjusted his electronic-integrated visor as the Target Designation Indicator lit up on his heads-up display.

The CIA had predicted a liaison meet between the Tehrik-e-Taliban Pakistan (TTP) and the Afghan Taliban warlords as a last-ditch effort to continue waging the war against foreign forces after the death of Osama Bin Laden. Frazer was ordered to bomb the location to disrupt the think-tank meeting. Not that he had any reservations about it, considering how the war on terror was proceeding. The Taliban had started using civilians as human shields of late and ordered the mass killings of civilians who had dared to question its authority. The command had slowed its offensive at first due to public outcry against collateral damage but that had proved to be counterproductive. Consequently, the command was told to crush the Taliban once and for all. With brute force, if need be.

His orders were clear: annul the meeting and any nefarious plans to counter-attack the last remaining International Security Assistance Force (ISAF) base in Afghanistan. Although peace was important, Frazer thought, freedom was paramount. A dead civilian, after all, was far less a threat to democracy than a terrorist alive and kicking. Every soldier involved in counter-insurgency operations knew that. No one wanted to kill—but it was better to kill than to get killed.

His radio sputtered and jerked him out of his reverie. His wingman awaited further instructions.

Frazer ordered him to fly another pass. He adjusted his aircraft's camera and started scanning for life forms. His search was abruptly broken when his eyes, which were focusing on every part of the street below, saw a ghastly, half-dead shape rise from the rubble and throw something towards him. Frazer, thinking it to be an armament, jerked his aircraft up in a steep climb, but not before firing at the location of his prospective assailant. Just then he noticed the projectile fall back to the ground in a pathetic, insignificant arc.

It seemed to be a handheld grenade. Grenades could not touch him where he was, even if he was flying low. Frazer pressed the trigger. He then confirmed that the street below had been blasted and that the group he had attacked was dead. He rechecked the image of the mangled bodies. The task seemed to be complete. He nodded in satisfaction. Then he checked his watch and motioned to his wingman. A bitter taste lingered in his mouth for long. Life was life. Bombing human habitation and killing people sometimes made him feel a little disoriented.

Frazer shrugged, trying to balance his conscience with his duty. It was time to return home. He wanted to be back on the ship to catch the day's episode of *The Simpsons*.

Part I
IGNITION

All warfare is based on deception. Hence, when able to attack, we must seem unable; when using our forces, we must seem inactive; when we are near, we must make the enemy believe we are far away; when far away, we must make him believe we are near.

—Sun Tzu

Outer Perimeter, National Missile Research Centre (NMRC)
Andaman and Nicobar Islands, India

Local time: 1100 hours
Date: 23 April 2014

Droplets of kerosene glistened in the sun and slipped down the smooth semi-naked body, hitting the ground with an inaudible plop. The parched grass absorbed them instantly. A tall, thin man, wearing nothing but a colourful loincloth, his head shaven the way rituals demanded, stood in the middle, screeching. His body shone with the fiery liquid all over it. He screamed — wild eyed, his breath coming in desperate gasps — in a voice that was a rasp of forced courage. With a heave, he hoisted the kerosene bucket and drenched every inch of himself in one quick, final act of defiance.

Others around him prayed; their heads bowed, their eyes scared. They looked on as their chief muttered an incantation, lit a dry shrub and walked towards the man. Cameras started to click and whirr as two German linguists, currently in the Andamans to study a local language, jostled for perfect shots. Someone shouted in ecstasy.

A golden flame had subsumed the man.

The crowd rushed towards him. The chanting got louder, frenzy was setting in, and tempers were beginning to flare. As if in response to the prayers of the mob, the massive doors to the complex they were protesting against flew open and berets, boots and bayonets forced their way through the living mass to the burning bush of a man, dousing him with fire extinguishers and putting out the flame.

The crowd howled in protest. The linguists shook their heads at losing the opportunity to get some Pulitzer-winning shots. The onlookers sighed, their fists clenched, and then caved in. The boots became softer in their blows, and the tribals covered their eyes with their hands to erase this sacrilegious intervention from their collective memory. Yet some amongst the crowd, who had until then shown no interest in the proceedings, and who were covered in blankets despite the hot weather, swiftly inched closer to the uniformed men who were spoiling the party, their dead eyes suddenly animated by the sight of olive green.

Another contingent emerged from the gate, with fire-control equipment ready. The security in-charge of the base had given the order to save the man trying to immolate himself outside the main gate. Force was not to be used. These men were tribal farmers after all, protesting against the missile tests. The gods were angry, the tribals had realized lately and were now trying to make amends. The outworlders had halted their sacrifice to pacify the gods. These mean men did not allow their tribe to complete the ritual to re-infuse their lands with prosperity — that the outworlders themselves had taken away by shooting huge metallic arrows at the gods. All was lost now. The land would be forever fallow.

The tribals knew that someone would pay, and that it would not be them.

◆

It is a truth universally acknowledged that an Indian in possession of an upper-middle-class stature must be in want of an anti-government demonstration, for Indians are immensely proud of their country but extremely critical of their government. Likewise, an Indian with an empty belly must be in want of a square meal, apart from a pair of Levi's jeans, a fancy sports bike and Ray-Ban sunglasses, though not necessarily in that order. Yadav thought and chuckled, putting down the earmarked copy of *Pride and Prejudice* he had borrowed from the base library.

Yadav had already ordered the man to be hospitalized. He had suffered third-degree burns. There was little Yadav could have done for him, apart from intervening at the moment he set himself on fire. He mournfully shook his head. He did not expect these tribals to be capable of such barbarism and abnegation.

Lieutenant Colonel Ankit Kumar Yadav of the Indian army, on deputation to the Central Industrial Security Force (CISF) for the past two years, was a slightly balding man with a prominent nose and an even more prominent senex complex. He pondered over the paradoxical dichotomy of the inherently reactionary nature of the Indian middle-class and its often quasi-revolutionary manifestations. He shook his head, casually adjusted the 5.56mm MSMC, an INSAS sub-machine gun, slung over his left shoulder, and tuned his ears to the noises again.

He made his way towards the scene of commotion. He saw his junior, Sandeep Rathi, an assistant commandant freshly out of the academy, approaching the scene cautiously from the other side of the fence with a sullen expression on his face. Rathi saw the lieutenant colonel and saluted midstride, to which Yadav simply waved. He hoped Rathi did not notice his suppressed rolling of the eyes. Not good for the morale, he thought.

They met and made their way towards the gate, Rathi trailing slightly in deference. 'This should not be happening, sir,' he said in between his lanky strides and pointed at Gate No. 1 of the complex, 'this is a restricted area. They should not be here! In fact, no one should be here but us.' He added as an afterthought, 'We allowed them to protest and look! One of them almost killed himself if it was not for our timely intervention.'

Yadav wondered if Rathi had always been like this. Yadav did not blame him, though. Not really. Yadav had served from Doda to Silchar and had realized that when one's life hung on a fine balance, everyone was a potential saboteur, and one needed to be on one's toes constantly – a lesson drilled home by military training academies all over the world.

Paranoid megalomaniacs, the grand old critical insider thought, cannot ever comprehend that the actually dangerous civilians do not look dangerous and the lethal-looking usually turned out to be quite harmless. After fourteen years of counterinsurgency operations, he had realized that classifying civilians based on their appearances was futile. They often reacted contrary to his expectations, throwing the entire system in disarray. The Wellington administrator at the back of his mind whispered, 'An unstable environment passes on its flaws even to a stable system, which is why the system needs to be inherently iron-willed and fortified by discipline and espirit-de-corps in order to survive.' Unfortunately, this very discipline acted as a limiting factor on the adaptability of the system against the environment's onslaught, thereby rendering it ineffective in the end.

Catch-22.

Morton's Fork.

Hobson's choice.

Yadav's mind raced to find suitable words to encapsulate the paradox. A long time ago, so long ago that it seemed almost like another lifetime, he had read sociology at a university before sitting for the Combined Defence Service Examination. He had wanted to join the air force but flunked the Pilot Aptitude Battery Test, and was offered a permanent commission in the army instead.

He had joined, though, with a bitter taste in his mouth. He had now realized how the outcome of a simple joystick simulator test almost two decades ago had changed his life forever. Instead of a fancy suit and a fluffy uniform, all he had was combat overalls soiled by mud, and a stupid gun that never jammed.

Yadav wondered if there was a God up there, toying with people like him. 'Think as much as you want, dear believer, but just when you think you have it all figured out, I am going to change the rules a little bit. There you are, my boy, now bow before me and donate munificently. And don't forget to organize a riot and a bombing now and then, my child. You may go.'

A gentle yet firm voice interrupted Yadav's reverie, 'Sir, shall I have them dispersed? More of them could try to immolate themselves right in front of our nose,' Rathi said, trying to delve into what he perceived to be his superior's stoic, calculating silence.

Yadav landed back to earth, shook his head, and said, 'Come on, Rathi, these guys are just tribal farmers.'

Rathi snorted, 'So are the Naxalites,' and kicked a pebble with his left foot. It landed in a puddle, splattering his trousers with mud.

'My, they really are thorough with training these days, aren't they?' Yadav looked at the poor indoctrinated chap with pity. If only he knew what *they* were doing to him. They were trying to get his soul. They were trying to brainwash him. They were trying to make him, Yadav gasped, paranoid. Yadav puffed his chest out with pride at the realization. He was not a mindless automaton. He knew the faults in the system. Or at least he thought he did.

Rathi looked at him, trying to find any sarcasm. He decided that silence was the best course of action. Let the senior continue, they like preaching sometimes. It is not enough to be in command; people need to *feel* they are in command.

Yadav continued, 'If some people want to protest against the evil effects these missile tests are doing to their lands, let them… Dharna and protests are an integral part of our national ethos.'

Rathi opened his mouth to speak but the lieutenant colonel, expecting his objection, continued, 'As long as they do it peacefully and do not hamper our work, which I do not think they are doing. This is a democratic country after all.' Yadav spread his arms wide and shrugged helplessly at the word 'democratic'. He added, 'I know a little bit of their history. As per tradition, only one of them can immolate himself, or at least try to, and offer oneself to God every year. The quota for this year is complete so all is well. Secondly, we need to have them here to give them immediate medical care, or else they will die.' Yadav's eyes were suddenly sad.

'But, sir, just look at them! Some of them do not look like tribal farmers at all. Just hear their slogans. Bourgeois aggressors...neo-imperialist reactionaries? Where did they study? Stephens?' Rathi pronounced it with a 'v' instead of a 'p'. Clearly, he was a man of breeding and much learning.

Yadav decided against craning his neck and looked upward prophetically, 'Hmm...*times they are a-changing*, boy. It is fashionable for our bourgeois to apply for ten days' leave after an important business deal, pack their American traveller bags, fly to a hotspot, stay in a four-star hotel, and join the local protests with their intellectual inputs. Sometimes they even join the protestors in solidarity. If foment does not exist, then create one, for governance is all about hiding things from the people, is it not?' This time the sarcasm was unmistakable, Rathi noticed, and heaved a sigh of relief. Better that the lieutenant colonel indicted the Indian middle class than his henpecked subordinates.

Rathi merely nodded, prodding Yadav to continue, 'Such is the system here, yaar. Let them do it, it keeps them sane and guilt-free. Otherwise the great Indian dream will come crashing down.' Yadav mimicked an airplane crash with his free hand as the INSAS on his shoulder twitched due to his sudden movement. I am good at this, he thought, and made a mental note to picture him in this pose for his Facebook profile. Let Sunita see this!

Rathi looked up, visibly relaxed. 'But, sir, the security concerns...' he said.

Yadav gave Rathi a look almost similar to the one he used to give his nine-year-old son when he insisted that Yadav sit away from the window seat in an airplane because the kid thought that it would make the plane change course to Dhaka.

'Believe me, Rathi, I have been posted here for the last six months and these poor tribals come here every week from the adjoining island. A witchdoctor had told them that our presence will ruin the crops, stop the rains and make the earth barren and so on. However, they are entirely peaceful. They just come here, raise a few slogans and go back. Moreover, nothing untoward has happened so far except today. But even then we need them here. The situation is under control.'

Rathi did not sound very convinced, 'But, sir...'

'Fine!' Yadav snapped, fed up of the trigger-happy punk. 'Go ahead, open fire or do what you feel like. Go on, do it, but be prepared for tomorrow's news — '500 crores of public money down the drain!' Our special correspondent reports that the Indian government's multi-crore Jarawa Tribal Welfare Programme that was launched to protect tribal heritage, came to a sudden and tragic demise yesterday as the CISF opened fire and killed the last members of the last native tribe of Andaman. Now the government plans to appoint a commission on how tribal heritage can be saved when all the tribals are dead. CISF expels the erring assistant commandant and he faces severe charges.'

Rathi opened his mouth to say something but stopped himself. He thought of his mother watching the news and hiding in embarrassment from their talkative neighbour whose son was a deputy collector by now, and then writing a letter to Rathi, groaning, *'Kyun beta...kyun! Humne kya kiya tha jo aise din dekhne padhe?'*

Rathi, fully convinced, barked orders to the sentries to let the protestors be, and withdrew to a distance where he could ponder over his narrow escape from the unrelenting and brutal media coverage. No longer will the bearded freak on the famous crime news show scream, '*Yeh dekhiye khooni* assistant commandant *ka asli roop, Vardi main chhupa jallad,* CISF *ka vehshi chehra'*, and flash Rathi's smiling gun-toting picture on national television.

Rathi smiled weakly at Yadav, thanked his wisdom, saluted him, and started walking back towards the base. Yadav watched the receding figure of Rathi against the sun. Poor kid, he thought. He is upset about being away from home. He wondered how he himself had been able to stay away from home for so long. Thankfully, he was no longer posted in the volatile regions of Kashmir, the Red Corridor* or the Northeast. He was now in the Andamans, a peaceful and serene island chain in the Bay of Bengal. Nothing ever happened here. No gunfights, no encounters, no raids, nothing at all. It was like a very long holiday. Perhaps this was the reason why the Andamans was chosen as the site for the newly instituted NMRC. For the safety, secrecy, and virgin testing grounds it provided.

Yadav enjoyed being the security in-charge of this base. It gave him a sense of direction in life. Just hold your line and make merry drinking beer on moonlit beaches. It was true that a very important project here was nearing completion, but he did not sense any danger. Who would want to attack this ultra-secret base designed to build a prototype that might not work when there were other more accessible targets like SHAR and VSSC?

He was so lost in his thoughts that he did not realize he had reached the main gate. He peered out and scanned the

*The Red Corridor refers to the region in the east of India that experiences considerable Naxalite-Maoist militant activity. It can be said to roughly run from Pashupati (Nepal) to Tirupati (Andhra Pradesh).

area. He saw some forty-plus farmers shouting and chanting at the gate. Yadav did not try to talk to them. There was no use of any dialogue. No one, absolutely no one, could make these people see sense, except of course a good old AK-47, as he had learned from experience.

God, I am talking like them, he thought. They are succeeding, but another voice muttered, who exactly are they? He ignored it.

Yadav had a problem. He thought too much. Sometimes way too much. However, the detached observer in him liked to watch these protests and later the romantic in him used to imagine himself in the crowd as he stood waving a protest banner and raising his hand as if reaching out for the future. And the next moment he would laugh at the futility of such attempts. Might is usually right, he had learned with age. The poor can only protest. Rarely is their voice heard. Rarer still the powerful pay heed to it.

He stopped brooding. Soon he would be promoted to a full colonel, and with his hard area posting over, he would reunite with his family. He flopped down into a chair overlooking the gate on one side and the dense forest on the other. Yadav closed his eyes and started to think about what to gift his wife, Sunita, on their forthcoming anniversary.

Research Laboratory Alpha, NMRC

Local time: 1100 hours
Date: 23 April 2014

A blank expression on his face, spectacles delicately perched on his nose, Dr AA Suryakant, Scientist-D, cocked his head to one side, his tongue protruding from between his teeth, the way it always did when solving a complex problem, and stared at a tiny point on his office notice board. Finally, when he could bear it no more, he sighed, scribbled something in his notebook and closed it shut with a dull thud. He had been awake the entire night. Not that he regretted it. He was a scientist, and any scientist would happily sacrifice a night's sleep for a day's work. Or a day's sleep for a night's work.

Nishachar, that was how he was known. But he was not to be blamed. This is how we do things, he mused. The class of 1985. IIT Kharagpur. Suryakant still had the class picture taken at the graduation day ceremony, with him standing in the last row alongside Wali, Bhau and Ray. In fact, he did not merely have it, he had it pinned on his notice board.

Those were the times, he reflected, *the* times. His batch was one of the most politically active batches to graduate from IIT after the fiery Naxalbari movement of 1969. Engineering, education, and life had no longer been the same. The people of this country deserved better than nepotism, corruption, hunger and poverty, he had realized. Suryakant unclipped the photo and slid it lovingly into the pocket of his overcoat.

History was all that he had. After a first-class degree in aeronautical engineering from IIT, Suryakant chose not to go abroad as many of his fellow IITians did. He wanted to serve his country. Serve in the real sense, not like those who went to the US, raked in tons of money, donated some to religious and political charities back home, started an online political party, and bought mangoes and gifted them to relatives in India. Suryakant was not one of those who would go settle abroad at the first chance they got. 'Hell, my English is not good enough for converse with people there,' he used to lightly remark, until he actually started believing it.

Therefore, after IIT, he decided to enroll for MTech at the Indian Institute of Sciences, Bangalore, and followed it by a doctorate in cryogenic propulsion. Suryakant was immediately spotted and offered a job in the Defence Research and Development Organisation (DRDO) with an attractive grade pay and soon, amidst much fanfare, the path-breaking CE-7.5 was operationalized.

Suryakant had toiled hard to become a team leader (Guidance Systems) in the Pralay-LGMS project. The project aimed at the production of a solid-fuel, stealth, intercontinental ballistic missile that was capable of being fired at a very short notice, and that too from mobile platforms. Pralay was the code name of the missile, the 'L' indicated that the missile was supposed to be silo-launched; the 'G' meant it was designed to attack ground targets, the 'M' reflected that it was a guided missile, and the 'S' referred to it being a stealth design.

Pralay was regarded as a natural extension of India's Integrated Guided Missile Development Programme (IGMDP) that had given her a lot of teeth. India now had potent surface-to-surface missiles such as Prithvi and Shaurya (tactical) and Agni (strategic); surface-to-air missiles like Akash and Trishul; an anti-tank missile Nag, not to mention Pradyumna (ballistic missile interceptor), apart from Sagarika and Dhanush, the naval variants of Prithvi.

IGMDP had given India a leading edge over the Pakistani Baaz-V missile, developed by the National Engineering and Scientific Commission (NESCOM), that copied the North Korean Taepodong design, and kissed a range of 5,500 kilometres. However, policymakers on both sides of the border knew that the difference in ranges of the premier missiles of the two countries was not what mattered. With Agni-VI, India was able to take out any Pakistani city. With Baaz-V, Pakistan was capable of crippling any major Indian city. However, India's defence policy was no longer Pakistan-centric. Though Pakistan still had to contend only with India, making its delivery systems based on threats from the Indian mainland. India, on the other hand, had to handle two potent threats simultaneously during the past three decades — Pakistan in the west and a belligerent China in the east. Moreover, China was working diligently on Songfeng, the 9000-km ranged beast that was capable of being launched from under water, striking any Indian city any time.

Although things were changing, boundaries were dissolving by way of the creation of Economic Cooperation Zones, nations were coming together, even old foes, but it was better to be prepared for the time when things went sour and past bitterness surfaced. Suryakant never forgot lines from a Dinkar poem he had read as a child:

Kshama shobhti us bhujang ko
Jiske paas garal hai
Usko kya jo dantheen
Vishrahit vineet saral hai

(Forgiveness is becoming of
The serpent with venom
Not the toothless,
Poison-less one.)

Pralay was to be the feather in the cap of IGMDP. From the moment orders came to fire, Pralay-LGMS could be airborne in about eight hours, including the time it took to assemble it from its core constituents. For that, its components were kept in a semi-assembled state and solid fuel cells were attached to the main body. Harmless canisters and parts were capable of being integrated and becoming deadly in just eight hours — from the scratch — in the shape of Pralay.

Suryakant was proud of it. He believed that only with military self-reliance could the foreign policy of a country be truly independent, and only with such a policy could there be economic development. Multinationals, FDI, FIIs, and oil politics led to the creation of two Indias, and the majority remained poor and at the mercy of a small elite. Things had to change now.

Suryakant wanted to pay the bad guys back in their own currency. However, what constituted bad guys changed shape in his mind every day. Today, it was the mess manager. How can they have a Delhi-wallah supervising mess workers cooking sambhar? It is monstrous! It is a travesty of the natural order of things! It is just not meant to happen! It is as efficient as him working as a fashion reporter in Milan, he thought.

Then he calmed himself. He had lived in Delhi and sambhar there was not half as bad as chapattis down south. He grinned at the irony.

Back to work, you foodie, the buzz at the back of his head grew stronger. He shrugged. This was usually the time he logged into the mainframe to play Counterstrike. Techies loved LAN primarily because it gave them a chance to kill each other in various shooting games. However, he had no time right now. The directive from the Ministry of Defence was clear; urgent. Build. One Missile. Sleek. Shiny. Kick-ass. Now.

Funny how a babu with absolutely no idea of how much time and energy it took to build a new missile, that too with an absolutely new concept, would run to his honourable minister and utter gibberish with key phrases like 'strategic, deterrent, incursions, policy, epistemological shift, technology, budgetary allocations, DRDO head, non-recurring expenditure, zero-based budgeting, lapse, global terrorism' thrown in. Funny how it earned him the task of the execution of such a policy at such a short notice.

This was the reason why Suryakant was here in the state-of-the-art laboratory of NMRC in the Andaman and Nicobar Islands, working sixteen hours a day for the past thirteen months. His team was charged with successfully integrating and installing the propulsion and guidance system in the missile—a task which they had almost completed.

Funding was not a problem. Time was. The catch was to get Pralay operational before the government was forced to formally abandon such projects due to international technology transfer deals in areas like nuclear energy. Therefore, here he was, slogging. Fortunately, things were not as bad as they could have been. He was assisted by the 'best brains in the galaxy', as he fondly put it.

The computer buzzed. An Instant Message had arrived from the central lab. It read: 'Project nearing completion. On schedule. No anomalies reported.' He chuckled and logged off, and started walking clumsily towards the central lab singing *Jaise Beemar ko Bewajah Qarar Aa Jaye*. He did not lock his office door.

The corridors of the complex were lit with jolly spirits. There was an aura of happiness about the place. Suryakant himself could not believe it. He passed a couple of scientists who smiled at him and waved. At last, after years of sweat and hard work, they had finally been successful in creating the 8000 km-ranged intercontinental ballistic missile, code-named Pralay. Having a CEP* of just 25 m, its accuracy was almost perfect. Its submarine launched version was also on the verge of operationalization. Next week was the D-Day — its demonstration to the prime minister himself. Suryakant imagined the moment of glory and smiled.

He reached the central lab and stared intently at the missile like a paleologist who had just found an egg. A dinosaur's egg. One that was about to break.

From the inside.

'Is everything ready?' Suryakant enquired, feeling unusually buoyant.

'Yes, sir. Everything is going as planned. The parts of Pralay are in the process of being assembled as we speak. We

---

*Circular Error Probable is the radius of a circle within which half of a missile's projectiles are expected to fall and thus is an indicator of the delivery accuracy of a weapons system.

have briefed the project directors. The testing will begin on schedule,' replied a fellow scientist.

Suryakant nodded in approval. For safety, the missile was not to be assembled until the very last minute. The military did not want to bring Pralay under open skies. That would have risked satellite detection and led to international pressure to abort the test. To avoid that, it was housed in a specially designed silo.

'Tomorrow would be the day of Pralay. It would go down in the history of India...and so will you,' Suryakant said prophetically, addressing a bunch of eager scientists expecting to be fathers soon. Little did he know that the next day would actually be the day of Pralay in many ways. And the scientists there, were to become history.

North Gate, NMRC

Local time: 1200 hours
Date: 23 April 2014

Lieutenant Colonel Ankit Yadav felt his guardian angel trying to snap his eyes open with a rusted car jack. He sat up and looked around, his neck bobbing as if on danger-activated springs. The sea breeze gently ruffled his collar and the sky was still a clear sparkling blue. Wisps of clouds were swimming towards him.

The clouds. That was what had made him sit up as if electric current was disrupting his synapses. He had seen such a cloud formation earlier in his life. The shape was ominous, almost… sinister. His eardrum popped. He shuddered involuntarily and was thrown years into the past. A gory past that he had desperately tried to forget. And failed.

An ill-kempt house, hidden in a dingy alley, overlooking a valley, illuminated by pale moonlight. Silence broken sporadically by boots on asphalt. Suddenly Yadav was swept off his feet by a hurricane, as if a bottle of champagne was uncorked inside a very small closet. He was drenched. White wine was all over him. Except that it was not white, it was red. Blood red. Someone screamed.

A loud whoosh. An RPG slammed the rear of the FV432 Armoured Personnel Carrier (APC) he was in, spinning it like a toy and setting it on fire. The driver sat still with his head drooped, his eyes unblinking, his face bearing a nasty grin — and blood spurting from his forehead, drenching Yadav.

That was 1998.

21A, Model Road, Srinagar. Reports had indicated that heavily armed terrorists planning to strike at Radio Kashmir, had holed themselves up in that house, shooting everything that moved. The Kilo Force of the Rashtriya Rifles* had been ordered to sanitize the area.

Cut.

Captain Yadav lay paralysed in his armoured personnel carrier with his driver bleeding all over the vehicle's floor. Wake up. Wake up! He came to his senses. He heard a steady rat-tat of machine gun fire as units surrounded the house. He climbed out, shaking but unhurt, and allowed his training to take over.

What...? What?

When under fire, first find a safe location, regroup, communicate and counter-attack. A fine commander he had been, he cursed himself, he had walked straight into an enemy trap. The house reported to be taken over by the terrorists was not this one — 21A, Model Street was empty.

27B, however, was not. This was the house where he had planned to set up a sniper and reconnaissance base to launch the first wave against the occupied house. The house where they were headed. The house that was raining death on them.

Bastards! They fed us false intelligence, thought Yadav. The house further down the road, the one they were planning to raid was empty. They knew we would try to set up a base at a strategic location nearby to assess the situation. 21A, the target, is empty. 27B, our to-be-base, is not ours. It never was.

---

*A counter-insurgency force in India.

At least five heavily armed terrorists were hiding inside the house, wielding one sniper rifle and two RPGs and were shooting at his column. Two APCs were on fire, caught fully unaware; screaming and barking soldiers ran helter-skelter trying to be heard over the din of moans.

The stench of charred flesh was all around him. He took aim from behind a corner of a building and started firing. He heard a dull thud and a shriek. He hoped it was a vital organ. Still, bullets kept coming from the other end. As if this was not enough, his AK-47, the most reliable gun in the world, jammed. Bad ammo! Yadav gritted his teeth. He took another weapon lying nearby, its owner being in no position to use it anymore.

Yadav ordered his squad to regroup and counter-attack. He rushed to the back door and peeked in. Suddenly, he felt ants crawling over his leg. His feet were no longer able to bear his weight as he sank to the ground. A small red hole appeared in his trousers. Yadav had been shot.

He opened his mouth but no sound came out. He felt no pain. Shock was all. He felt the ground rising to meet him as a sub-inspector of Jammu and Kashmir police dragged Yadav out of the firing range. He was laden into a waiting ambulance. The last picture he remembered from that day's operation was the moon shining behind 27B, making it glow like a surreal yet immensely attractive Venus flytrap. Another APC exploded as the ambulance sped away.

Blackness. He woke up screaming. The cloud...the approaching cloud. The shape of this tuft of cloud, closing in fast on his present location, NMRC, was strikingly similar to the shape of the house 27B in Srinagar a decade ago.

Yadav stood up and ran towards the gate. With his INSAS rifle in his hand, he scanned the entire area. It seemed as if the ghost of Christmas past had returned to haunt him. He looked all around again. All he saw were some peasants protesting. He lowered his gun but not his guard.

Then almost in slow motion, he saw a Heckler and Koch 9mm MP5SD sub-machine gun emerge from beneath the garb of a farmer; others followed suit. He immediately lunged for the nearest cover, his gun thundering even before he reached it.

Yadav did not panic. With cold efficiency infused in him by the rigorous army training, he kept firing at the attackers. He saw two tribals fall to his bullets. The two sentries also saw the unusual weapons of protest and their rifles returned fire.

Damn, why did I not ask for additional protection? Yadav mused. As if to answer him, the two Browning M2 machine guns from the two watch towers located nearby started chattering. Bless the Americans, he thought. He reached for his communicator. The base had to be warned. The sky thundered. It had started to rain.

In between reloading his INSAS rifle, Yadav's mind was working furiously. With the main facility three kilometres further inside, he was sure the gunfight would not be heard there, at least not over the raging storm. Security around this isolated base was pretty light and superficial, as no one expected much trouble round here. One could easily get in, but getting out was impossible. Who would be mad enough to do it?

Somehow, he had to raise an alarm. Before he could think further, or bark a command, he heard a familiar whine and saw two white streaks tearing towards the watchtowers. He felt his stomach drop. He knew what was coming. Before he could react, a barrage from 85mm RPGs had reduced the watchtowers and the gate to rubble. Yadav merely stood there, his mouth agape. How did these tribals get their hands on something as sophisticated as a rocket launcher? Now that he thought of it, where did they get the MP5s from?

He was so absorbed in his thoughts that he almost missed the attackers clamber over the smoking remains of the gate. It was then that he noticed the corpses of the sentries. There was no use running back. He would be shot in the back. He waited for them to come inside, hidden for most of them to come within their killing range. With a growl, he started to fire.

Yadav lunged out of his lair and cut three attackers down before he was shot in the head. Wrong technique, Yadav-ji, this is not *Border* nor are you Sunny Deol, was the last mirthless thought in his head before he hit the ground.

◆

Ignoring their dead and moving forward with the efficiency of a well-trained army, the 'tribals' split into two groups. The gate was clear. Barring the attackers, everyone at the gate was already dead by now. No one would know what had happened here, until it was too late. One group headed inside towards the main testing facility and the other stayed behind at the gate, fortifying it. The facility was surrounded by hills on three sides; this gate was the sole entry to the facility. Now they controlled it.

From the trolley of a tractor in which they had arrived, they took out bunches of P5 MK1 versions of M18 Claymore mines. These mines were capable of firing steel balls within a 70-degree arc in front of them to a distance of 150 metres. Soon, everyone from the group that stayed back at the gate was busy digging the earth or looking for trees to plant these mines. These directional anti-personnel mines formed a barricade that was almost impenetrable. From now on, no one and nothing would be able to pass this gate without their consent.

This is precisely what the plan had been all along.

◆

MH Kutty was dying.

He moaned and tried to stop the bleeding by covering the wound with his shaking hands as he slithered to safety. Blood gushed forth, falling on the green leaves, brown earth and the white tiles, leaving behind a colourful mosaic.

Kutty clenched his teeth and got to work. He had to survive. He expertly wrapped the gaping hole with a cloth and tried to minimize the bleeding by exerting pressure at the right points. Although his I-card identified him as an administrative officer in DRDO's Material Management Directorate, his acts were of a seasoned combat veteran. Kutty was far from a smug file-pusher. He was an Assistant Central Intelligence Officer (ACIO) with the Indian Intelligence Bureau (IB), and was working undercover to assist in the security of the base.

Kutty had been unlucky enough to be at the wrong place at the wrong time (or lucky enough to be at the right place at the right time). He had been shot in the legs. He had dropped to the ground the moment he was hit and was taken to be dead. His training at IB had taken over. The words of his drill instructor rang in his head. When in trouble, run. His job was to warn others on time—not fight back. There were others better trained to do so.

Ignoring the pain, he had dragged himself to a safe spot. Kutty had to inform of this breach to his superiors. He knew he would soon be breathing his last due to excessive bleeding and he could manage only one quick, terse broadcast.

He reached for the radio and in a spluttering voice, began his ultimate message.

Kalaiya, Bara District, Nepal

Local time: 1645 hours
Date: <u>25 March 2014</u>*

Run, Basheer, run for your life.

Yasser Basheer instinctively looked around. The voice seemed to emanate from all around him. He shook his head and sniffed — as he always did in any sticky situation — struggling to fathom what the air was trying to tell him. He casually tried to glance around again but was met by questioning glares. Evidently, it was his brain playing tricks with him.

His two aides steadfastly at his side, Basheer felt the dozen men surrounding him were gently yet firmly prodding him to walk in a particular direction. No, not only men, but also a woman. She wore combat fatigues like the rest of them. Her lips were cruel and her eyes cold. Barbarians, Basheer thought, his mind revolting, what kind of man allows a woman to fight for him?

Basheer looked at his men, who, as evident by their expressions, shared his disgust. He was, however, intelligent enough not to voice his concerns out loud. He kept walking silently. The jungle party kept looking at Basheer cautiously —

---

*Dates when underlined imply action having taken place in the past rather than during the linear timeline of events.

unsure of how to respond in case he turned on them — and stole a glance at their comrades every ten seconds. They were emaciated, tired, shoulders drooping, but their hands were steady on their guns. The leader of the party wore spectacles and had a pedantic look. He seemed well educated. Ha! Basheer thought, what is the use of such education? In the afterlife, only deeni-taaleem* will matter.

The guns were not pointing at Basheer or his two burly companions, but he knew those surrounding them would not hesitate to fire if need arose. His aides had been asked to surrender their firearms when they had rendezvoused with this group an hour ago, making them uneasy with the realization that they lacked any means to defend themselves. These people had no imaan, Basheer thought. They could not be trusted, but he needed them, just as they needed him.

The group entered dense foliage, butting their way forward with their guns. Basheer followed. He was good at tracking and navigation, but now even he was beginning to falter. Deep down he knew he was safe…as long as they made a deal at the end.

Their pace fastened. It was getting darker; the sun was about to set. This infused in the group a renewed zeal and quickened their pace. Basheer found himself panting. Age was catching up with him. He shook his head wistfully. Gone were the days when he started with a five-kilometre jog. Basheer was beginning to get tired of the jungle.

Soon, they stumbled across a clearing. Ah, sanity at last. Makeshift tents were scattered throughout. Some were dark, some had light flickering inside. Music emanated from a nearby

---

*Religious education.

tent, two men were bandaging a third's wounds and singing. They looked at him, their expressions vacillating between curiosity and hostility. Basheer hurried forward.

He was led to a tent. It was shabby, torn at places, smelt strongly of sweat, blood and gunpowder. The recent ride through the fresh jungle air made this smell even more intolerable. He heard voices inside; an argument was on.

His mind immediately got to work. There were at least three men. One sitting on a stool in the centre of the tent, one standing near the entry and the third was lying on the floor at the rear end of the tent. He tried to triangulate their position. An old habit. Observe, triangulate enemy position, shoot, and disappear. He hoped that particular skill would not be required here.

Basheer stood at the entry of the tent and glanced at his escort. Go in, the man motioned with a slight tilt of his head. Basheer nodded and stepped forward. His aides tried to follow him but were stopped by the same man. They looked up at Basheer questioningly, and he merely shook his head. Relax; keep your calm, stay where you are. I will be back. All of this conveyed with a single glance. Basheer stepped into the tent.

He did not expect what he saw. The tent was clearly more comfortable than it looked from the outside. In a corner lay a king-sized portable bed with a thick mattress on it, though the sheet was a bit dirty. Right next to it was a fully stocked bookshelf and a writing table. A TV, three laptops, a satellite phone, and some personal firearms were kept nearby. Chinese assault rifles, Basheer could make out from the markings. He knew them well.

'Welcome, Basheer sahib. Hope your trip was not uncomfortable. Comrade Agyaat thanks you for your visit,' the man standing near the entry said, and extended his hand to Basheer.

Basheer took his hand and shook it nimbly. 'Are you Agyaat?' he asked.

'Er...no.' The man coughed, visibly uncomfortable under Basheer's inquisitive gaze. He was saved the trouble of further explanations as the curtain parted.

A wiry bespectacled man walked in from the rear of the tent, wiping his hands with a towel, and said, 'I am Agyaat.'

Basheer nodded. Is this how a typical guerilla fighter looks like? He wanted to ask, but all he said was, 'Uhm...interesting place you have here.' Even a warrior needs some comfort, he thought. No, a warrior especially needs comfort. For other parts of his life were not easy.

'It has to be interesting,' replied Agyaat. 'It is also the headquarters of the Coordination Committee of the Maoist Parties of South Asia.' Agyaat threw his arms open *a la* SRK so grandiosely that it almost looked comic.

'Let us get down to brasstacks, shall we?' Basheer wanted to leave as soon as possible. He was not too comfortable in the jungle at night. Agyaat's pathetic sense of humour did little to ease his discomfort.

Agyaat shrugged, 'Yes, but first I need to handle some unfinished business.'

He parted the curtain to go to the rear end of the tent. He motioned Basheer to follow him. A man lay tied, blindfolded and bleeding. Agyaat rasped, a note of glee creeping up his voice, 'Basheer sahib, meet Javed Mandal, a zonal committee member of the Marxist party.'

Nice move, Basheer thought, to show a potential collaborator your fangs apart from your loving licks so that he thinks twice before backstabbing.

'Why is he here?' Basheer inquired, a little interested in this new charade.

Agyaat replied, 'Mandal has been on our radar for quite some time now. He fed intelligence to the armed forces that led to the capture of a number of our Maoist comrades, apart from our Mrinatool allies. We caught him when he came to Nepal for a friend's wedding. Well, seems this enemy of the people will not trouble us much longer, will he?' He chuckled.

Basheer looked at him again. Mandal opened his eyes and looked pleadingly at him to end his misery. Basheer forced himself to look away. 'Aren't you two supposed to be on the same side? You both are Communists, are you not?' he asked.

'We are, but I can't say the same for him,' barked Agyaat. 'He is as much a Communist as…Israel is Islamist. His people merely use the concept of Communism for selfish ends. He is a bourgeois spy, a class-collaborator and a traitor to the aspiration of people. He's the murderer of tribal rights, of equitable development, of the voices of hoi-polloi.'

Basheer nodded. Comrade Agyaat's tone was pretty agitated by now. Best to keep up with him, he thought. 'How is he different from you? How is his brand of Communism varied from yours? I thought you were all the same!' he sputtered.

Ha! Ignorant fool, Agyaat thought, and suppressed a smug smile. What else could he expect from a madrasa-educated, gun-toting religious fanatic? Basheer's class-consciousness and knowledge of contemporary political discourses was as developed as that of the participants of *Rakhi ka Insaaf*. Agyaat let out a sigh and began, 'Well, firstly his people,' he pointed at

Mandal, 'are as Muslim as you regard the Ahmadiyas to be.'

A flicker of comprehension played on Basheer's face. Agyaat congratulated himself for giving the jihadist familiar yardsticks for comparison. Agyaat considered himself to be an expert in dumbing down. When with people, talk of their problems, their aspirations, their prejudices. Talk like them, but think like a leader. This simple mantra of success had got Agyaat where he was today.

He continued, 'Moreover, his people, instead of an armed revolution, believe in people's democratic revolution. You do know what that means, don't you?' Basheer merely shook his head and tried to look interested.

'It means they want to achieve power by participating in democratic elections! Traitors! Cowards! Fools! They have turned their backs on the teachings of Mao, Marx and Lenin. True equality can only be achieved by an armed overthrow of the bourgeois state! Only with the establishment of the dictatorship of the proletariat can we all prosper.'

Basheer nodded as if urging him to continue. The last thing he wanted was a mad comrade.

Agyaat continued, 'From Pashupati to Tirupati, our cadres have been under constant attack by the capitalist state. We have to defend ourselves. Thus, we have started targeting the people. We fight them ideologically and physically. Why, as we speak, one of our best assassins is on the trail of another pseudo-Communist Politburo member of his party. Let's see how soon he gets a Lal Salaam from us here! Haha!' He chuckled at his own joke, unsure of whether Basheer would get it at all.

Agyaat took out a Chinese-made 7.62mm Tokarev Model 213 and toyed with it, pointing it at the pathetic figure at his feet. He bent down and pulled at the tape covering the mouth of the stirring man, gently, almost lovingly, as if enjoying every bit of it.

Mandal's temple was caked with blood. The figure took a few moments to come round and reorient himself to his ghastly surroundings. He groaned, 'Leave me... Please let me go...I have done you no harm...'

'You have not, eh? What about the revolutionaries you betrayed to the police? What about Singur and Nandigram? What about your class-collaboration with the reactionary enemy?'

'How...how am I to blame for what happened there? I am as pained as you are. Stop exploiting it for political gains,' Mandal managed to say, and spat blood.

'What! Political gains?' shouted Agyaat, 'The only gain we want is to make New Delhi hear the voices of the exploited... a sigh that has been suppressed since time immemorial by the feudal and now capitalistic world orders. Tribals die as you create your special economic zones. Peasants and nature suffer as the effluents from your bourgeois factories ruin their land. Workers are exploited and labour laws violated everyday by your democratic governments. Those with money snatch freedom from your quasi-free countries. Global corporations dictate your developmental policies. Still you expect us to remain silent?'

The look on Agyaat's face convinced Mandal that there was no escape.

'We want their voice to be heard, that's all. Even Comrade Bhagat had to turn to violence...to create an explosion to make the deaf hear,' Agyaat repeated softly, as if to convince himself more than his interlocutor.

Mandal shot back, 'And this is how you tackle voices who are different from yours? By kidnapping and torturing them? I hear your supporters plead for the ethical treatment of tribals, Maoist prisoners, and speak up for the dignity and human rights of all in courts and on TV shows back in Delhi. However, in Dantewada and Jhargram you negate the very principles you claim to fight for! People who dare oppose you and your methods simply "vanish", even if they are collectors or social workers! Then you accuse the state of clamping down on you, even if you are the ones who refuse a dialogue. Hypocrites! You say you are not against the country but the system. So why don't you sit and talk? Now is the perfect time for it—a time when the entire country is willing to listen to you.' Mandal stopped; breathing was becoming harder for him.

He looked up and continued, 'And don't even bring Bhagat Singh and other extremists of the Indian freedom struggle into this debate. They despised taking innocent lives. You seek to emulate their methods in a way so perverse that it would have made them throw up. How many more will you slaughter for the establishment of your new system? You do not want the betterment of the proletariat. All you want is a civil war for you to lead your escapist...romantic lives.' Mandal sank back, totally spent by this sudden outburst. Even he did not know he had this in him.

Agyaat was livid, 'Don't tell me what I want. You have been brainwashed by the West for too long. Go and see the living conditions of people. A kilometre away from every mall is a slum. While you feast on burgers, pizzas, fries and coke, people do not even have water to drink and a chapatti a day. Your children go to public schools; their children can do nothing but work as bandhua slaves on a piece of land. You have sold your soul to these capitalist compradors. You are a disgrace to the rights and aspirations of the oppressed of this country. You! And dare you accuse us?'

Mandal saw the Tokarev loom closer. Spent, his tone turned soft, almost pleading, but Basheer had a feeling it was not his own life that he was pleading for, 'Listen to me, Comrade. I beg you, please reconsider what you are doing. What do you plan to achieve by blowing up trains and killing innocents? Your left-wing radicalism is doing to the grassroots movement what,' Mandal's eyes flicked from Agyaat to Basheer and back, 'what Islamic terrorism is doing to Islam. You think you are fighting for something dear, but you are only distorting it and making it a subject of ridicule and hatred. You are just what the right-wingers want. They already want to see us in a bad light; your actions give them a reason to further their prejudices. You are to Communism what Osama bin Laden is to Islam. You are…'

Agyaat did not let Mandal complete his sentence. His mouth contorted with anger as he kicked Mandal and then, without warning, he shot the man lying on the floor. Point blank. Twice. The moaning stopped immediately. It was replaced by a gurgling sound as a mixture of blood and air oozed out of the two punctured holes the bullets had inflicted on Mandal's body. Sound strategy, Basheer realized. Not only was it a display of power and effectiveness, but also of resolve. He let Agyaat be for a minute, and then broke the silence, 'Nice shot. The poor, indoctrinated, brainwashed bastard.'

Agyaat looked at him for a second. He realized that Basheer was there too, a fact he had almost forgotten. Oh yeah, as if he is any less brainwashed, thought Agyaat.

Basheer sat on the bed and asked, 'That done, tell me, why did you call me here?'

'Why do you think I did it?' Agyaat counter-questioned, his mood still damp. Being compared to Bin Laden rather than Guevara was not something he fancied.

Basheer thought for a minute. He had to be very careful of how he put it across, 'To ask for help? You are losing your battle against India. The new state offensive against you has taken the wind out of your sails. You need supplies, weapons, and men, don't you?'

'Yes, though men are in plenty still,' Agyaat stopped as an orderly peeked in, saw the body and dragged it out.

'But I fail to see why you're contacting us this time instead of the Inter Services Intelligence (ISI),' Basheer asked.

Agyaat let the question linger for a while before replying, 'I was hoping you won't ask me that. The ISI officials said they could not help us any longer. Change in policy. The hanging of the 26/11 kid, the war in Khyber, and Pakistan's internal disturbances has made it more cautious for the time being. Although they have assured us that they will back us up very soon, but not now. However, we need the supplies the most right now. If we do not get the supplies soon, then god help us all.'

Basheer smiled in spite of himself, 'You believe in him?'

'In what?' Agyaat could not understand for a moment.

'God.' Basheer pointed a finger upwards.

'Sometimes. Those in power have used the name of god to keep the masses backward and docile. Opium of the masses, you see. But that does not mean revolutionaries like me cannot take that opium once in a while to counter the angst generated by the capitalistic mode of production!' Agyaat confessed, a smile spreading across his lips.

Basheer snorted. He imagined Agyaat, along with all his comrades, being roasted over a pit of fire in hell and screaming, 'A spectre is haunting us—the spectre of sin!' Basheer smiled at the image.

Agyaat's voice cut into his vision, 'We are losing the battle on all fronts. I had to cross into Nepal to meet you. The high command never would have even thought that we would be asking you of all people for help...if you do not mind me saying it, despite some of our earlier joint operations. But if we do not get the supplies now, even God will not be able to save us.'

'He can save anyone! This is sacrilege...please mind your words. I am here for negotiations, not to listen to your insults,' Basheer retorted, his temper rising, fully convinced that this godless Communist was doomed to rot in hell, people's messiah a rat's stinking ass.

Agyaat realized the man he was talking to could not take any denials of the existence of god. Fanatic, he mused. A narrow-minded, short-sighted, anti-positivist fanatic.

Basheer too was having similar thoughts. He did not like these godless, wretched automatons. He had beaten these Communists once in Afghanistan, and he could do it again but he was here to forge a common bond of trust and respect, not antagonism. Tread carefully, Basheer, he thought, the success of your mission depends on it. Calm down, Jung-e-Badr was won not only by brute force, but also by meticulous planning. Basheer inhaled deeply and looked away, trying to rein in his raging emotions.

'You do not like me,' Agyaat said evenly.

'No.' A terse reply came from Basheer.

'Might I ask why?'

'Just…' Basheer had no idea where to start. Also, he knew he might get carried away. Better to shut up than be shot.

'Can I be frank?' Agyaat asked.

'Please do,' Basheer said.

'I do not like you either. I think you represent all that is bad in this world. You are parochial, non-rational, unscientific and opposed to women's liberation. You are an icon of the past, cling to old values and are unsuited to a democratic, free and fair world. You have refused to change with the times.'

'The same can be said of you. This is not 1949 China either,' Basheer cut in.

They both eyed each other, sizing the other up. Then Agyaat broke into laughter. 'Hmm…so we agree on one thing at least. We are different, and we know it.'

'I am not sure I want to agree on that. I know how you tackle the different,' Basheer nodded in the direction of the dead Communist.

A dark cloud passed over Agyaat's face. 'Your way of tackling the other is not very pleasant either,' he countered. Then all of a sudden, the menacing look was gone and was replaced by one of sheer angst and fatigue. 'What do you want?' he asked; he was beginning to get tired of this blame game.

'Maybe exactly what *you* want,' Basheer replied. 'We have a common enemy. The Indian state is killing you in Orissa, Chattisgarh, Jharkhand and so on. The Pakistani army is attacking and finishing us. Our common enemy? The state. A democratic, bourgeois, secular state. Cannot we unite?'

'How? By signing a Memorandum of Understanding?' the Naxalite mocked.

Basheer was not so easily swayed, 'No. Something else.'

'You have a plan?'

'An understanding will be enough for now solemnized by some supplies from us to you,' Basheer said realizing the iron was finally hot, 'on the other hand, maybe I do have a plan.'

Agyaat responded, 'Go on, I'm all ears.'

'You know what the source of our recent troubles is? India and Pakistan have been doing what they probably have never done before. They have started to move away from xenophobia and external prejudices. They are beginning to look inward to create a "better" system. A bit too inward! Bad for us, bad for you,' continued Basheer.

'Ah,' Agyaat said as realization dawned on him. 'So all we have to do is to give them a reason to look at each other again, so that they forget the domestic tangle for a while.'

'Exactly. A while that is enough for us.' Basheer laughed.

'Can you think of something important? Something strategic?' questioned Agyaat.

'Indeed I can.' Basheer took a diary out of his pocket and gave it to Agyaat. He sat down and started to browse through it.

For about ten minutes, Agyaat lay immersed in his reading and Basheer sipped tea that an orderly had brought in. Agyaat finally looked up, shook his head and said, 'NMRC sounds good to me.'

'It is good. Okay, so here is the deal. You provide men and external intelligence, I know you have some factions near Port Blair, the civil society…the oh-our-government-indulges-in-war-against-people types,' Basheer continued almost triumphantly. 'We, on the other hand, will provide leadership, equipment, and even some specially trained officers.'

'Done, but two things… External intelligence? Incidentally, I have a source who is far more valuable,' Agyaat looked at a framed photo kept on his study table and smiled. 'Secondly, you don't really think that we Naxalites need specially trained officers? For every one of us killed, we have killed one civilian or security personnel. It is better than your record in Kashmir. For every four of your men dead, you killed just one.' Agyaat guffawed, his mind racing to arrive at suitable tactics.

Basheer breathed in deeply. They were supposed to be allies, and if this man wanted to derail the train before it started, well, he just would not let it happen.

'It seems, dear Agyaat, you do not know about the Black Storks. The Special Service Group. We do not have their institutional backing, but I have just the man to lead this mission. He is a recipient of Sitara-e-Jurat, four commendations for valour, a former Special Forces commander who has trained with the British Special Air Service, and has operational experience in organizing such raids ranging from the deserts of Somalia to the jungles of Peru. Think you can beat him at his own game?'

'I do not have to. He is on our side,' Agyaat said, realizing the faux pas he had earlier made and trying to make amends, 'it will be a pleasure doing business with you, Basheer sahib. I hope you will be kind enough to ship us some supplies with this understanding?'

'It will be my pleasure, Comrade.' There was no malice in Basheer's voice this time. He had struck a deal. An important one at that. 'I will see what can be done.'

'Mahto will show you out. Nevertheless, Basheer sahib, please dine with us before you leave. Allah Hafiz,' Agyaat remarked, this time almost chummy. Basheer nodded and started to walk out. He stopped midstride, turned back, and smiled. He clenched a fist, raised it towards Agyaat and said, 'Naxal salaam, Comrade.'

The flap of the tent was sealed again.

Research Laboratory Alpha, NMRC

Local time: 1240 hours
Date: 23 April 2014

Dr Suryakant rushed out of his room at the first sound he heard. A sight of frenzied people running about greeted him. His brain struggled to make sense of the situation. It was then, in an incandescent flash, that he understood why the sensible scientific community, rarely shouting when no invention had been made or no one had his birthday, had gone inexplicably mad.

No! This was not supposed to happen! They had promised the base would never be compromised. They had said no harm would come to any man or apparatus. They had assured him it was merely a precaution. They… Before Suryakant could think further, he heard it again and flinched.

The sound of gunfire was new to Suryakant. Funny, how these small projectiles, a nano of what he designed and breathed, freaked him out. He wondered how he was able to withstand the sound of rocket engines when he found the sound of mere guns unnerving. It was probably because he had never heard a missile being launched. Yet.

Suryakant saw a group of his colleagues running away. His first instinct was to duck back into the room and hide. Then he realized it. Oh God, they are after the missile!

His mind seemed to go blank. He ran out of the corridor and tried to sneak past the assailants, or at least past the positions where he thought they were firing from. Firing at him. The golden words of Dr Leonard McCoy — 'I am a doctor, not a commando!' — started to echo in his brain.

As he rounded a bend, he saw two of his colleagues fall to bullets. They screamed. The handful of security personnel in the inner facility were being easily overpowered. It was a sensitive location, not many were cleared to serve here. For that reason, the security had focused on defending the outer perimeter. Why defend the nucleus when nothing can get past the outer periphery? The logic had been sound, only now did Suryakant realize that it was backfiring.

He saw blood splattered on the white-tiled floor, making it slippery. He started to sob, his tears coming fast as he ran. Someone shouted. He stopped and peeked over his shoulder, it was a friend. The man motioned with flailing hands and whispered hoarsely, 'Get away, doctor sa'ab. Run!' Suryakant stood rooted to the spot. He was a man of thoughts, not a man of action.

A voice shook him up. It was his superego. Without thinking, he climbed atop the nearest table and shouted in a scratchy but surprisingly loud voice, 'Stop! Please stop. Who are you? What do you want?'

He heard the guns stop for a moment. He saw a ray of hope shining through the dark. Then, without warning, the guns started firing again. This time he felt the bullets ricochet near him. Suryakant did not have time to think. He jumped off the table to run for cover. Then, with a loud bang, he felt the world explode in a thousand brilliant colours...before it started to go dim. Time seemed to slow down.

He looked down to see his lab coat was stained with blood. His blood. A volley of bullets had found their target. Suryakant felt no pain. His knees buckled and his lifeless body crashed to the ground.

◆

The second group continued its advance towards the main facility. Three sentry posts and four barricades had been overrun even before the security forces had time to mount a defence. No alarm had been sounded in time. The attackers had had no trouble overpowering stray pickets and routine patrols.

Their strategy was ruthless. The attackers opened fire the moment anything or anyone moved. The atmosphere reverberated with the din of MP-5 suppressed sub-machine guns, SA80, Kalashnikovs and M16s. The attackers had been clearly briefed on the layout and the security drills. The heaviest concentration of security was around the perimeter. Once that was neutralized, getting in was a piece of cake. The forward teams had already sabotaged the lone MI-35 Hind Gunship assigned to the base. It would be flying no sorties to defend the perimeter.

They entered the inner facility with surprising swiftness, and divided in sub-groups, each with a particular area to secure and sanitize.

The leader of the group ran towards the flight lab; resistance was sporadic and scattered. However, the resistance had another deadly flaw that doomed its effectiveness, the leader thought. Fear.

The security here was caught unawares. They did not know who they were facing. A holiday posting had suddenly gone horribly wrong. The first teams to enter the facility had destroyed their contact with the outside world, they faced innumerable odds, and to top it all, most of them were civilians, unsure of what to do in such crisis situations.

But we had been thoroughly briefed, trained, re-trained and perfected, the leader thought and chuckled. Trained to kill.

They saw a man shouting for order. The leader turned around. The man, trying to exude confidence, surrendered. 'Yes, let us talk, shall we?' the leader muttered under his breath, grinned, and shot that man in the chest the very moment. He moved on almost callously.

Their guns kept firing. Their hands were aching by now because of changing magazines continuously. They left no one alive. Dead men tell no tales. Researchers, security personnel and maintenance workers, all lay dead, blissfully ignorant of the impending doom. Finally, when all proof of life had been eliminated, they stopped firing.

Stage One was complete. Time for Stage Two. Soon they would have India at her knees. The world would follow.

◆

The intruders got to work immediately after firing the last bullet. Each one of them had been assigned a specific task to complete. They did not run around or fret to locate their objectives, like the disorganized tribesmen they earlier posed as, would have. They were familiar with the entire area. They had been made to memorize its map—locations, tunnels and landmarks—in painstaking detail.

The men streamed into the assembly room where the components of Pralay were kept. The ultra modern equipment did not perturb the farmers. They did not hesitate. In fact, they felt more at ease. Technology was roughly the same across nations and cultures — it provided them common ground. With extraordinary focus, speed and finesse, they started assembling the missile. As was the case with the base, it was the same with the missile. They had absorbed its blueprints and the technical know-how required for the launch to such an extent that they could have assembled it even in their sleep.

'How much time will it take?' asked a heavily-built man with a rough military demeanour. This was the first time someone in the group spoke. No one looked up but the one to whom the question was addressed.

'Seven hours, sir. Just as we estimated it will,' he replied.

A brief flicker of relief played on a few faces. 'Hurry up!' Thereafter, silence resumed.

The leader whipped out a radio and a short coded burst followed from the sole operational radio on the base. Piercing the atmosphere, it headed for a Chinese military satellite passing overhead at that precise moment. The transponders realigned themselves and passed on the message to a secure location in the North West Frontier Province of Pakistan.

The leader smiled. Glory was coming to them on the wings of death.

Army House, New Delhi, India

Local time: 1430 hours
Date: 23 April 2014

Bloody hell, thought General Rohit Malhotra, chief of army staff and former chair of the Strategic Forces Command, as he placed his coffee mug on the dining table and reached across to receive the hotline his deferent orderly held out to him. General Malhotra's face had a vacant expression. Something had been gnawing at him for a long time. It was not exactly painful, but it made him restless. He felt incomplete; something was missing in his life. Not even the medals and decorations bestowed upon him could give him a sense of satisfaction now. Nor did the status of the 'most-liked' general of the Indian army given to him by the press do any good. Malhotra was thinking of doing something constructive, which would make him feel alive again. He wanted a new goal, which he could pursue the rest of his life.

Handling calls was the last thing in the world he wanted to do right now. Nevertheless, the call was very urgent and unwillingly Malhotra had to break his chain of thoughts. He answered it, 'Yes...what?'

Exactly seven minutes later his car was speeding towards the PM's residence. Sitting glumly inside the car, Malhotra wondered what had happened. He was not told much over the phone, only that an incident had happened, a big one at that, and he was immediately required. He tried to guess what it could be — the Directorate of Military Intelligence had predicted no major development.

He had been ordered to report immediately to the PM's residence for an emergency National Disaster Response Council (NDRC) meeting. Malhotra would have been looking forward to another fruitless discussion on tackling infiltration in the Kashmir Valley or violence in the Northeast had it not been for the urgency in the PM's voice. Well, this was surprising; he rarely used to get calls directly from the PM. Usually his secretary would call. It implied something big had happened — or was about to happen.

Malhotra hoped it was not the prime minister reversing his earlier anti-Naxal policy. That was one of his biggest concerns these days. For Malhotra, Naxalism was probably the greatest threats to Indian national security. Despite the announcement of multiple Integrated Action Plans (IAPs) by the Centre and state governments, the money allocated for the development of the affected districts had not reached the grassroot level. In cases where it had, subsequent implementation was rendered impossible by the total domination of Naxalites over land. The condition got from bad to worse, for any remedy, even when properly administered, failed to cure the menace of Naxal hegemony on the minds of people.

Finally, it had happened — the Big Putsch of encircling urban centres and laying siege. A couple of months ago, the Maoists-Naxalites had overrun and taken de facto control of a number of district headquarters in four Indian states. They isolated civilian administration, paralyzed governmental machinery, looted armouries and banks, indulged in executions of public functionaries and were almost on the verge of declaring their states liberated Red Republics when Malhotra had decided that the army could no longer fear bloodying its hands.

The political executive had taken no drastic steps to counter this situation and had stuck to their wait-and-watch approach to Naxalism, an approach that they had followed to the letter since the past four years. The army too, for various reasons, had not been keen to engage in proactive steps to wrestle control back from the Naxalites. The reasons were many. One, it was already bogged down in Kashmir and the Northeast. Any more theatres of engagement would have led to more casualties; the morale would have sagged further. Two, the terms of engagement in the impenetrable forests made the Red Corridor a prospective Dien Bien Phu for all the sanitizing forces. An armed Naxalite was the same as an ordinary villager — travelling through fields on a bicycle carrying a stick or a concealed gun. Identification was next to impossible. Air attack was not only useless but also increased the chances of collateral damage. The army wanted no Vietnams to its discredit and chose to stay away.

Thirdly, and most importantly, Malhotra's corps commanders had raised serious concerns, though in private, about how the army jawans could easily have been brainwashed and converted to follow the Naxal cause by the wily propaganda machine of the extreme left. The last thing the generals wanted was to have battalions deep inside hostile territory reading Naxal pamphlets on Marx and Lenin, interacting with 'liberated' tribals, and be indoctrinated by the Naxalites to turn against the Indian state itself. 'Hmm... class-war? This Marx seems like a decent chap. What he said makes sense...Why should we fight our poor brothers and give away our lives for 5000 rupees a month?' was not what they expected to hear from their jawans. If some captured Naxal commanders were to be believed, the sudden spurt in kidnappings of government officers and killings of tribals was meant to be the bait. It displayed the inability of the state police and the Central paramilitary forces to tackle the Naxalites — thereby forcing the Centre to deploy the army in combat zones. This decision would have given the Naxalite command direct access to the lower ranks of the army, in the red terrain, away from their bases, and exposed to a sustained ideological attack through propaganda and psychological warfare. This would have been the ultimate victory for the Naxalites. The hounds of state turned on the state itself.

However, things had to change one day. It was then that Malhotra, along with the then home secretary (and now the current Cabinet secretary), Ajay P. Mishra, an IAS officer of the 1982 batch, had decided to pick up cudgels to make the political leadership listen. They had convinced the PM to implement an integrated anti-Naxal action-plan prepared by the Institute of Defence Studies and Analysis (IDSA), the Institute of Peace and Conflict Studies (IPCS), and the Special Centre for Internal Security of the Jawaharlal Nehru University.

The report called for a multi-staged, multi-pronged operation consisting of three stages. Stage One proceeded by notifying severely Naxalite-infested areas in the Red Corridor as 'Disturbed Areas' and brought them under the purview of the Armed Forces (Special Powers) Act (AFSPA) that conferred special powers upon the armed forces to restore law and order. The purpose was to regain physical control of territory by utilizing the army, Cobras (CRPF), Jaguars and Greyhounds with close-air support provided by the Indian air force gunships operating from the Anti-Naxal Joint Operations Command

(ANJOC) set up at Raipur. ANJOC worked under the direct supervision of the Special Secretary (Naxalism) at the Ministry of Home Affairs. It aimed to flush the Naxalite-Maoist combine out into the open, strengthen the law and order machinery, run a sanitizing operation, and thereby pass control of the affected districts back into the hands of the civilian administration.

Stage Two required to isolate covert and overt political support to the Naxalites, negate any foreign aid to their cause, and de-doctrinate (but not de-politicize) the lured away youth.

With the rule of law thus established, would begin Stage Three. It aimed at consolidating the victories of the army by pacifying the people of the region and promptly initiating schemes for equitable socio-economic development. This was to be achieved by zealously fortifying the Panchayati Raj Institutions with regular meetings of the sarpanches with the chief minister and chief secretary of the respective state, apart from a representative of the Central government. Grievance redressal was to be the focus and the judiciary was to act as an effective appellate authority in the guise of fast-track courts. Steps were to be taken to ensure that the decision-making became bottom-up, participative, accountable and transparent to the people, and red-tape was minimized.

Presently, Stage One was well under way and the Naxalites-Maoists were about to be routed — their command and control structures smashed, their communication lines cut, their supplies depleted, political and foreign support quashed, and their morale crushed.

Convincing people to do it had not been easy. The prime minister had called a national-level high-powered meeting. The chief ministers of the affected states, when asked for their opinion on the implementation of the report, had been the biggest obstacles. They had vehemently protested against the use of force to dislodge the Naxalite-Maoist combine from their hold. Elections were coming, they had argued, and to strike out at their own people was far more dangerous than just sitting on files. The states did not like military action to be initiated against the insurgents at such a grand scale. As long as the people of their state voted for them, the Centre could keep barking.

The chief ministers also knew that allowing the army access to their states in combat operations would not merely turn their home turfs into active war zones and thus cost precious lives but may also cost even more precious votes. They had howled in protest and tried to convince the PM to give the Naxals another chance and to let things be.

'We cannot send the army against the Naxals, they're not… terrorists (gasp!), are they? They are our own people, forced to turn to violence by want and hunger. It is an internal matter! Let the state police deal with it' was the argument put forth.

The top bureaucrat had heard them out patiently and retorted, in the unctuous civil way he was known for: 'So why use the army against terrorists in Jammu and Kashmir or the Northeast? Are not they our own too? Where do we draw a line between external aggression and internal disturbance?'

The chief ministers had looked at each other, confused and shocked. The prime minister, briefed by the wily Ajay Mishra and the resolute Rohit Malhotra, had given the chief ministers a simple choice — agree with the PM in public and allow the army in, or the PM would be forced to act as per Article 356/365 of the Constitution and recommend the imposition of President's Rule in the rebel state, thereby dissolving state legislatures. If even then leaders at the state-level fostered discord, the PM, with a clear mandate in both the Lok Sabha and the Rajya Sabha, would turn to Article 3 of the Constitution and change the boundaries of the states to the disadvantage of the party ruling the state at the time.

The chief ministers were away from their party high commands, their voters and the briefings of their conniving political secretaries. They had no option but to bow down to such cowboy tactics, simply because they were up against a unified military and bureaucracy, both supported by the supreme political executive, the PM. The chief ministers had babbled amongst each other. They were unsure of what to do.

Taking advantage of the vacuum, Mishra had continued, 'Yes, I think you are right. We do not need Central forces in states as the state police are more than capable of handling threats. Thus, we do not need the presence of the Central Paramilitary Forces in the states. We should withdraw regular army and all Central forces from all these locations. Let the states deal with such law and order problems themselves. We can start by pulling out all the Central paramilitary personnel from unwilling states, including those engaged in VIP protection. NSG, CRPF, CISF, BSF. All out.'

His proposal was met by a ghastly silence. Someone coughed uncomfortably. The CMs were livid. How could it happen? National territorial sovereignty was above all! The ploy had worked. The prime minister, Bipolab Roy, a young dynamic reformer, the first member from a party overtly left of centre to rule India, had agreed and declared with his trademark charisma, 'Gentlemen, we are a union, not a federation. The army moves in.'

Fifteen days later, the Maoists were on the run.

By now, the army chief's bulletproof black, shiny ambassador had reached the PM's residence. Like other cars going in and out of the PM house, his car was thoroughly checked. Though he was the chief of the Indian army, the Special Protection Group (SPG) took nothing for granted. Moreover, security had been beefed up after attacks on the high office holders of the country by terrorists disguised as Red-beacon functionaries.

Malhotra had no problems with the security checks. What he had problems with was what unfolded after that.

Model Town, Rawalpindi, Pakistan

Local time: 1500 hours
Date: <u>07 April 2014</u>

'So even a patriot like you would spill your own blood rather than that of the enemy?' demanded Yasser Basheer, his fists clenched, face red and eyes wide in disbelief.

He was addressing a middle-aged man with salt and pepper hair. Basheer had spent most of his army life with Asif Hussain Chowdhury. Both had been brother officers: promising, young and talented. It was said that Basheer, if he continued the way he was, would go on to become the chief of army staff of Pakistan one day. All had gone well, until that fateful day, years ago.

It was a routine operation in the Federally Administered Tribal Areas (FATA) against holed-up jihadists. These two friends, both of them lieutenant colonels, had been supervising counterinsurgency units when tribesmen unhappy at Pakistan's role in the Allied invasions had attacked them. The units commanded by Basheer and Chowdhury came under heavy fire, and were pinned down on all sides. Chowdhury had retaliated by calling in air support. Basheer did not. In fact, he asked the troops under his command to stand down.

Basheer was caught, taken to a remote seminary and assimilated by the Islamists. Six weeks later, the Allied forces had rescued him, but the damage had been done by then. Basheer was a shattered, indoctrinated and bitter man. Consequently, he had to spend the next six months in a mental hospital abroad for rehabilitation counselling and medical assistance, so jolted had he been.

When Basheer finally returned to Pakistan, he was court-martialled for disobeying a direct order, and for putting lives under his command in danger, but that mattered little to him. He was now accustomed to look at the bigger picture. His newfound mentors had told him about what a waste infighting was. The enemy was always changing his face, and one needed to adapt with him to be able to defeat him. Some lives had to be sacrificed for the betterment of the entire world. How could he have forgotten such a crucial fact? How could he have allowed jingoism to dictate his actions and prevent him to work for the greater goals of humanity? Basheer had changed that day. He had distanced himself from the army — which had been his life for over twenty years. He went closer to God instead.

Basheer's mind came back to the present. He may have been disgraced by the army, but there was no dearth of his followers in Pakistan, even though the new government distanced itself from him. However, to the people, he was a hero. When a hero asks for an audience, even a lieutenant general has to relent. Especially the one who wished it was he who had had the courage to halt strikes on his brothers that day. Their cries still returned to haunt Chowdhury at nights — was there a chance to make things right? He really hoped there was.

The two men were sitting in the plush drawing room of a three-storey villa in the high-end locality of Model Town. The villa belonged to Basheer's friend. Basheer spoke aloud again,

'So you would rather kill innocent women and children than the actual enemy?'

Lieutenant General Chowdhury merely shrugged, surprised at the accusatory tone, 'I had no choice. No one wants to kill. But sometimes it becomes necessary. What these people are doing leave us with no alternative. We kill by profession, not by choice.'

'Why are you of all people talking like this, Yak? The jihadists are fighting against the Westernization of Pakistani society in the name of modernization. This country was founded in the name of Islam and would always remain an Islamic country. Pakistan will and should never become a secular state. These people are Ghazis, fighting for the will of Allah,' Basheer retorted angrily.

'Allah has nothing to do with it. Their driving force is vengeance, narrow-mindedness and greed,' Chowdhury muttered evenly.

Basheer flared up, 'Quaid-e-Azam never envisioned a secular Pakistan but laid the basis of an enlightened and modern Islamic state. Our leadership chose Pakistan to be like that. Who is this new government to question the words of our founding fathers? Yak, you think you are serving Pakistan by killing people in indiscriminate attacks? By supporting the West? By selling our people to Western multinational corporations? By allowing the Americans to blast our sovereign territory to take you-know-who out right under our noses?'

'That is the policy of the government. What I want is irrelevant…We had to make that deal since bigger things were at stake…' Chowdhury did not know what he was supposed to say. All he knew was that he did not want to make the same choice that he had made years ago.

'A civilian government, corrupted by Western hypocrisy, cannot impose itself on the Pakistani people. We have defended Pakistan against all odds, and now we are on the verge of disintegration because of our infighting! Can you live with that? Not long ago, I remember you were a fiery young captain who wanted to make Pakistan a superpower. Is this your resolve?' Basheer asked.

'Listen, Basheer, these people leave the government no choice. Do you remember how local bazaars used to be when we were young? How they were filled with rounaq until late at nights? How the common Pakistani was a carefree citizen who wanted to enjoy life to the hilt?' Chowdhury counter-questioned.

'What is your point?' Basheer asked patronizingly. Poor Westernized fool, he thought, refusing to see that he is just a pawn in Western hands who is made to believe that he is serving the interests of his own nation.

Chowdhury wanted to make his stand clear. He said, 'Go and see the bazaars now. They are empty. After seven in the evening, shopkeepers start downing their shutters. Lahore is no more the cultural capital. Culture has fled away, fearing the wrath of the fundamentalists. Peshawar seems like a war zone. Karachi lives in perpetual fear. Islamabad shudders at every loud noise. A Pakistani feels threatened at all times. Pakistanis have become the objects of suspicion, ridicule and fear all over the world. Such is the mahaul these people have created. Bomb blasts, suicide attacks, assassinations—they have not even left mosques and schools! No one can speak out for freedom, democracy and secularism. One is publically gunned down if one does. Remember Salman Taseer? You expect the government to give them leeway?'

'They were provoked, you know. We do not want to attack civilians, but we need to send out a strong message. You were the ones who attacked us first. The Soviets, the Americans, and now our own army.'

Basheer sighed and continued, 'You think it is easy for us to see our women and children die helplessly when death rains from Allied bombing missions? You think we want to kill our own people? No! But we have had enough. We seek to return to the original path. We want to create a Caliphate governed by just, humane and equal rules and where hedonism would be crushed. We are willing to lay down our lives fighting, but we are not terrorists. That is what the larger army calls the smaller army. We are freedom fighters.' Basheer had a strange fire in his eyes.

Chowdhury caught him. 'We?' he asked.

'Yes. I was court-martialled, remember?' Basheer responded, 'I consider myself closer to Allah now and work with like-minded people to spread his word. However, you... just look at the direction in which you are propelling Pakistan! Tell me, are you happy?' Basheer asked.

'Happy? With what?'

'Are you happy with the army killing its own people?' Basheer asked, his voice indicting Chowdhury for all these years of inaction.

'Of course not! But what can I do?' Chowdhury tried to defend himself.

'You can do a lot. You want to prevent a civil war, right? We cannot have another 1971, can we? We cannot have any more divisions of Pakistan,' Basheer said emphatically.

'No, we cannot, ' Chowdhury conceded.

'Don't you want to bring back the good old days. We on our side…they on theirs. No quarters given or taken. Fight and die honourably like men, not rats.' Basheer seemed unstoppable. He started pacing up and down in front of Chowdhury, his voice raised, his eyes burning.

'Uhmm…yes' was all a surprised Chowdhury managed to say, the portals of time being opened to him for one last chance to correct his past mistakes.

'Don't you want to regain the lost glory of the Pakistani military? Don't you recall how the last attempted coup in early 2012 made Pakistani people so hostile towards the army? Don't you want to get back our lost respect? The army getting its rightful powers back from this pathetic civilian government? ' Basheer was not done yet enticing his old chum.

'Of course!' Chowdhury felt better all of a sudden. A part of him, a part that he had suppressed for long, was speaking through Basheer. Hearing him made sense. He sounded soothing.

'Don't you want to show India her place?' Basheer asked.

'Yeah,' responded Chowdhury, his voice rising. He realized he was no longer Basheer's equal, and that he had to follow what Basheer told him to do.

'And if along with all this, you get promotions, glory, riches and fame, would you mind?'

Chowdhury managed a smile; this was not as hard as he had thought. This time, he would choose his own master. He would be an old man soon, and old men needed to go closer to god. Or cash. Lots of it.

'Try to look at the bigger picture, Yak. If a tremendous plan were to come knocking at your doorstep, would you be foolish or cowardly enough to send it away?' Basheer cooed.

'Ha ha! Spoken like a true siyasatdan. I have heard you are into politics and all. Jolly good, old boy!' Chowdhury tried to lighten the conversation now that the deal had already been made by Basheer and accepted by Chowdhury.

Basheer smiled and remarked, 'Politics is just the means. Salvation is the end.'

'Is that what you wanted to discuss with me?' Chowdhury felt stirrings of adrenalin after a long time. Action at last, after all these years of mindless paperwork.

'Yes.' Basheer relaxed. Calm descended over him. He sat in front of Chowdhury and looked straight into his eyes. He kept quiet, giving Chowdhury time to absorb what he had said.

Chowdhury was cautious, 'What exactly do you want from me, Basheer?'

'That you be true to yourself, my friend, make the right choice this time and atone for your earlier sins.' Basheer patted his friend's shoulder as he went stiff with the memories.

'How?' Chowdhury needed guidance. Deep down he knew what the truth was — that he *wanted* to be convinced by Basheer. He wanted to be persuaded, to be shown the right path.

'By helping us…' Basheer kept driving him towards what he wanted.

'But how?'

'We want equipment and supplies,' disclosed Basheer.

'What for?' Chowdhury was suddenly on his guard.

'Don't worry. Not for use on the Pakistani soil. We plan to raid an Indian base,' Basheer assured him.

'What!!' Chowdhury suddenly did not know whether to feel happy or be alarmed. 'Which one?'

Basheer handed Chowdhury a file. He took it and read it, his eyes widening with each line he read. 'This is big!' he said.

'We need it to be big. Operation Tupac* has failed. We need to launch another offensive. The bigger, the better. Think of the blow it will be for the Indians...' Basheer's voice was distant by now; he was lost in imagining the glory the future might bring to both of them.

Chowdhury whistled softly. 'Men and material?'

'Material more than men. Men we already have. A gift of some Indian rebels.' Basheer smiled.

'It is difficult. I am bound to raise suspicion because of my requisition orders. How can I...?' Chowdhury asked him, though in his heart of hearts he knew his mind was made up.

'You will find a way,' Basheer assured him, 'you will save Pakistani lives, prevent a civil war, frighten India and show her the Pakistani might. It will be back to the good old days when politics had not corrupted us. What more do you, a loyal Pakistani citizen, want?'

Lieutenant General Chowdhury studied him carefully. He thought for a few seconds and said, 'I will see what can be done,' and then looked away.

Basheer smiled. The die was cast.

---

*Operation Tupac was an action plan initiated by Pakistani President Zia Ul Haq in 1988 to disintegrate India by exploiting porous borders with Nepal and Bangladesh to set up spy bases and engage in strategic sabotage.

7 Race Course Road, Prime Minister's Residence, New Delhi, India

Local time: 1500 hours
Date: 23 April 2014

The black car swerved and came to a halt, as the pilot vehicles drove tangentially. A guard opened the door even before the car engine went off. General Malhotra was greeted by a whiff of sizzling air the moment he stepped out. His life in an air-conditioned atmosphere had almost made him forget how cruel the Delhi summer can be. Moreover, this year was hotter than usual. Must be because of the weapon discharges all around the world that contribute to global warming, he mused. After a long time, Malhotra felt like he was back in Rajasthan. I hope all these years of babu-giri have not made me soft, he thought, and smiled to himself.

The minute from the car to the main door seemed like a long trek across the Thar. He cursed himself inwardly as he was ushered by the deputies directly to the conference room. He saluted the already sitting ministers and took his seat. He saw some other additions apart from the regular members of the National Disaster Response Council. It seemed something big was afoot. Next to him sat CR Prasad, director of Research and Analysis Wing (RAW) and Akash Gupta representing the Intelligence Bureau (IB). The naval chief Admiral Yashpal

Sapra and Air Chief Marshal Vikramjeet Sharma sat huddled in deep conversation with Ajay Mishra, the cabinet secretary. Dr Amrit Pal Dhillon, the head of DRDO was a special invitee, who was nervous as hell, as evident from his frequent glances at Mishra.

Mishra may have been a civilian, but RAW reported directly to the Cabinet Secretariat — that is, to him. Although the control of the cabinet secretary over RAW was limited to administrative and financial matters, with very little say in operational and policy matters, Mishra was an extremely important cog in the hierarchy, and an intelligent one at that. No wonder, the defence chiefs, though already briefed by their directorates of air and naval intelligences, sought him to clarify any doubts.

To the right of the PM's chair sat the home minister, the defence minister and the external affairs minister. A couple of other ministers were present, apart from the two Leaders of the Opposition (from Lok Sabha and Rajya Sabha) and some party functionaries. The elections were close; they certainly did not want anything to upset their apple carts.

'So, what is the matter?' asked Malhotra, guessing if anybody present had any idea about what inspired this untimely meet. Heads turned to look at each other. Shrugs were forthcoming but answers were not.

With the quorum now complete, the door opened and the PM entered. He scanned the room, his eyes boring into the persons in attendance. After a long wait, the man spoke. Bipolab Roy, a young Stanford-educated reformer who led his party to a landslide victory in the previous general elections, was not easy to tackle once he had made up his mind. And today, he had decided to be pissed with everyone present.

'You want to know what the matter is, Malhotra sahib,

then ask him,' the prime minister replied having overheard the question, and jabbed a finger at the director general of DRDO, who had a beam-me-up-Scotty expression on his face. Oh boy, he looks enraged, thought Malhotra. He had learned that one should never let a neta not blame people around him, for it was the neta's pet alibi.

All heads turned to Dhillon, the director general of DRDO, who squirmed uncomfortably in his chair. He was as aghast at what had happened — and was desperately hoping to think of something brilliant to rescue him from the soup.

'Tell them,' hissed the prime minister.

Dhillon began addressing the gathering as keen faces turned to watch him. 'Well, I hope you know about the development of our new missile Pralay...which was to be test-fired soon at NMRC in Andaman.'

'Yes, and you also assured me it was off the enemy's radar,' the PM butted in. Dhillon fell silent, his eyes downcast.

'Please continue,' the defence minister spoke up.

Dhillon waited for some time and said, 'So, the missile programme has developed a...snag.

'A snag?' the home minister asked cautiously.

'Yes, snag,' Dhillon managed to squeak.

'What is it?' the Leader of Opposition, who was observing the proceedings finally jumped into the conversation, his interest piqued by the opportunity such a development provided.

'Why is no scientist present here then? Call the Pralay mission directors. We need their inputs,' the naval chief also chipped in.

'They are...er...inaccessible at the moment,' replied Gupta, speaking up for his assailed counterpart. It takes two to tango. He knew they must hang together, or they would have hung separately.

'Stop beating around the bush, will you? Tell us what the snag is. Magnitude?' The defence minister was almost hysterical. I am not losing the next election because a scientist forgot to put the bolts in the correct spots, he thought furiously.

'A rather large one, sir,' Prasad said.

'How large?' Air Chief Marshal Sharma asked.

'Depends on how you look at it, but I reckon...quite.'

'For God's sake, are we getting any straight answers from you two?'

Malhotra knew about that missile, of course. What happened to it? Malfunction? Any other technical snag? He was hoping that Pralay would join his arsenal at the earliest.

'We have reports that the missile centre has been taken over by hostile forces,' Prasad formed the words slowly, as if that would help the information to sink in.

Malhotra's jaw dropped open. 'Taken over? What do you mean by that?'

'Yes, allow me to explain. It was taken over. To be precise, overtaken by someone.' How droll, Mr Thompson! Gupta saved Prasad again.

'But how? And by whom?' Malhotra said.

'It is your job to find the answers to those questions, General. This represents one of the biggest failures in the history of Indian intelligence. It is one of the most grave threats to our national security,' the PM retorted. He may have been speaking to Prasad and Gupta in particular but everyone in the room seemed to cringe at the tone. The PM looked frustrated. Of course, he should be. His biggest achievement in the field of defence was on the verge of biting dust.

'What else do we know?' the defence minister asked, trying to put the shock behind.

'The infiltrators are armed with automatic weapons and there are around twenty-five to thirty of them, though that's an approximation,' the RAW chief replied.

'What do they want? Ransom? I must appreciate their choice. We could not have complied if they had captured our people. Some lives are dispensable. Whilst Pralay is not. Definitely not,' the defence minister thought for a moment and spoke again, quite needlessly, 'please do not quote this outside.'

'How did they manage to break in?' the PM asked.

'The complex was lightly guarded, sir. We thought assigning more guards would attract attention. Therefore, we let its remoteness be its primary defence. We assigned a regular CISF guarding contingent led by a lieutenant colonel on deputation,' Prasad said.

'The question, right now, is not how they got in, but what do they want,' Malhotra asked.

'But what if they do not want ransom? Maybe they want something else. Who knows, they could even try to destroy it. Hell, they can even smuggle it out!' the defence minister told the gathering.

'They cannot,' said the head of DRDO. 'I just had a word with the key DRDO personnel responsible for erecting the security apparatuses on the base. They assured me that Dr Suryakant had himself devised the security measures and his skills with computers and designing are almost unsurpassable. The hardware and software of Pralay is locked inside a blast-proof chamber, the entry to which is protected by a biometric thirty-two character random-shifting key. Access to the main silo containing Pralay or the master control facility is next to impossible for anyone not knowing the password or not having proper identification. They may use TNT on those chambers without a scratch. So the missile is, for the moment, secure.'

'Are you sure?' asked the PM again and then looked at his intelligence heads, 'do you concur?'

'Yes, sir,' the heads of IB and RAW said in unison, 'the HUMINT from DRDO was pretty specific about this. Almost everyone believes that access to the missile is impossible for those with no idea about the passwords'.

'What do you suggest we do?' the PM asked the service chiefs.

'As far as I know, sir, by now the enemy should be well dug in there. We should first study the situation. The centre has only one entrance. The hills block entry to the complex from three sides and I presume the sole entrance will be well-defended. Moreover, they will not be going anywhere nor can do anything since their quarry is sealed behind closed doors. They are trapped,' said Admiral Sapra.

'It was the same case when we were in control of the centre. If they could easily barge in, so could we. What is the difference?' asked the home minister.

'There is a very big difference. In our case, we were not expecting anything to happen. We thought the secrecy maintained about this project and the remote location of the centre would shield it from prying enemy eyes. Nevertheless, we were wrong. We did not expect to be attacked. That is why our security there was so relaxed. This was the best way to fool enemy intelligence. But now, on the other hand, I am sure they will be expecting us,' replied Sharma.

'Can't you do anything?' the PM addressed the air chief.

'What do you want me to do, sir? We cannot bomb the centre and possibly risk the destruction of all our missiles and warheads. Sorry, this is not my cup of tea. Rohit will have to help you there,' Sharma replied pointing at General Malhotra.

'Malhotra, move your troops, storm the place, I want the missile centre sterilized. The test will happen as scheduled. More importantly, I am not going to a United Nations meeting to talk about India's permanent membership in the Security Council when a vital missile base of ours is in the hands of terrorists. Such a scenario is precisely what we accuse our neighbours to be capable of. I have to leave for the UN General Assembly tomorrow night, and by then I want the facility to be ours again,' the PM made his decision. It was no longer about the next elections, but about the future of his country vis-à-vis its image at the global forum. He had to convince the world that India is a safe destination not only for foreign investment but also for nuclear commerce. It would be a slap on his face if the news of what had happened broke out when he was addressing the UN General Assembly. 'Secure the base. Now!' commanded the PM. His order had a ring of finality to it.

'I repeat, sir, that can cause massive casualties among our men. The infiltrators must be armed to the teeth. Moreover, they cannot damage the missile parts or even copy its plans. The base is under an ultra-safe security net. The attackers may have gained entry to the base, but they can never gain access to the central silo. Even with the personnel neutralized, the software programme will defend itself and refuse to divulge any information to all but who have the security password. Let them rot there while we plan to smoke them out!' Sapra gently reminded the PM of an alternative action plan.

'Let there be casualties. The test should take place tomorrow as scheduled. Do it. This is what you are paid to do,' thundered the PM, in perhaps a momentary lapse of control.

Malhotra, who until now had remained a tight-lipped spectator in the discussion, spoke, 'Sir, my men will need time to observe and evaluate the enemy. I suggest we slow down the pace of this operation based on the assurances of safety we have from DRDO.'

'Time is something that I do not have right now. The test...' said the PM impatiently.

'...can be delayed for a few days, sir. So can the trip. It will not harm anyone. I am sure the Ministry of External Affairs can come up with some good reasons to postpone your meet. In addition, I too feel that time is of the essence, but let us not rush hastily into a hornet's nest,' pressed Malhotra.

This really led PM Roy to fume, 'Look, General Malhotra, the military does not dictate policy in New Delhi. You have been given a direct order.'

'I am not refusing to do as you say, sir. All I am asking for is a little time so that we can understand the terrain and precious lives can be saved. We already are suffering heavy losses in the war against Naxalism. Operation Green Gold is tremendously successful, but at a terrible cost. Every fourth soldier in the Red Corridor either does not make it back or is disabled, sometimes permanently. There is resentment brewing amongst the ranks.'

'India is a democracy, General, not the military. You fight to save democracy, not to practice it,' the PM said.

'Perhaps we should...'

Others sitting in the room watched with keen interest the verbal sparring between the PM and the general. The military men heard the heated discussion with an air of rebellion and the politicians with growing disdain. Even the faces of Gupta from IB and Prasad from RAW, both IPS officers rather than military men, showed that they were siding with one lot more than the other. Only a certain creed of the civil servants showed no overt reaction and refused to take sides. Perhaps that was why the IPS was IPS, thought the cabinet secretary. Too much thinking affected their brains and hampered the cold, rational and emotionless demeanour required of a true administrator, as their IAS counterparts would have said. The cabinet secretary and his bureaucratic buccaneers were expressionless, silent, and guarded in their involvement. The reason: whoever was to win this debate today, the IAS had to ensure it was on the winning side. Like always.

'I order you to move your men to NMRC and punish all those who dared to rise against us, even if it means the loss of some of our men. The nation will never forget their ultimate sacrifice for the country,' screeched PM Roy.

'Do not teach me what my job is,' said Malhotra in a steely voice. 'I cannot risk the lives of my men for a mere speech at the UN.'

The prime minister was shocked. He opened his mouth to say something but then decided against it. He leaned back into his chair, closed his eyes for some time, rubbed his temples and then stared at the general. The PM actually smiled as he spoke after what seemed like a long time, though the smile did not reach his eyes, 'Very well, I call these creative differences. How unfortunate, General. But the show must go on. I am sure your resignation will be on my table by this evening.' The PM got up, signalling the end of the meeting.

Malhotra stared at him for a long time. Then, in a low voice, he said, 'Yes, sir. As you wish.'

'What about the press. What do we tell them? Sooner or later, they will come to know about this,' asked a worried minister.

'Not a word of this to anyone. This is an ultra-secret location we are talking about. OK, not so secure, but what the hell! I hope that by this time tomorrow we will be standing over the remains of the infiltrators. Then we will break the news. Thank you for your time, gentlemen.' Roy left the room.

Malhotra shuffled his papers and folded them, ready to leave. This would be his last day as the chief of army staff. He was going to resign. The insolence to disobey an order would not be tolerated in a democracy, even if it meant saving lives. He had initiated the anti-Naxal campaign, and the deaths of his men fighting in the Red Corridor weighed heavily on his conscience.

He shook hands with the bunch and left. The service chiefs realized he was in a rotten mood and kept their distance. Malhotra walked out towards his car. His driver opened the door and he climbed in. At a distance, he saw the Indian flag fluttering. This is all, he thought, a Neruda poem...*This Being the Last Pain She Makes Me Suffer* occurred to his mind. The car started and moved out of the gate.

Barely a couple of minutes later, at a signal, Malhotra saw a little girl, begging and jumping through hoops to please motorists. Another begging girl, hardly seven or eight, knocked at his window. She was holding a little brown pup in her arms that looked at Malhotra with hauntingly cute eyes and whimpered hungrily.

Suddenly an inspiration struck General Malhotra. A plan seemed to take concrete shape in his mind. The cloud of doubt vanished. 'The sovereign,' he recalled Sun Tzu, 'must not always be obeyed.' He had taken a decision. Malhotra, at last, had found his goal. And like many of his earlier missions, he was willing to pursue it to death.

Army General Headquarters, Rawalpindi, Pakistan

Local time: 1530 hours
Date: 23 April 2014

Footsteps echoed throughout the deserted corridor as Captain Jehangir Malik, trying his best to hide his excitement, skidded to a stop outside the office of the military secretary to the Pakistani army. The aide-de-camp dusted his uniform and walked the last few steps towards the office of his mentor and superior. Calm needs to be maintained, even in the most agitated times.

Malik reached the ornately carved door, knocked and entered the room a second later. He was one of the few who could walk in that office anytime. A privilege he understood all too well. There was another thing he understood well enough—that failure, even a small one, will make him fall down the long ladder of command and in the blink of an eye, will earn him a posting in NWFP. He winced and looked at the general, trying to focus on his fears to prevent himself from looking over-zealous.

The general looked up and smiled, a cigarette dangled from his lips. Lieutenant General Asif Hussain Chowdhury was of average height but with shoulders broader than normal. He was a dexterous field commander, a former head of Pakistan's elite Special Service Group and a major mover of the nuclear weapons programme. The youngest military secretary in Pakistani history, General Chowdhury was a Saraiki Bhutta Jatt from Bahawalpur and as loyal to his state as to his nation—a man forever confused where the boundaries of Punjab ended and where Pakistan began. It was a common feeling amongst Pakistani officers from Punjab. There was a well-known joke, if it could be called one, that Punjab was Pakistan and Pakistan was Punjab. If in a conflict Punjab fell, Pakistan fell and if Punjab survived, Pakistan survived. Punjab gave the Pakistani army around sixty per cent of its officers whereas its contribution to personnel below officer ranks was just about twenty per cent. However, as long as the Punjabis dominated the hierarchy at the top, other denominations like the Sindhis, Balochis and Pashtuns could do little. The army controlled Pakistan, and the army, in turn, was controlled by Punjab.

Chowdhury kept looking at Malik but did not say anything. Silence, he knew, brought out the best and the worst in men. He had learned to exploit it. Inwardly, however, he was dying to know the result of the mission that could very well immortalize him in the Pakistani history. However, he did not want his aide to know how desperately he wanted this mission to succeed. A commanding officer must always seem in-charge of the situation, all-knowing and all-powerful.

Chowdhury had personally supervised this mission, a bit too personally, and had used all his contacts to keep this mission a secret. When the time was right, he would himself tell the chief of staff and even the president. Until then, he had a secret to keep.

He could not believe his luck. Some days ago, an old pal contacted him and offered to liberate his soul and return to the good old days. A suggestion to which he had happily agreed.

Malik smiled. 'They are in, sir. All opposition neutralized. No casualties,' he said.

Chowdhury smiled at the news, although he knew the result the moment Malik stepped confidently into his room.

'Our men will not be returning. I want the army to provide whatever assistance we can for their families. Tell them they were killed in the Indian firing across the LOC and that their bodies will not be coming home as they were buried on site. Destroy all records of this mission, if they exist. Malik, see to it personally. Keep updating me with the latest developments on this mission. I do not want anything to go wrong,' Chowdhury ordered, then sat back and smiled serenely at him again.

Good going, thought Malik, as he nodded. 'Yes, sir. It will be done,' Captain Malik replied, saluted, and walked out of the room.

He was happy about how things were shaping up. If it went on like this, he knew that he would soon be Major Malik.

Lutyens' Delhi, India

Local time: 1200 hours
Date: 24 April 2014

It was a strange sight for Delhi. Office-goers stopped in the streets to stare at the columns of monstrous tanks lazily prowling around. Apart from the Republic Day parades, the people of Delhi never saw armoured columns in the heart of their city. General Malhotra, it seemed, had been busy on calls for the past few, frantic hours.

Men in olive green had cordoned off Parliament while the budget session was still in progress. Movement of civilians had been restricted, though with much civility and leeway. For what he was about to do, Malhotra expected neutrality at least from the public, if not overt support. He knew politicians and certain elements of civil society will oppose his move vehemently, but he was ready for them. He had a plan to make them cooperate.

The army was with him. Even though some corps commanders did not agree with the decisions of their respective General Officer Commanding-in-Chief (GOC-in-C) to support Malhotra, it mattered little. The Western Command had promised to back Malhotra up to the hilt, so had the Lucknow-based Central Command and the Northern Command at Udhampur. Moreover, if the guardedly zealous response of the GOC-in-C of South Western command was an indicator, another tactical command was on the verge of compliance. The Eastern Command Kolkata was presently non-committal, but likely to come around to see his viewpoint. The only tactical command openly against him was the Southern Command headquartered at Pune. It seemed Malhotra had to keep the non-cooperative command's Jodhpur-based XII corps, the Desert Corps, in mind when making any plans.

The air force was in, too. The Western Air Command (WAC) of the Indian air force was firmly with Malhotra, the air marshal being a chummy squadron mate from his NDA days. Other Air Officers Commanding (AOCs) were also ready to rise to the occasion. Thankfully, WAC, the only IAF command already on-board, was headquartered at Subroto Park, New Delhi, and was ready to fly sorties out of the Hindon Air Force Base located at Ghaziabad, a suburb of Delhi, to augment Malhotra's maneuvers, if the need arose.

As if to bear testimony to the air warriors' word, a couple of Mi-25 gunships flew over Malhotra at the precise moment, more to intimidate hostile personnel than to enforce a no-fly zone.

Unfortunately, the navy had unequivocally refused to go along with Malhotra, which meant that the Coast Guard and the Sagar Prahari Bal (SPB) was out too. However, Malhotra knew that the action would take place here in Delhi, and the dissenters sitting far away mattered little now, for he also had the support of IPS. It was siding with the military for one simple reason—it promised them more control over their territories—especially when it was at the expense of IAS . The Central paramilitary organizations, headed by IPS officers, adopted a wait-and-watch approach. Most of their middle-level officer cadre was drawn from the army. The Strategic Forces Command too did not openly oppose him. The way ahead was clear.

Malhotra's car cut across the barricades and reached the Parliament House through Gate No. 1. General Rohit Malhotra stepped out of his car in ceremonial uniform. Bound by his nature cultivated over years spent in field duty, he scanned the entire area the moment he stepped out. Precaution was better than a bullet between the eyes.

Scores of T-90 Bhishma tanks were lethal predators stalking the Delhi roads waiting to unleash their firepower in environs where it would have been disastrous. The few Delhi police and CRPF personnel who had tried to resist his men were overpowered and transported long before he had arrived. His men now operated the sentry posts.

Although a majority of commands backed him, he had asked units of the Rajasthan Rifles to form the core of the first wave of assault. This served a dual purpose. One, Rajasthan Rifles would have a base in Delhi Cantonment, and that amounted to quick mobilization. Two, he was commissioned in that very infantry unit. He had served with officers and men for long, hard years; they knew and respected him.

Consequently, Malhotra's orders were obeyed without any of his men protesting. From a watch tower, one of his men raised his gun in salute. Malhotra smiled. He went up to the Parliament entry. The doors had been locked from outside. A JCO opened them for him. Malhotra motioned him not to follow and stepped inside the Lok Sabha hall, alone.

An angry roar greeted him the moment he stepped in. He spotted the PM and moved towards him, smiling serenely. The PM was perplexed at this sudden turn of events. 'What are you doing here? You will not escape after this attempt,' a visibly shaken prime minister, Bipolab Roy, managed to sputter with great effort.

Malhotra ignored him and made his way towards the speaker chair. He had to convey his message. The speaker stood up and joined the protesting MPs.

'Silence...please,' Malhotra cried in the coldest voice he could muster. The noise receded though it did not stop entirely. 'Respected Members, may I have your attention please. I will put it in the least possible words. As of now, the military has taken over. Martial Law has been imposed, but for a temporary duration. I had to take this drastic step for reasons I will disclose soon. I request you to cooperate. You all will be escorted to your houses and no harm will come to you. However, any special privileges and legal immunities will be withdrawn from those with criminal charges. Comply, and no harm will come to you.'

There was a sudden howling and banging of desks. The usual Parliament procedure, Malhotra mused, to express dissent. Had it not been for his men standing guard, he would have expected mikes and objects flying at him. Again, not uncommon for these people, he thought loathingly. That was why he had given specific instructions. Sometimes the mere sights of poisonous fangs work, but when you bite, bite deep.

He savoured the look of bewilderment and shock on the faces of the MPs. Malhotra hated their lack of decorum, integrity and inability to follow orders. They were not able to adjust to new situations, which is why politicians, individually or in a group, were unable to take quick decisions. He was counting on this trait of theirs for his plan's success.

The PM walked to him and spat out, 'Listen, General, for your own lust for power, you cannot disband people's democratically elected representatives. We represent the people of this country and speak for them. We are the ones who take decisions for the country. You can't dare to overstep your authority.'

Malhotra retorted, 'You can't seem to think of anything else apart from power and politics? I am doing this for the betterment of this country. This uniform does not merely imply serving political masters. I serve my country, not any political party or ideology. For more than the last sixty years, the military has never interfered in the political affairs of this country. This is just a temporary shift from the routine—only to make you understand the value of what you have got...so you might use it wisely when all of this is behind us.'

No one interrupted Malhotra. He wondered if this was due to his gun-toting guards who were eyeing the MPs with increasing antipathy. The PM sank down on a chair, unable to believe what was happening.

Malhotra went back to the speaker's chair again. He glanced at the sceptical hordes in front of him, adjusted the mike, inhaled deeply, and started speaking impromptu, 'Ours is a great country, with a great polity and people, but for the past few decades we seem to have forgotten the ideals our founding fathers fought for. No longer do you, in whom the supreme power is vested by the people of this country, abide by the Constitution and respect its ideals and institutions. No longer do you cherish and follow the noble ideals that inspired our national struggle for freedom. No longer do you defend the country and render national service when called upon to do so. No longer do you promote harmony and the spirit of common brotherhood amongst all the people of India transcending religious, linguistic and regional or sectional diversities.

'You sell the products of your office to the highest bidder instead of helping the poor Indian through it, someone who needs it the most. Money has become your sole guiding principle. You buy votes, you horse trade your kith and kin, and you even take money to ask questions in Parliament! You have not even left defence deals alone, buying substandard equipment only because it gives you a higher cut. You conspire to appropriate the wealth and welfare measures meant for martyrs and war widows. You and your politics. It ends... here,' he almost choked with anger, 'and now!'

He spotted increased frenzy and flurry of activity amongst his audience. The MPs were furious! They seemed to have forgotten the fact that there were guns pointing at them. This arrogant lot knew nothing could happen to them as long as they were elected from their constituencies.

Malhotra knew he could not convince these unruly ministers and he had very little time. He had other things pending. He came down and started walking rapidly towards the exit. A hand grabbed him roughly. A group of four to five MPs surrounded him. Fat bellies, gold chains, arrogance in their stride.

'Abe General, *aukaat main reh, pachtayega,*' someone hissed at him. Malhotra recognized the MP. With more than two dozen criminal cases levelled against him, he was a well-known don from a cow-belt state. Nevertheless, since he had supported every successive government in the state since then, his cases had been pending in court for the past fifteen years without a hearing.

Another voice was more civil in criticism, 'General Malhotra, do you know your attack on Parliament could result in your execution? Wait until the people of my constituency hear this. I will make you pay for the embarrassment you caused me and the other national leaders. The international community...' the voice continued.

Some other MPs rushed and mobbed Malhotra. His guards moved to intercept, but they had to force their way through a raging mass. In addition, they had special orders not to open fire inside the Lok Sabha hall until it was absolutely necessary.

Malhotra realized it would take the guards a couple of minutes to get to him, and by then it could be too late. He had to send out a strong signal. However, before he zeroed in on a course of action, the don MP who had earlier blocked his path, came dangerously close to him and took him by the collar. Malhotra opened his mouth to say something but he felt a sharp thwack on his left cheek.

It started to sting. He had been slapped. A corrupt, criminal MP had just slapped General Malhotra, the chief of army staff. The people around him stopped in their tracks. The noise of the slap seemed to echo through the hall with the triumph of a wrong done right.

Malhotra's jaw dropped open. Never, never ever in his thirty-year long combat career had he been slapped like that. He had been fired upon, mortared, shelled, punched, pushed, shot at, bayoneted, thrown, kicked, but never ever slapped this way. He felt a wave of anger swell inside him. The MP had a smug smile playing on his lips. He looked at Malhotra for a full minute, savouring the attention he was getting. He was already thinking of what he would say to the news channels.

The general shook his head, not being able to believe what had just happened. Then a thought struck him, challenging him. He tried to force it away, but it came back stronger like an irresistible urge. Absentmindedly, he felt his firearm. He decided not to feel guilty for his actions now. Till then, he was playing the game of talking, which these people were good at. Soon, he would start the game that would be played by his rules—a game which he was expert at. Another final show of strength remained.

Malhotra realized that the decision to fire or not was yet to be taken. The next moment, he took out his personal sidearm, a Glock-17 C and shot the erring MP in the chest. From conception to execution, the entire process took a total of 2.5 seconds.

Malhotra watched him struggling to utter something as he was thrown back on his party colleagues by the sheer force of the bullet. Those who were nearest to him were unable to take the impact of his lifeless body hitting them. They fell down with the MP's body on top of them, groaning in shock. His blood started to seep down and red blotches appeared on the green carpet. Pin drop silence swept the hall as others looked agape at Malhotra and the dead body in horror and disbelief. Apart from strengthening his position and cause, Malhotra wanted the politicians to understand how it feels when one loses one's comrades. He went to the bleeding man, looked in to his eyes, and shot him again…in the head.

A mosquito was heard angrily buzzing in the far end of the hall. Coup-de-grace.

Malhotra started walking away from the mob. They lowered their eyes and let him pass unchallenged. He came out of the complex, moist eyed. They formed a line and without speaking a word, were escorted to the waiting buses to carry them to their destination — the Tihar prison complex — where after detaining those who had criminal charges against them, the rest were to be taken to their official residences.

He knew this part was not going to be easy. Hell, any part of it was not going to be easy. The most difficult would be to convince the public. But he knew the Indian public had an uncanny way of adapting to the changing circumstances. The famous Indian 'jugaad' was as much a socio-cultural concept as a technological one.

Malhotra boarded a waiting car and left for the Akashvani Bhawan that was situated at about 100 metres from the Parliament building. He entered the gates and went straight to the studio, where a production team of All India Radio, the national radio broadcaster and its sister TV service Doordarshan, was waiting for him, courtesy his persuasive staff. Although Doordarshan had the maximum penetration amongst all the TV channels in India, he knew he had to utilize the radio too — for a significant part of rural India, radio was still the life-line of communication with the rest of the country. His staff had blacked out private channels temporarily for Malhotra did not want them to break into a frenzy as they usually did. That meant he had to use this weapon well — his success hinged on a speech that would get him the attention and support of the people of India.

Malhotra's address to the nation was upfront and measured. The military had seized power temporarily until the country was ready for another election, which would be held soon, though civil liberties would, of course, not be curtailed.

This done, he quickly moved to the integrated defence command headquarters to set up his command and control base. Malhotra knew he had a war-like situation on his hands and that he required expertise, tact, and sheer luck to pull it off. However, what General Malhotra did not know then was that not only would he have to face a war-like situation, but also an actual war.

Topi, North West Frontier Province, Pakistan

Local time: 1700 hours
Date: 24 April 2014

The heady smells and sounds of the bustling market slowly receded into the background as Yasser Basheer made his way to the second storey of the non-descript building. He climbed the stairs with practised, quick steps. He may have become old, but old soldiers did take time to fade away. The winding staircase was, Basheer counted, currently home to a total of five people—lying, sitting, conversing—trying their best to resemble people in casual, slothful conversation. Their Kalashnikovs may have been out of sight but were well within reach. To a casual observer the group would have looked normal, but not to trained eyes.

Basheer saw their itching, quivering fingers, their frequent glances at the entry of the building, and their unnatural twitching. He saw the carefully wrapped headgear concealing their crew cuts. Good, he thought, the five guards assigned are present at their posts. All of them had served under him at the Parachute Training School, Peshawar. This made Basheer feel a lot at ease. He passed by and the men saluted with slight but noticeable tilts of their heads. He felt even better.

Basheer reached a door, this one guarded by a different species of men altogether. Two burly men blocked his way, holding far more sophisticated weapons. Their guns were in plain sight and held without any intentions of hiding their lethality. Basheer shook his head. With each passing day spent with such people, he felt more disgusted by their crass attitude towards combat where no quarters were given or taken. It was a no-holds-barred, free-for-all, dishonourable fight. For them, war was merely a means to an end — in this case, global retribution.

The men scanned Basheer from head to toe, nodded curtly, looked away, and stepped aside casually. For a former military man, this was an insult. Sentries acting like this. No salutes, no respect! They should learn from the others, he thought. It struck Basheer then that apart from faith, he had nothing in common with these men. Nothing at all. But then faith was all that mattered.

'Colonel sa'ab,' the man sitting on a radio acknowledged and stood up, hands clasped behind his back. A good old former subedar. Basheer consciously halted the flow of thoughts in his mind. As the military commander of TNSM*, he had to ensure his personal feelings did not get in the way of the completion of the mission. He was a commando first, a vain human being later. He rubbed his temple with his right hand and glanced at the equipment.

It was out of place. The room was sparsely furnished; paint was peeling off its yellowish walls, a cot was kept at a corner, and at the other corner lay an ultra-modern communication console. He made his way towards the radio.

'What is their status?' he asked for the nth time in the past hour.

---

*Tehreek-e-Nifas-e-Shariat-e-Mohammadi: Movement for the enforcement of Islamic Law.

Perhaps he was getting too emotionally involved in this mission. He knew there was nothing he hated more than the command's constant requests for field updates from combat units, especially those on dangerous missions, for they had to operate with utmost caution, stay alive, stay sharp, and report back when things got a little normal. He was doing precisely the same thing now. Being a pestering desk jockey.

He was old now but still displayed the same impatience of his youth. Such is the cycle of karma, as the Bamiyan Buddhas he helped destroy would have said to him. His silent mirthless laughter echoed in the room.

'All going as planned, janaab. The units are in. Proceeding to the next stage,' the subedar replied quickly, alarmed at his boss' sudden fit of laughter.

'Good,' Basheer sat on the cot and reached for a glass of water, and after gulping the water down in three measured, deliberate sips, said, 'I promised General Chowdhury plenty of action. Let's not keep him waiting, shall we?'

The subedar grinned, 'We should not. Shall I send our agent the final set of instructions, janaab?' Basheer thought for a few moments. There was no coming back from this, he said to himself. What he had planned was bold, in some ways reckless, but only a pest killed a pest.

Basheer sighed and muttered, 'Do it.'

Integrated Defence Command Headquarters,
New Delhi, India

Local time: 1300 hours
Date: 24 April 2014

For the first time in independent India's history, the military had come to the political centre stage. Malhotra, along with key personnel from the military, sat hunched over the console, reading reports. The cabinet secretary and secretaries for home affairs, defence, and external affairs were on their way. Malhotra knew it would be foolish not to utilize all the resources of the state to counter the threat they faced.

The war room was a blast-proof structure located two floors below the ground. It served as a command, communication, and control platform for the most important operations of the Indian defence forces, especially during wartime. The room spanned an entire floor and contained not only computer labs, conference areas, a cafeteria and a dormitory, but was also equipped with state-of-the-art communication devices, transponders, jammers, and survival kits. Digital maps of India's neighbours were displayed over huge screens. Currently, the Andaman and Nicobar Islands were zoomed in to show the Garrison Island — the island that housed NMRC.

'I hope you all are aware of the seriousness of the situation,' Malhotra formally initiated the meeting. 'But first, I want your comments and ideas on the question: who are these people and what do they want from us?'

'One thing is for certain, sir, they are not protesting farmers,' said Admiral Sapra.

'But what do they want? People do not attack and capture a military base just because they feel like doing it. I smell something bigger than that,' Air Chief Sharma ventured forth. He was stopped from making any further remarks as the door opened and a group of bureaucrats walked in and took their seats.

'The information on Project Pralay was top secret. I do not know how it leaked out.' The defence secretary shook his head.

'And the base was attacked just when the missile was ready for testing. Is it a coincidence?' The home secretary raised his concern.

'The attackers have been in for quite some time now. If they had wanted to disable the missile they could have done so and tried to escape. The fact that they still are in there reveals much more sinister designs. I strongly feel they will try to steal its plans. Maybe they are making a copy. That is what is taking them time. The concept ...eh...will be new to them,' said the director general of DRDO, a special invitee.

'This is the most stupid way of stealing plans. Especially when they know they will not escape alive after trying it.'

'All right, get your point. But now we have to decide what we should do. How to respond to it?' General Malhotra asked.

'Rohit, we cannot enter the facility through land or water undetected. The facility is a fortress now. But we can at least know what's going on inside through an aerial survey,' the admiral replied.

'Vikramjeet,' said Malhotra, addressing the air chief, 'what do you think?'

'IAF is already flying reconnaissance missions over the island. Fighters have been scrambled from Kalaikunda Air Force Base. I expect Intel soon. However, even then I will only be able to give a rough idea about the situation. I fear I cannot be very accurate. As you must know, to avoid detection by American satellites, most of the facility is planned in such a way that it is hidden from aerial sight, especially the silo containing Pralay, the test lab and the main control facility.'

Malhotra wanted more accurate information. He asked, 'What's the position of RISAT?'

The ISRO-built Radar Imaging Satellite was a series of Indian radar imaging reconnaissance satellites. On 20 April 2009, PSLV launched the 300-kg RISAT-2 before RISAT-1 into orbit because of the 26 November 2008 Mumbai attacks and the fact that the indigenous C-Band Synthetic Aperture Radar (SAR) to be used for RISAT-1 was not ready. The IAI-built X-SAR in RISAT-2 gave it an all-weather spatial resolution of about a metre, making it effective for border surveillance in anti-infiltration and anti-terrorist operations as well as disaster management.

'It will be passing overhead soon. I will consult with the planners of the base and align the satellite so that we can scan the areas at NMRC that are more prone to imagery intelligence. I am sure we could get a more detailed picture. Until then, we will have to wait,' volunteered the director general of DRDO. The air chief, under whose aerospace command the satellite actually functioned, gave him a dirty look.

'Is any satellite of a friendly country passing over the island?' asked the defence secretary.

'I do not think so. However, presently I am working on the definition of a friendly country. Our friends may not want to help us the moment they know we are clandestinely working on developing an ICBM,' shrugged the secretary to the Ministry of External Affairs.

'I understand. Whatever be the case, I do not want the news of the attack on NMRC to reach the press. They know how to make an issue truly burn. We will handle it on our own,' commanded the general.

'Well, Vikramjeet, see to it that I get the information ASAP. Sapra, send a ship to the island and quarantine it. Take care that no merchant or civilian vessels escape the blockade. Meanwhile, I want 201 Paratrooper Battalion to be deployed to NMRC and surround it. They are supposed to be jungle warfare specialists, let us see what they can do here. In addition, have 901 Paratrooper Battalion reach the surrounding hills and await further orders. Let us wait for data from RISAT and the reconnaissance sorties of IAF and then formulate a plan of action,' Malhotra said.

'Yes, sir.'

'We will meet again when we have more information. Dismissed.'

Malhotra strolled out of the room. He fancied a game of golf right then to soothe him. It always worked.

Master Control Facility, NMRC

Local time: 1600 hours
Date: 24 April 2014

The intercom of the team leader, Major Masood Rana, formerly of the 4th Commando Yalghar Battalion of Pakistan's Special Service Group, beeped the moment he came off the long range radio, having received the final set of instructions from his handler.

He checked the intercom. It was one of his men stationed at the air defence console. 'Sir, the radar has picked up an IAF formation approaching the base 30 degrees west of south […] four hostiles […] about 2000 feet AGL.'

'It could be an enemy bombing mission,' a shaken voice was heard in the background.

'Nah,' Rana replied, wondering how soon this soldier had cracked. Next time he would ensure that this man never got on-board for any important mission. Or better, any mission. If there was a next time.

'The Indians simply cannot bomb the fruits of a decade-long research project. We should be expecting a reconnaissance sortie. You know what you have to do.'

'Right, sir. Will do. Out,' the voice at the other end said, sounding reassured.

No one but Rana had looked up when he was talking; everyone else was busy in their tasks. They had been given specific instructions to talk only when asked, and to focus on the task at hand. Rana looked around, almost paternally, and then got back to work.

◆

Wing Commander VV 'Sanyo' Nayar was cruising serenely in a four-finger formation of Su-30 MKIs belonging to No. 30 Squadron Rampaging Rhinos. The super flankers, having punctually reassembled in reconnaissance formation at their Initial Point (IP), scrambled towards the target, constantly checking for any signs of trouble. Speed was of the essence. Sanyo swung and aligned his Sukhoi-30 MKI in a direction parallel to the missile base, the machine responding superbly to his touch.

Custom-made for IAF by the Sukhoi Company, Russia, and Hindustan Aeronautics Limited (HAL), the Su-30 MKI integrated Indian, French and Israeli subsystems and avionics to create a heavy class, long-range air superiority fighter that also doubled up as a multirole strike fighter aircraft, making it a feared adversary in the skies.

Sanyo craned his head and spotted a couple of Mi-8 choppers of the HU 122 Dolphins Squadron already hovering around his target. Apatsu mitram, indeed. He focused further and saw numerous yet tiny dots of land-masses approaching, like glittering jewels on the smooth skin of a sea nymph. The voice of the fighter controller cackled over his RT, 'Target [...] eleven o'clock [...] fifteen nautical miles [...] RV Dolphins [...]'

Sanyo, the flight leader replied, 'Roger. I have visuals...'

Sanyo then glanced to his left and saw three accompanying crafts in a sparkling blue sky with unending visibility.

He spoke to them this time over his RT, 'This is red leader to red team. Red two, stay at my side. Red three and four, follow from another vector. We will not go in together. Red two and I will fly very low and cover the northern area. Red three and four, you have the southern sector. Go!'

The Su-30 MKIs slowed their speeds, activated their cameras to record the proceedings below and commenced a dive down to 250 feet. Sanyo saw his number two swing to the north to cover the respective sub-area allotted to him. Three and four were already behind them. Adrenaline pumping through his body, he lowered the altitude of his plane to record even the minutest details on the ground.

The reason why Sanyo was there instead of a Searcher II Unmanned Aerial Vehicle (UAV) from Car Nicobar Air Force Station was that a manned reconnaissance mission was preferred — simply because of the human intuition to focus on what *looked* important. From his briefing, Sanyo and his team knew about the vital areas of the installation they had to cover, hidden from sight though they were.

The cameras had started clicking when the RT spewed some not-so-good news. 'Red leader…sensors detect a ground based SAM launcher powering up at bearing 099…repeat 099… Exercise caution.'

'Roger,' Sanyo replied.

Hell, who was operating a Surface-to-Air Missile (SAM) launcher here, he thought? He had been told in his briefing that the security apparatuses of the base were under lock-and-key and access to them was impossible for any hostile forces. How did they bypass security and manage to activate a launcher?

Sanyo pulled his craft up in a steep climb and told others to follow. The command would most definitely not approve his data collecting efforts if he lost a plane.

He was climbing when he heard a scream over his radio. 'Number three under attack,' shouted his wingman, 'twelve thousand yards.' At the same time, a proximity alarm went off in his cockpit.

His number four whispered, 'Visual contact with an incoming bogey!'

'Request type...' said the fighter controller and Sanyo almost together.

'SAM...SAM...SAM!' replied number two, his pitch rising.

Sanyo heard the scream on his radio and saw the white streak of a SAM almost simultaneously. The missile angled away from him, missed him by a couple of metres and went back. It was on top of him even before he realized; it was fired from so close. Heat-seeking, he thought. Instinctively, Sanyo turned back to see where it had gone. He pulled the nose of his craft and pointed it to the sky, somersaulting and trying to avoid contact as it made another pass at him.

'SAM on your tail, repeat, SAM on your tail, red one,' he heard his radio utter. Damn, Sanyo released decoy flares and chaff. The missile was not deterred. It continued following his plane like a hawk preying on a sparrow.

This time too, it came dangerously close to him. Nevertheless, he was lucky again. Suddenly, the missile swerved sharply, as its sensors got a lock on another target and it veered away from him.

Sanyo sighed involuntarily. The missile was gone. But where? A SAM does not leave its prey for another. What was it? Some technical malfunction in the SAM...or in his own aircraft?

Sanyo's reverie was broken by a harsh moan, 'Ahhh...I am hit...I am hit.'

'Number three, you are on fire, eject, eject!' another voice said on his radio, almost pleading.

Sanyo had until now been so absorbed in his miraculous escape, he did not see where the SAM had gone. He looked back to see a ball of fire in the sky. He was no longer the target. It was number three. The missile had found its prey. Thankfully, number three had time to eject. His white parachute was slowly drifting down towards the ground by the time others came to their senses. A life was saved. Machinery, on the other hand, was not.

Bitter with the way the events unfolded, but content that the task was done and pictures taken without any loss of life, Sanyo found himself ordering everyone to return to the base, as the Indian Coast Guard units swung into action to intercept the falling parachute.

◆

Finally, a member of the infiltrating group exhibited the first signs of unprofessional behaviour. He looked at his friend and touched his fingers to his lips, grinning sheepishly. The meaning was unambiguous. Care to smoke?

The friend shook his head and looked away. Give a dying man some leeway, he then thought, and tilted his head a little in the direction of the door. Go ahead, go out and have a smoke, I will wait, the look meant. The man got up and exited the room. He walked down the corridor, stopped at a door, checked if he was being followed, opened it and went in. It was the Auxiliary Launch Navigation Control Station (ALNCS), meant for manually programming the coordinates and flight path in case the more often-used, computer-operated Primary Ballistics Navigation System (PBNS) failed.

No guards were present. Why should there be? Thieves' honour, he thought. The base personnel had been neutralized and his own team was busy completing the tasks allotted to it, preparing for its part in the grand scheme. Access to this room came much later, if at all. It was only in case of failure to access PBNS that this room was to be used—unlikely given their initial success in gaining entry to the PBNS itself. Therefore, other priorities needed to be addressed first.

For them, he thought. Not for him.

This room was vital to him. He re-read the final set of instructions again. He did not know what they meant, but it mattered little. He booted the machine, opened a program and with quick, deft key strokes, modified the programming. He then took out a pen drive and installed a program into the mainframe, as he had been ordered to do. This done, he exited the room and joined his mate at the end of the corridor.

He smelt of smoke.

Bay of Bengal, India

Local time: 1630 hours
Date: 24 April 2014

The crew thronged the deck of the tiny, dingy fishing trawler and stared agape at the sleek, shining convoy. They were all young, sturdy village lads who depended on fishing for a living. Every second week, they used to set out deep into the sea. A few months ago, they decided to go even deeper into the sea and hunt for lobsters, and if time and tide permitted, pearls. Inflation was at an all-time high, and the thekedar who bought fish from them was giving them lesser and lesser cut. Drastic times called for drastic measures to earn. This was one of them.

What they saw right now was greater than a thousand pearls. A carrier group of the Indian navy proudly sailed at their side. The boys waved at the passing ships — majestic, shining and radiating power. One of the village boys, who had gone to the recently opened school in the nearby village, knew how to read. The crew thrust him to the portside of the trawler and gesticulated wildly.

His duty was clear. He mustered all his learning, squinted at the largest of the ships, one that carried aircrafts on it, and tried to read, 'I...N...S...Vi...Vismaya...' Everyone looked at him with expectation. He turned to another ship, smaller than the first one but still managing to look as impressive.

'I...N...S...D...Dharti.' The elders looked at him with visible pride.

There were other ships too, helicopters strapped on their decks, waiting to rain fire. The elders shuddered, the young suppressed shivers of excitement running through their bodies.

A crew member shouted. He had seen a whale! Yes, a whale! It had surfaced for a brief instant and then dived. It had been following them for a while. However, he was too experienced to feel afraid. Whales seldom attack people, contrary to the Hollywood movies. Though the thought never struck him, simply because he did not know what Hollywood was. He thought the whale was merely playing tricks with them, though not with any malicious intentions. At least, he hoped so.

At an expletive-ridden shout from the leader, the trawler crew stopped gawking at the task force and got to work. They were here to feed themselves, not to ogle at these monstrous pieces of machinery, the leader made it evidently clear with his words.

The leader of the trawler then took the wheel and started laughing all of a sudden. If piloting this little thing is so hard, he thought, he was glad he had nothing to do with those mammoth ships. He shook his head, still laughing, and concentrated on catching some lobsters. His daughter wanted a new pair of shoes. There were many ways in which he might have got them, but staring idly at ships passing by was not one of those ways.

◆

'Get me to periscope depth,' a harsh voice cracked like a whip in the confined spaces of a submarine's bridge, knowing that no one would be able to hear them over the din the fishermen were making.

The battle-hardened captain whispered again, '10 degrees rise on bow planes [...] 5 degrees Up Bubble [...] on my mark [...]'

The orders to the helmsman were coming directly from the master of the boat, instead of via the executive officer and the diving officer. Clearly, the chain of command on that submarine was more flexible. The executive officer (XO), if he could be called one, was away attending to an important guest. The diving officer, if any, was handling the sonar equipment as he was the best submariner of the crew after the captain and was required to focus wholly on his current quarry at the precarious moment. The sonar operator, on the other hand, merely stood on the bridge, doing nothing. Sonar was all he knew, rest everything puzzled him.

As a result, orders were flying directly from the top to the bottom. Though it punctured the pyramidal chain of command, it also ensured that the orders be followed to the pith and substance, in the minimum response time and to the best efficiency a crew can muster in the circumstances.

'Up periscope,' the captain said. The crew and the boat rushed to comply.

The captain was given orders to minutely observe the happenings around them and then inform his master of every development that was to take place. The master was keen on it, which came as a surprise to the captain as his superior rarely took interest in such small matters. Which meant only one thing — what was about to happen was not small at all.

The captain had done well by staying hidden under the nose of the Indian fleet, or at least the belly. It was not too difficult, he thought, thanks to the Indians' lousy anti-submarine warfare capabilities, but he had to be vigilant. Vigilance leads to victory. Brazenness leads to death. Many had paid in blood to realize that.

He knew he would be engaged the moment he was spotted, and he had no wish to battle an entire carrier group, not to mention the nasty Sea King anti-submarine helicopters comfortably strapped on the deck of a ship, especially not with whom he was carrying on-board. History would never forgive him if he did.

He had utilized the signature of the fishing trawler, staying near it, and trying to merge with its readings to confuse sensor sweeps by the Indians so that his presence might not be detected. Not very difficult, he thought, especially when the Indians were not looking for him. They had other things to do.

He too had other things to do. He coarsely whispered to dive deeper and change course; the boat still rigged at silent speed. Again, the boat complied. Its tanks started pumping water in, and silently, the submarine disappeared into the depths of the sea.

Launch Silo 01, NMRC

Local time: 1700 hours
Date: 24 April 2014

The second in command gave the leader a zealous thumbs-up and grinned from ear to ear. Highly out of place, thought Major Rana, but it showed good spirits and that was a good sign.

Rana looked up from his watch. He knew they were behind schedule, if only a little. He controlled his anxiety and did not tell them to hurry. The men were already under pressure, but that did not matter. Pressure was a part of the game. Errors were not. It was a delicate task, and having a superior breath down on your neck all the time was not only disturbing but also irritating. The last thing he wanted was to have the missile change its target by a couple of miles. That would have been disastrous.

He barked orders to begin the final assemblage. The men rushed to comply, their muscles paining and sweat glistening on their faces. Their eyes were thin slits of concentration. They closed the silo doors and started to assemble the parts of the missile in launch position. God bless the Indians, Rana thought, for creating a missile that was so easy to assemble.

The silo was lighted and ready for action. The men took their positions. Some faltered at the sight of the huge monster.

Those who did were guided by those who did not — with encouraging whispers and gentle nudges.

Pralay was taking shape.

Meanwhile, the man deputed to handle the pre-flight sequence made his way to the propulsion guidance lab and started working, this time on PBNS. There was no need to lock the door to execute his task. Others were busy and no one would come checking until the time came. He focused on the task at hand. First, he had to encrypt the target coordinates. He did. Secondly, he had to upload a program for the remote guidance of the missile. Check. Third, he had to install safeguards to prevent unauthorized access. Complete. He smiled and let out a sigh.

He had done it all in record time.

Andaman and Nicobar Islands

Local time: 1900 hours
Date: 24 April 2014

His heart thumped furiously, beating against his chest with an almost painful regularity, as he followed his lieutenant. He was glad at being tethered to the line. The light above the aircraft door was a soothing green by now. Funny how this shade of green was now associated with such an event that it neither soothed him, nor looked green in the first place.

The line ahead of him started to move, slowly yet decisively, and disappeared into nothingness. Havildar Sumit Shinde looked down at his restless feet. He was outfitted for a High Altitude-Low Opening (HALO) parachute jump: he was wearing a black jumpsuit, helmet, wrist altimeter and square canopy parachute. Shinde gulped, focused on the rope, fondly patted the SIG P226 9mm semi-automatic pistol and TAR-21, for one last time and followed the lead.

The air rushing in was getting stronger as he neared the gate, pushing him back towards the rear of the craft, vacillating between whispers, 'No! Do not Jump! It is dangerous' in his mother's voice, to screams 'Move it, Commando. *Kood!*' in his CO's. Intensity and proximity won again. His CO was with him in the aircraft; his mother was not.

Shinde took a deep breath and jumped down. His legs felt the nothingness and he started to fall into the vast, empty belly of the hungry sky.

It is strange how the first reaction of any paratrooper when he has just jumped off an aircraft is of relief at having had the courage to jump, despite the fact that he is hanging kilometres above the ground. Shinde felt relieved simply because from then on, he had no choice. All he had to do was to follow his training, survive the landing and then follow the instructions given to him.

No more choices. Choices made him anxious. Shinde knew that an existential crisis was not good for the military. Let the officers grapple with the larger questions of life, he thought. He would handle the smaller questions about who to shoot and when.

That is what made him a good soldier. Alas, he was not an officer. Shinde didn't like to look at the larger picture. He lacked, in short, officer-like qualities, he thought ruefully, trying to position his body to slow his fall. The ground rushed to hug him.

Breathe. Take a deep breath. He forced himself to breathe long and deep. The impact would empty his lungs of air. Better hyperventilate now, he thought.

Then suddenly, the constant falling motion to which Shinde was slowly getting accustomed, stopped abruptly. He had hit the ground with a soft crunch, and his heart almost stopped for a second as he made contact. He buckled under the impact, but not before he had mentally braced himself for it.

Inertia battled gravity as he rolled over and detached his parachute from his body, hoping for the sensation to delay itself. His parachute flew off the cliff, still propelled by a strong wind. Shinde had landed on the side of a steep mountain. He clung to the rock near him and balanced himself. He closed his eyes and waited for it.

It was then that pain struck Shinde. It felt like someone was sawing his feet away. He moaned and started counting to ten. With the count, he slowly began to feel his legs, and with it, pain. He tried not to focus on his legs. Instead, he forced his mind to go blank and imagined he was back in his native village, walking through the fields. He looked up at the sky.

The sky seemed to be dotted with umbrellas of various colours and the horizon looked like a big rainbow stretching to infinity. He started counting to divert his attention. The parachutes were colour-coded, a new experiment by DRDO, he mused. He saw the white parachutes of the 901 Paras mingle with the green parachutes of the 201 Paras. Shinde thought that perhaps it was done to make their parachutes easier to hide in the terrain when they landed, 201 being experts in jungle warfare and 901 being their mountainous counterparts. Damn, he was already thinking like an officer; he allowed himself a self-congratulatory smile.

The pain had started to diminish. Shinde got up. He grabbed his Tavor rifle, checked his compass and started trudging carefully towards the rendezvous point. He knew that their task would be easier from now onwards. The facility was surrounded.

The grey thunderbirds flying above continued to drop their cocoons that metamorphosed into colourful butterflies at a certain altitude. The first wave had already landed and formed a defensive perimeter to protect the airborne troops from any ground assault.

The stage was set. They had landed.

The men were not law enforcement agents, nor were they plain infantry units of the army. With their gleaming balidaan badges, these men were the Special Forces, the crème de la crème of the Indian army. They were charged with intelligence collection, sabotage of vital enemy infrastructure through surgical strikes behind the enemy lines, apart from covert and overt counterterrorist operations within and beyond the Indian territory. They had seen combat not only in times of conflict, but also during peace, that too in all terrains and climes, owing to the ever-present insurgency and extremist movements in India. These men had not just trained; they had been in the thick of almost continuous combat for over two decades. It not only made them dangerous but lethal as well—for only the quick and the deadly survived to go on another mission.

Currently, the Special Forces were engaged in hounding the Naxalites out from the Red Corridor. Apart from regular combat, 201 Paratrooper Battalion, a former unit of Maratha Light Infantry, had been coordinating with the Border Security Force (BSF), utilizing its Tehri Camp to train officers and men of regular army in counterinsurgency and jungle warfare. The other premier facilities of Counterinsurgency and Jungle Warfare School (CIJWS) and Narayanpore Jungle Combat Academy (NJCA) were also operating at full capacity. Sending only specially equipped and trained men into the Red Corridor had been a policy decision as early endeavours had resulted in heavy casualties. They had almost finished the task when they were mobilized for operations in Andaman.

Word went around of what was afoot. Their briefing said they needed to secure the area and sanitize it when the order came. Until then, they had to keep constant watch.

Shinde intended to do more than that.

Integrated Defence Command Headquarters, New Delhi

Local time: 2100 hours
Date: 24 April 2014

'Shall I report the bad news first or the horrendous news?' Air Chief Marshal Sharma's face was grim, the ever-present twinkle in his eyes had vanished.

'Give us the bad news first. We need time to brace ourselves for the worst,' Malhotra replied evenly.

'They hit a reconnaissance sortie of ours. A SAM launcher seems to be the villain. Or the one holding it at least,' the ACM divulged the reason behind his glumness.

'What the...' Malhotra's jaw almost touched the polished tiles of the floor.

'Yes. We lost a plane... Su-30 MKI. The pilot is safe, though.' ACM Sharma lamented the loss of a million-dollar state-of-the-art machine. 'No more will Sukhoi-30 MKI be considered invincible,' he continued, anger seeping into his voice. 'Weren't we told that the attackers did not have access to any security systems on the base, least of all a SAM console? Did they not need an unbreakable password to get into the mainframe to access and activate such a system?'

'It seems the attackers were well-equipped and they somehow managed to get the air defence systems online. This is bad news indeed but how could they? DRDO had assured me that no one would be able to get through the system. Only three individuals knew the proper coding and unlocking sequence and all of them were fully reliable!' The IB head shook his head and slapped the table in a bout of disbelieving anger.

'Well-equipped? If they got through that system then they are surely more than well-equipped!' snorted the defence secretary. Malhotra had a fleeting vision of the defence secretary's head in place of a golf ball as he hit the stroke of his life.

'And what is the horrendous news?' the cabinet secretary, who was quietly studying the situation with practised ease until now, asked.

This time Admiral Sapra spoke up, 'It is based on the ill-fated sortie and fresh images from RISAT.'

'Ah good. Now we will have some answers. Go on.'

'They...they plan to launch Pralay,' the admiral, who was earlier talking with the chiefs of ISRO and DRDO, tried to keep his voice as even as possible. The room suddenly fell silent as hearts stopped beating for a moment to process this information.

'They plan to WHAT?' Malhotra could not believe his ears. He was livid.

'You heard me right. They plan to launch Pralay.' The admiral looked down and started fiddling with the water bottle for the lack of anything better to do.

'But how can they? Even if they got past the security, how come they can get through all the software safeguards we installed? How can they override the safety mechanism? How can they get past the hardware lockers?' Malhotra was jumping all around the room.

A chorus played. 'They got past our security forces,' the defence secretary said, realizing the implications, his face carved out of stone.

'They got past the software locks that our brightest had installed,' said the foreign secretary.

'They found the assembly plans and hardware storage bunkers of the missile,' Air Chief Sharma muttered softly.

The naval chief remarked, 'They cracked the code the missile defence system employed.'

'All within record time!' echoed the RAW head and the cabinet secretary, sealing the eulogy with an acceptance of the veracity of the claims.

'If only we had employed them instead of DRDO for our weapons research program. Hell!' Malhotra said and looked at them incredulously. Sometimes the most serious of all situations could be the most funny. Like a Pakistani soldier shot in his bum while peeing. Malhotra knew it. He had fired the shot. However, this was not funny. Not one bit.

Malhotra began, 'I can understand them getting past the light CISF cover, but how on earth can they beat a complex computer program? It was specifically designed to prevent anyone from launching the missile without prior permission. All our strategies until now were based on one underlying assumption—that they could not fire the missile simply because they could not gain access to it, and that they were there to merely attract our attention. Hell, they could not even have, as I was briefed, copied the plans or sabotaged the missile. It was a futile, suicidal mission. How can they…fire it!'

'I can think of only one explanation,' the cabinet secretary volunteered, his lips pressed in a thin line, his eyes focusing on the far end of the wall.

'What?' asked Malhotra, a bit too vehemently.

'If one eliminates all the options, then the one remaining, no matter how unlikely, has to be the correct explanation,' said the cabinet secretary as if to provide rational credence to what was about to come. It not only made the listener think twice before doubting the source of information, but also made him accept the viewpoint at face value, and thus the conclusion and the action plan, of the speaker. A typical, by-the-book, IAS maneuver.

'What do you mean?' The general was on his guard. If this babu so much as hinted at his boys' incompetence or passed the blame to the sentries guarding the centre he would have had it. The dead should be respected. Their mistakes analysed, yes, but they should not be disgraced. They died fighting for the nation. The military, after all, took a different view of the errors committed in the line of duty. A reprimand, a show-cause notice or a transfer to a distant town were half as heartbreaking as a funeral. They can never understand this, the general thought. He sized up the cabinet secretary from head to foot. He thought he saw him twitch. That made him feel better, all of a sudden.

'Yes?'

'General,' offered the cabinet secretary, 'it seems that we have been betrayed.' It might have been Salma Sultana announcing that the new development schemes initiated by the government were having the desired results.

'What!!' the general bellowed, bewildered.

'Are you sure, Mishraji?' he asked the cabinet secretary incredulously.

'Yes, I am,' came a terse and infuriatingly calm reply.

'So are you suggesting that someone from amongst our staff passed on the schematics and the master code to unlock the hardware chamber and propulsion laboratory to the terrorists?' the admiral asked. Someone gasped.

'Hmm... Now that I think about it, I concur with Mishraji. There is no other explanation. One of the three scientists who had the password and the biometric key must have sold us out.' The RAW head jumped into the conversation, suddenly aware that only such a turnout of events could save his job now.

'It is betrayal! Our intelligence did not fail. Our own people did. We just did not think anyone could betray our motherland!' he said further.

'Yes, this seems far more plausible. There is no way on earth they could have hacked into our database in a matter of hours—a database guarded by a safety program that took the IIT five years to manufacture. They most definitely had insider support,' his counterpart from IB had similar thoughts. His and RAW chief's eyes met for a brief second. A feeling of empathy passed between them, like two drowning bees who had just realized that the water was not wet at all.

The air chief marshal opened his mouth to say something but was cut off by Malhotra's sharp voice, 'Order them to move in!' The rest of the men looked at him, realization dawning on them.

'Attack!' Malhotra shrieked at the top of his lungs, his face puffed and his hand pointing to a red spot on the displayed map, 'Tell our forces to attack and recapture the base. Now!'

Part II
LAUNCH

War is a game both subjectively and objectively.

—Carl Philipp Gottlieb von Clausewitz

Launch Silo 01, NMRC

Local time: 2200 hours
Date: 24 April 2014

His infrared scope settled on the lone gunman guarding the entry to the complex, trying to hide though the gunman was. No other enemy units were in sight. Pity, he thought, the gunman must know he will be the first one to go in case of a counter-attack, but had agreed to guard the gate to protect his comrades so that they in turn could complete their mission, whatever it was.

Lieutenant Dilip K. Dey felt a tang of regret. People like them were unique. But then the very fact that they needed to kill each other to survive was what gave them this rare character in the first place. Birds of a feather roost together. And kill together.

It was not that he was sitting idly as his mind brooded over the similarities. He had been cleared to engage. Another part of Dey's brain was busy receiving visual inputs and trying to find correlations in order to target him successfully. He noticed the gait, the rare stretching of legs, the speed of walking, and the weapons on the gunman, trying to find a pattern.

The weapons, he thought. The gunman was not using an AK-47 or its Chinese variants like the Naxalites did — weapons he had seen enough of in the past few months. The gunman was holding a Heckler and Koch MP5. A commando's gun.

He increased the magnification on his scope. Like always, he avoided focusing on the face.

Later faces would return to haunt Dey. Shooting in the face was not his style, even if it was the standard operating procedure in such operations. This designated marksman preferred going straight through the target's heart. Armour or not, no Kevlar was strong enough to stop this baby's vomit. He caressed his semi-automatic 7.62x54mm RSVD Dragunov Sniper Rifle, felt the wind velocity and direction and modified the settings again.

One shot. One kill.

Dey focused his scope on the man. He seemed to be agitated. His pace had increased and he was trying to duck and find a safe location. Perhaps he had realized that the base was about to be attacked. Run wherever you can, Dey mentally conveyed to his prospective target, but you cannot run fast enough to dodge a bullet.

Dey sucked in a deep breath and held it in, squinted again and finally squeezed the trigger. The gun recoiled, and his eardrums popped with a loud thwack that scared away birds on a nearby tree. He looked through the scope.

The gunman was no longer standing.

◆

'Major, the perimeter has been breached. We lost contact with number 6,' the man reported, shuddering as he broke the news. 'It seems that the Indian forces are at our gates. They c-c-c-can burst through anytime.'

Rana shot an irritated look at the visibly shaken man. Not a commando by a long shot, nor commando material. He was not happy with the choice of men supplied to him. Manifestations of frustration of a rural populace at underdevelopment, acts like pelting stones and grenades at army convoys passing through a jungle and then disappearing, were much different from the actions expected and characteristics required of a paratrooper. The people supplied may have been the best as per his superiors, but this was a different ball game altogether. These people were trained to operate in their terrain—their jungles, towns and villages. A paratrooper like him, on the other hand, operated deep inside the enemy territory. Cut-off from all routes of supply or escape, possibly even communication. That alone gave him greater adaptability, courage and resourcefulness. However, this was a time to neither differ nor debate. This was a military operation and he had to make do with what was given to him. Otherwise, would there be any difference between his people and the Lahore police?

Major Rana's mind digressed even further when he saw himself holding a gun. It made him realize the difference between the law enforcement agencies, the military, and the intelligence community. The law enforcement agencies often whipped out their firearms, but rarely used them. The military always had to keep their arms in sight; chances to use them were not that often, especially in civilian postings. The intelligence agencies, on the other hand, rarely brandished weapons. However, whenever they had to reach out for their weapons, it usually meant an impending death. A commando was a perfect synthesis of the military and intelligence men.

He smiled, more so at the thought than at the man bearing the news. Rana's smile seemed to have a calming effect on him. Rana always tried to understand the men under his command, like all officers worth their salt. These men were picked from the jungles of Orissa and Jharkhand. They had grown battling hunger and want. Later, indoctrinated by the Maoist cadres, they had turned their ire against the Indian state. First, they attacked the police, then the politicians and then the people, which was when the tide started to turn against them. Most of them had never seen a missile in their life, or even dreamt of seeing one, until his bosses handpicked them and sent them to train in China. A crash course later, they were ready to assemble and launch a deadly missile in a matter of hours. Ah! The wonders of liberal education. He turned towards the group.

'Men, we are very close to what we want. Do not forget how this act is going to benefit our brothers and sisters fighting all over the subcontinent. Never forget the sacrifices they made for you. Now it is time to repay them.'

He paused, giving it time to sink in; most of them knew this mission came with a one-way ticket. 'How much time will it take?'

'Five minutes maximum, sir,' his second-in-command answered.

He sat down. No use hurrying them. A single error and the missile will explode somewhere over the Bay of Bengal. What a waste would that be. He heard gunshots in the background, and the faint whirring of a chopper. 'Do not panic,' he told the others. They were well dug in. All the entries had been sealed, mined and secured. No doubt, the Indians would make their way in, but not without massive casualties — if they hurried. And if they did not hurry, it would be too late. He just hoped the Indians had not realized by now what they were planning.

Rana recited Sun Tzu in his mind to boost himself up: 'Whoever is first in the field and awaits the coming of the enemy, will be fresh for the fight; whoever is second in the field and has to hasten to battle will arrive exhausted. Therefore the clever combatant imposes his will on the enemy, but does not allow the enemy's will to be imposed on him.' He did not realize he was speaking it aloud and others could hear him. The others did not pay heed to him at first, but then a bespectacled man nudged another and whispered, 'He was Chinese, you know.' Then everyone listened to Rana in rapt attention.

Minutes ticked by. When Rana's watch uttered a short crisp beep, he turned towards the concerned section heads and barked, 'Status of the assembly?'

'Complete,' a man looked up to reply, his face proud with the satisfaction at a job well done.

'Fuelling?' Rana asked.

The section head merely nodded, his face showing signs of exhaustion.

'Warhead?' Rana was hesitant to ask this.

'As ordered,' came the reply.

This was where Rana differed with his superior. If we were to fire a missile at the enemy, that too his own, then why not let it be nuclear, especially when it cannot be traced back to them? However, he had explicit orders to activate a conventional warhead from his superior. Well, so be it.

'Silo?' he asked.

'Cleared.'

'Launch doors?'

'Open.'

'Coordinates?'

'Check,' a scratchy voice said and immediately looked away. A wall had started to shake.

The Indians were trying to blast their way through. He had to hurry! He ran to the master control and barked at the technician 'Come on! Do it!'

The stocky man's hands shuddered as he hit the away button. Pre-flight sequence had been completed even before the checklist began. He was good at his work; holding an engineering degree helped in such matters. Perhaps that was why the most important part of the operation was entrusted to him.

'Missile launch in two minutes,' he chimed pleasantly.

The thumps and the explosions started to get louder as they got nearer. The group, apart from the one handling final launch propulsion and guidance, took out its weapons and positioned itself in key areas, taking orders from Rana. This was where his experience and tactical skill came in handy. Rana inserted his gun in a crack created by the explosions and fired a rapid burst. He heard a scream.

The countdown continued as the Indians made a desperate attempt to move in. They must have seen the launch doors open and realized what was about to happen.

'Missile launch in one minute,' a voice shouted.

It was exactly when the Indian forces burst in, using gas canisters. Paratroopers, as expected. They must take us for fools, Rana thought. He and his men had worn gas masks at the first signs of trouble. The faint hiss of the gas went almost unheard due to the steady rat-tat of automatic weapons fire. Rana saw two of his men fall. An Indian fell too. He kept firing.

No indiscriminate shots. Ammunition is always precious. He fired in single-burst mode at a target, incapacitated it, and moved to the next with a lightning reflex. He was well hidden behind a console and kept taking his attackers out as his men fell one by one.

He saw the man charged with guidance and propulsion working furiously at the console. He should have dispensed with all the tasks until now. Finally, the man, one of his own, a Soviet war veteran and the oldest man on this mission, completed his task, as evident from the smug look on his face, and started running towards higher ground. He was viciously cut down by enemy fire. Major Rana's mouth opened to utter a profanity but before he could, he heard the sweetest voice in his life.

'Missile launched,' the automated computer voice chirped, and was then blown away by a rapid burst from Rana's gun into its core processor.

Rana pulled back and muttered a short prayer. He fingered the bomb strapped onto his chest. He closed his eyes and saw his younger brother beaming at him. He saw their home in the lush green valley of Swat. He saw both of them playing together, going to school…and then his brother's lifeless body after he was killed by American drones.

The sounds were on top of him by now. He waited.

Someone was screaming at him, asking him to surrender. Absentmindedly, not wanting to snap out of his daydream amongst all this grime, smoke, and death, Rana pressed a button on the carefully concealed device that was mounted on his chest.

Then, in a swirling flash of colours, life, as he knew it, ceased to exist.

Integrated Defence Command Headquarters, New Delhi

Local time: 2215 hours
Date: 24 April 2014

'What!' The men were aghast, shocked and unsure of how to react. Simulations or drills, no matter how detailed, were never able to produce the same effect as actual happenings. 'They have launched the missile,' a voice announced, sombre and resigned.

The words sunk in slowly. Heads started to buzz. The light in the room became surreal. Hearts started to beat faster and then slowed down to nothingness. The missile. Away. Directed at god knows where. *Our* missile. *Their* target.

'Were not our forces supposed to stop them?' another voice asked, bitter and afraid.

'They set it off just as our men reached the control station,' the RAW head explained.

'Why did it take our men so long?' asked the external affairs secretary, desperately trying to find someone to blame.

'The entrances were mined and closely guarded. Seems they knew about all the possible points of infiltration. They had the detailed plans of the complex. They expected us. They even knew exactly how we would come in,' the admiral reported.

'Damn!' A collective sigh ran through the group.

'Status of attackers?' Malhotra, who had been listening quietly until now, spoke up. It was time to react. He knew that damage control should be the foremost thing on his mind now. There was always time for self-pity and denial later.

The general began to fire questions one after the other. The men around the table answered. It felt like a rapid-fire round in a school quiz. Nervous faces looked at each other, united by grief and determination. 'Tell me, what about the attackers? Did we find anyone alive?'

'All dead.'

'Pralay?' Malhotra asked.

'Airborne.'

'Warhead?'

'Unknown.'

'Target?'

'Presently unknown. Further information needed for calculations.'

'Estimates?'

'It has a range of 8000 km with a 500 kg conventional warhead. Pros for us: it is a test missile and can splutter and drop down in the sea any time. Cons: it is nuclear capable. 150 kilotons strategic yield,' sputtered the chief of DRDO.

'Damn!'

'And with a range of 8000 km, it can hit any city in India, including New Delhi.'

'Hmm… It is my opinion that we must prepare for the worst and hope for the best.' Who else but the cabinet secretary could have said that!

'Hang on. If the missile is airborne, all we need to do is use the guidance boosters to make it drop harmlessly in the Bay of Bengal,' suggested Air Chief Sharma.

'We have already tried doing that. The attackers have installed a program that locks and encrypts further modifications made to the trajectory of the target,' said the director general of DRDO, slumping in his chair.

'Are you telling me we are locked out of our own system?' asked an incredulous Malhotra.

'Yes, but we are working on it.'

'But how can they install such a program? Now that I think of it, how can they even build one?' The admiral was furious, 'Looks like the attackers had some backing from the Silicon Valley itself!'

'Oh come on...' the air chief stopped midway as he scrutinized a note thrust in front of him. 'Sir, this news is just in. We have calculated that the expected target of the missile, as per its current trajectory, is...' He looked unsure.

'Yes?'

'Delhi.'

Moans of 'Oh my God', 'Is this really happening?', 'This cannot be true!' rendered through the air.

'Time of impact?' General Malhotra asked, unfazed by the recent development, or at least pretending to be so.

'Unknown.'

'Unknown? What do you mean by that?'

'Pralay employs a multi-ring laser gyro-inertial navigation system Mark II. It keeps the speed of the missile and bearing constantly changing in order to confuse the enemy about its time and location of impact.'

'Gosh. We created that?'

'Indeed we did,' said the DRDO chief, unsure whether to feel proud or ashamed.

Malhotra started to give orders. 'Fine. Contact the Central Emergency Response Agency. Start evacuating Delhi. We can only speculate that the target will be Raisina Hill, which should be symbolic enough for the attackers. Start evacuating people to Gurgaon, Noida, and Faridabad. The farther they can go, the better. What is the status of our Strategic Forces Command?'

'It is still at Level 7, sir, all green,' the ACM replied.

'Huh? All green? What is that?' asked a confused administrator.

Sapra almost smiled before saying, 'SFC follows a prioritized seven-level alert that is based on the current threat perception. In the lowest, that is Level 7, the nuclear core is kept in secure and concealed storage facilities managed by the Atomic Energy Commission.'

'Ah. So what do we do now?' asked the secretary to the Ministry of External Affairs.

'Simple. We raise alertness from Level 7 to Level 5, Amber,' said the general.

'And that would mean?'

'It means that some of the nuclear cores are mated to the warhead by DRDO. Also, we review strike plans.'

'I have a feeling we might need it. It is better to bare fangs now than to bite later. If any country thinks it can attack our soil with our own weapons, then it is time to set things in better perspective.' A decision, huge one at that, was about to be taken. Despite the gravity of the situation, someone involuntarily yawned.

Launch Silo 01, NMRC

Local time: 0010 hours
Date: 25 April 2014

The dark shadows swept across the bleeding room. One by one, they picked up the moaning enemy targets, destroyed them with controlled bursts from their Micro-TARs and moved forward, unhindered by walls of steel or fire. They were tasked with reaching the centre of the missile complex — the main control lab — as soon as possible, and then retake the area.

Rush in, sterilize the area, and prevent the enemy from inflicting any significant infrastructural damage. Although they had been successful in neutralizing the enemy until now, they had been failing on the second front. The enemy had been able to block their path with mines and sharpshooters, not to mention the tactical positioning of their men that gave them an edge. To top it all, unlike the attacking Special Forces, the enemy had been using heavy weapons and anti-material weaponry, designed to cause maximum damage to personnel and property.

Captain Rajiv Thomas of the 901 Paratrooper Battalion moved forward, stealthily and steadily. As a battalion intelligence officer, his CO had ordered him to gather any clues to ascertain the identity of the attackers. Thomas was not active in combat duty on this mission, going by the real meaning of the term 'combat'. His task was to tag along his mates, observe enemy behaviour, focus on their dress, language, supplies, weapons, tactics and strategies and try to speculate on their intentions, goals, methods and of course, their parent body.

Thomas moved forward, acting as a staff agency, registering every minute detail. In the intense fighting that was happening all around him, he had not fired a single shot. He was there to act as a detached observer. An involved observer may miss crucial details. Thus, be detached and cold. It could save many lives in the future, at the expense of one life today.

He heard shouts. Thomas focused, trying to filter the words from background noise. It struck him. Kharia! They were talking in Kharia, an Austro-Asiatic language spoken by a tribal group living in the states of Jharkhand and Orissa. Thomas knew them from his counterinsurgency operations in the Red Corridor.

What were *they* doing here? The answer struck him like a newspaper roughly flung in through his second floor window early morning, and onto his sleeping dog. It was clear to him. Kharia. Jharkhand. Naxalites.

Precision firing had, by then, cut down the insurgents. They did not stand a chance. There were no jungles to run back into and disappear. Within minutes, three more attackers lay dead.

Another attacker came out, threw his gun down and surrendered. Operating under standard procedures, attempts were to be made to capture him alive, but not in all cases. Such men, even if caught, rarely sung. Why bother wasting men over such a source of information that might never talk? He was shot when he tried to throw a grenade at Thomas.

Thomas was assimilating the information when he heard another voice from the adjacent room. Radiating calm in the pandemonium, the voice sought to bring order to chaos. It barked orders in English with a heavy Punjabi drawl. And that pointed the needle of suspicion towards Pakistan.

Thomas saw the guns, the tactics, and was transported back to the days of his training in enemy identification. The Pakistani Special Service Group was working hand-in-glove with the Naxalites, he realized. His brain jolted at it processed this information, so did his body. Thomas tried to move forward when he was suddenly thrown backwards by an explosion. He was not hurt but two of his mates were not so lucky. Thomas looked back to see their guts sprawled open. They opened their mouth to moan but no sound came out. It seemed the last attacker had blown himself up, and a couple of Indian paratroopers and an entire wall went with him. Thomas was lucky to have escaped with minor injuries.

He shouted for the medic to attend to his fallen comrades and moved on. The radio started chattering. The facility had finally been secured. Damage assessment was under way. Thomas started scanning other rooms, quickly peeking in and ensuring that all was well—or not all that wrong, he thought wryly. His mind focused on only one thing—getting information, clues and answers to this riddle, so that whoever did this could be repaid in kind.

Integrated Defence Command Headquarters, New Delhi

Local time: 0100 hours
Date: 25 April 2014

The room was witnessing confusion distilled to its purest form.

Caught unprepared in an unusual situation, with no knowledge of what they were facing, the men present in the room had to rely on their experience, ingenuity and courage. They were expected to take shots at an elusive, invisible target, that too in the dark.

Because of their painstaking efforts, Delhi was a city in motion. The military and CERA had swung into action to implement their orders. Entire cantonments, air bases, the Central Paramilitary Forces and police lines had been mobilized for that. The authorities were busy goading people to initiate a quick evacuation of the city. Bus terminals were full of people assembled for transport to distant locations or to be shepherded into bunkers. There were long but well-managed queues as hastily recalled DTC bus drivers came running in their pyjamas, and sped their jam-packed buses away. Trains inbound for Delhi were stopped and unloaded at the borders of the National Capital Territory (NCT), sent forth empty, loaded with people at pre-planned intra-city stations and were rushed out. The smaller railway stations of Sarojini Nagar and Pragati

Maidan were acting as transit points where citizens residing nearby boarded the next train out of the city. The government had already issued instructions to the Delhi Metro Rail Corporation to divert all coaches to the Delhi-Meerut, Delhi-Faridabad and Delhi-Rohtak lines of the Delhi Metro.

Consequently, from every metro station in Delhi, an express train with seven overflowing coaches left Delhi for a station in another state every ninety seconds.

The plan to evacuate Delhi integrated trains, buses, metros and the Mass Rapid Transport System to empty the city into its surrounding satellite sub cities where the impact of the explosion would be less than in Delhi. Protocol-wise, units had swung into action to transport people, starting from the high and mighty to the aam-aadmi, to underground shelters and places far away. North Block, South Block, the presidential estates, residences of the top brass, the diplomatic enclave were already empty by now; crucial staff were airlifted to secure locations. The evacuation of others continued.

Malhotra read a status report of the process handed over to him, nodded in satisfaction and turned to the room.

'Estimated time of impact?' he asked.

'Two and a half hours, sir. Its speed seems to puzzle us. Perhaps it is the navigational system of the missile. The target is bang in the centre of Delhi—India Gate,' said the operations officer, not being able to believe the words coming out of his own mouth.

'Strategic and symbolic...but two and a half hours?' asked the defence secretary.

'Yeah. The trajectory of the missile is very irregular,' noted ACM Sharma and looked questioningly at the only man who could have answered that question satisfactorily—the head of DRDO who was also the scientific adviser to the Ministry of Defence.

The DRDO chief thought for a bit and replied, 'It was meant to be. The new guidance system we installed was precisely for this effect. But even I cannot say if it was meant to be this irregular.'

'This is extremely unusual. What should we do?'

'When in doubt, shoot,' whispered General Malhotra.

A sceptical cabinet secretary, Ajay Mishra, realized the implications of this decision and raised his eyebrows. He spoke, 'General, are you sure you want to do this?'

'Yes,' came a terse reply from Malhotra, and he nodded to the admiral.

Admiral Sapra got the hint, and in turn looked at the operations officer and said, 'As you wish, General.'

He then gave his order, 'Raise the SFC alert to Level 3. Mate the warheads to the missiles and let the military begin to move them into launch positions. Also, review and ready plans for Level 2. But take no proactive measures, OK?'

The operations officer looked at General Malhotra, and at a nod from him went out and began to comply by coordinating with the actual executors of the orders, passing on the specific codes required for the job.

Suddenly, an officer from DRDO, white as a sheet, burst in panting. 'Sir, we have developments,' he screamed, his spectacles almost falling off his nose.

'What? Is it going to strike sooner?' asked Mishra, rising from his chair.

'No, sir.'

'Will strike later than expected, then? Good for us. It will give us more time to evacuate.' Air Chief Vikramjeet Sharma heaved a sigh of relief.

'No, sir.'

'No? Are you telling me it veered off course and fell in the sea or in a forest?' enquired an agitated Admiral Sapra.

'Er...no, sir.'

'Then what are you trying to say, young man?' General Malhotra asked. Irritation oozed out of the room like a white frothing brook. The general's gaze was capable of melting steel.

'Based on the present calculations, the missile will...er... overshoot Delhi,' the DRDO officer managed to sputter.

He was not to be blamed, though. He was on deputation to DRDO from the Indian Space Research Organisation (ISRO). All this talk of missiles and violence made him sad. Not to mention scared. He was an explorer who had planned to devote his life to locate and communicate with extra-terrestrial intelligence. All this human infighting made him irritated. However, he chose to keep his irritation in check, for greater matters pestered him.

An incredulous general asked, 'What! Are you sure?'

'Yes, sir. I double-checked,' the man said nervously. The only thing that would have offended him was to have his calculations doubted. Thankfully, it did not happen.

'Ha! Thank God we have got the DRDO working for us!' the admiral said, sarcasm mingled with relief, as the DRDO chief gave him an angry look.

'Then where is it headed?'

'Er...this is only a rough estimate. The missile constantly keeps changing bearing but the most probable target as per its current trajectory is...' His voice trailed off imagining the kind of reaction his revelation would invoke.

The home secretary realized his condition. He said, 'Come on, beta. Speak up. Where is it going to strike?'

'Sir, based on its current trajectory, it will strike Amritsar,' the man from DRDO said and looked away.

Silence engulfed the room like a dark, icy sheet.

Master Control Facility, NMRC

Local time: 0200 hours
Date: 25 April 2014

As a hound on scent, Captain Rajiv Thomas kept searching room after room diligently. Salvage operations were under way. Based on what he had come across until now, the perpetrators were most definitely Naxalites, but with SSG guns, ammunitions, supplies and leadership.

Grapevine had it that India was officially moving to Red Deux, Level 2 of nuclear readiness. Preliminary action had been initiated to permit rapid transition to maximum readiness and nuclear capable missiles were being moved to launch positions.

Funny, he thought, how it was a missile that had started it all. He instinctively looked back at the empty silo. How could they have assembled and test-fired a missile? How on earth? He saw a dead attacker. He rummaged through his gear. Yes, definitely SSG standard issue equipment. However, the man himself was frail and emaciated. Moreover, he was wearing spectacles. Not the SSG-type at all, Thomas thought.

Thomas stumbled across another body, this one wearing a lab coat that was caked with blood. He must be one of the technical staff of the base, he thought. A postcard-sized photo hung out of the lab coat's upper pocket. Was it a picture of his family? Friends? Out of curiosity Thomas bent down to pick it up. It showed a man, most probably the one lying dead at his feet, on his graduation day. Weird scientists. Colleagues are their family, work their religion, he mused — is it any different from us?

Thomas was about to put the photo away but he decided to look at it once. The picture was clicked with an old Polaroid camera and was of the same man standing with a couple of his friends. He saw the picture and was about to respectfully stuff it back in the man's pocket when something caught his eye.

He looked at the photo again. A shiver ran down his spine. He shook his head forcefully and rubbed his eyes with his hands. Then he looked at the photo again. And kept looking, his mouth hung open, his brain refusing to work.

Jesus, is it possible? He flipped the photo over to read 'Surya, Bhau, Wali, and Ray — Graduation Day 1985, IIT Kharagpur' scrawled on it in wriggly handwriting. The man at his feet was definitely Surya. Or Suryakant, as the name tag on the lab coat said, something that Thomas had missed earlier. He chided himself. Such minute details were vital.

Thomas looked at the picture again. His mind started to whirr as he compared the picture he was currently holding in his hands with the sole existing picture of another individual he had come to fear. The photo that he had seen had been taken in Kathmandu about a decade ago. This one was, on the other hand, about thirty years old. A swear word escaped him as realization struck home. Mutual necessity, it seems, is the mother of strange bedfellows. 'O God, why hast thou forsaken us?' he said. From behind the face of a young, smiling Bhau thirty years ago, Comrade Agyaat's penetrating gaze stared back at him.

Integrated Defence Command Headquarters, New Delhi

Local time: 0300 hours
Date: 25 April 2014

'Sir, I am not sure whether this will make you feel better or worse...' The DRDO man was back again, his eyes carefully checking the data on the pad he clutched close to him, as if it was the only thing standing between him and the forceful personalities all around.

'Or mad?' Sharma, the cheeky joker, quipped.

'Or mad,' the man accepted gracefully.

'What is it?' asked Malhotra, who was, by now, getting extremely wary of the sudden twists in the tale.

The DRDO chief had by now stridden towards his staff member and was glancing at his data with the most peculiar expression on his face. 'Er...you are not going to like this,' he said.

'Come on, tell me. How can I like this if I have not liked an iota of whatever that has happened in the past few nightmarish hours of my life?' Malhotra was feeling on the edge.

'The direction of the missile has changed. Pralay has a new target again,' the DRDO chief announced.

'Oh how wonderful,' someone rued in the background.

'What???'

'Again!'

'No!'

Had the situation not been so tense, the chorus would have been quite aesthetic for its absurdist tautology.

'Yes, the variable target guidance system installed in Pralay just kicked in. The target changed at the last instant. The missile was twenty-three kilometres from Amritsar when it swerved in another direction.'

'Which direction? Is it doubling back on us now that we have stopped the evacuation of Delhi and asked Amritsar to be evacuated in turn?' Malhotra asked, horrified, and hoping that he was wrong. He was.

'No, sir.'

People in the room sighed collectively in relief.

'Then what is the missile's final target?' asked Mishra.

'It does not make any sense! I do not know what to make of it, sir!' The DRDO man holding the data pad was still shaking his head.

Poor lad, buckling under pressure, thought the civil servants, must be hard for him. Incompetent wretch, thought the military men, he should be shot for dereliction of duty at such a crucial hour. As ever, the two viewpoints clashed; one was hard when the other was soft, one was aggressive when the other was defensive. Between the civil servants and the military, no one way of life was either hard or soft forever—their perspectives changed with the context. The military was from Mars, and the civilian administrators from Venus, but for the fact that both of them frequently kept changing their home planets.

'Dammit, tell me where is the missile going to strike?' Malhotra screamed; he was fed up of the erratic missile.

The man stammered, 'La-la-la-Lahore, sir. The missile is headed straight towards Lahore.'

It seemed as if time stopped for a while. Then everyone in the room, from the battle-hardened warriors to the most esteemed rational, non-sentimental core constituents of the steel frame, went utterly mad.

Part III
IMPACT

We make war that we may live in peace.

— Aristotle

Ganda Singh Wala, Kasur, Pakistan

Local time: 0345 hours
Date: 25 April 2014

Corporal technician Rashid Haidar operating the air defence station in the twenty-four hours operational observation room was freshly hurting from a fight with his better half. His fondness for cricket clashed with his wife's love for reality shows, and he had just one television set at home.

An irritated Haidar stopped cursing the day he had said yes to marriage when he spied something anomalous on the screen. He bent to recheck as he felt his body shiver. He looked up from his console slowly and shook his head. He counted from one to ten and then looked down again, only to stare disbelievingly at the venomous information the console was spewing out. He scanned the scope for a third time, his eyes unable to believe what he was seeing. This was not possible! Where did it come from?

Haidar took a print out and ran to the officer-on-duty, Cecil Chughtai, a lieutenant recently graduated from the Pakistan Military Academy, and handed him the paper. Chughtai was, against regulations, listening to music on his iPod and smoking a Marlboro while still on duty. Night shifts, especially pertaining to watch-keeping and coordination, were immensely boring. Some leeway was granted to officers with regard to how they chose to spend their time. Listening to music, having a smoke and reading a book, generally qualified as one such illegitimate but acceptable time-pass.

Chughtai started as the visibly pale Haidar entered the room in a mad rush, as if rabid dogs were chasing him.

'Yes?' Chughtai asked curtly. He did not like being disturbed in the middle of Zaphod's daring escape from the Vogons.

'Sir...' Haidar pushed the paper towards Chughtai. He did not salute, an omission noted by the lieutenant. He will have to record it and discipline the corporal himself, the lieutenant thought. He never trusted these air force types with their inherent oh-I'm-so-better-than-you-bloody-earth-thumpers attitude. Leave officers, even other ranks were obnoxious. A pity air defence was primarily the responsibility of the Pakistan Air Force.

Chughtai looked up in time to see Haidar trying to steady himself on the table.

'*Oye! Ki hoya?*' Chughtai asked, suddenly cautious, 'You look as if you have seen a ghost! Are you all right?' He hoped the man under his command was not having a cardiac arrest. Such accidents tarnished one's record. Really. He knew a lieutenant general who did not make it to a full general only because he had given many under his command. Cardiac arrests.

'J-j-janaab,' Haidar pointed at the printout with shaking fingers.

Chughtai glanced at it, his interest piqued by such a queer anomaly. He studied the document further. It sunk in with the intensity of a sharp, heated scimitar. The cigarette dropped from his lips. He got up and rushed to the console to recheck the calculations and sensor readings himself.

Chughtai completed his calculations as sweat drops began to appear on his forehead. With a quivering voice, he called his superior at GHQ to inform him of the development. From there, the chain of command took over, until it reached and forcefully shook General Mohammad Akram Haque, the chief of Pakistani army, from his cosy slumber.

♦

The general was out of his bed and making his way towards the headquarters in almost record time. His farmhouse was not very far away from the headquarters. His cavalcade sped on the empty roads, sirens blaring at full. When he reached, his deputies who had already assembled in the war room waiting to be briefed, greeted him with worried looks. This was insane. This was so not happening.

'Status?' General Akram barked, as the doors to the conference room closed behind him.

Silence greeted him, followed by a wave of incoherent murmuring. He did not know whether it was the unearthly hours, low morale, trouble with enemy identification or lack of plain sleep that made his officers act like this. Or was it the anti-corruption cases lodged against them by the new government?

'Come on, men, pull yourself together. We have a job to do. We have planned for such eventualities, right? We always knew India would attack us one day. Today we prove to the Pakistani people how much they need us for their safety. Brief the president and the PM.'

Akram knew well one of the basic rules of command. When in a sticky situation, distance oneself from urgency. Behave as if nothing is wrong. Act almost casual. That everything is well under control. Or soon will be. Just keep a cool head, use your training and follow orders. Otherwise, all is lost in the first few hours of combat itself.

There was a murmur of agreement. People started falling in line.

'Target?' General Akram asked no one in particular.

The men understood at whom the question was directed. The commander of Army Air Defence Command said, glancing up from his notepad, 'The target remains the same, sir. Lahore.'

'Have you tried to take the missile down yet?' Akram asked.

A major general reported, 'We have, sir. We have activated the Missile Shield System and locked on Interceptor and S-75 Dvina missiles, but the oncoming missile is highly agile. Almost invisible. It fools our counter-attacks.'

The air vice-marshal of the Air Defence Command, Chaklala, ventured forth, 'Yes, sir. We have also launched three unsuccessful waves until now with MBDA Spada 2000. All failed. This is highly advanced enemy technology we are dealing with. We cannot even lock in on the heat signature of the missile about to hit us. The speed and bearing keeps changing with every moment. This is absurd! It is Op. Geronimo all over again!'

Akram responded, 'This is irritating indeed. Launch one more wave. The intelligence reported that Indians were planning to do something similar, did it not? Did we not create battle plans for such a contingency? There has to be something that we can do!'

His question was met by an awkward silence. Of all the battle exercises and plans, none had prepared them for an attack with an invisible missile.

'Warhead?' Akram asked.

'Indeterminate,' came the reply.

God, I hope it is not nuclear. He gritted his teeth, 'Evacuation status?'

'Lahore is being evacuated, but it is bound to take time. It is a big city, after all. The delay lay in locating the incoming missile,' said commander north of the Pakistani navy.

Others jumped to his defence. 'It seems to be a new stealth design, sir. Even our newly acquired American radar sensors were unable to pick it until it was almost on top of us.'

'Yeah, even the American technology failed to detect it!'

'Even now, it disappears off the screen now and then. We can only hope it reappears. We know one thing—the flight path makes it clear it originated from the Indian airspace. It was launched from India.' Perhaps this was the only thing that everyone present in the room fully agreed to. It was all India's fault. As always.

Akram swore and turned to face his most trusted aide, who had uncharacteristically remained silent until now. How very curious, Akram thought, and opened his mouth to say something to him. Lieutenant General Asif Chowdhury sat gazing into the distance, drumming the table with his fingers. His face was unreadable.

Integrated Defence Command Headquarters, New Delhi

Local time: 0400 hours
Date: 25 April 2014

'If deep shit qualifies as this much...till here,' General Malhotra made a gesture of the depth of the entity he was talking about, 'then I reckon we are in deep shit to the power of n, where n equals the number of battle plans we have drawn up in case of opening up of hostilities against Pakistan.'

'And it is time for legs up-hands down drill,' muttered ACM Sharma, his NDA days flashing back in his mind all of a sudden.

The war room was abuzz with voices. The cabinet secretary leaned forward as the defence secretary whispered something in his ear. The military men sat huddled together, pondering over the near miss, some even savouring the visible discomfort of the Secretary to the Ministry of External Affairs. Clearly, someone had a lot of explaining to do to the world.

The home secretary broke the silence, 'What do we do now?'

'What do you think we should do?' shot back General Malhotra.

'We should tell the Pakistanis they have an inbound missile. Give them the target and any information they need.

Tell them that the missile is…er…rogue and was launched by non-state actors.'

'I am sure they will understand the terminology all too well,' said Air Chief Sharma, his tone acerbic.

'And hope they believe it.' The Secretary to MEA was already thinking of a list of possible excuses that ranged from equipment malfunction to a terrorist takeover.

However, Admiral Sapra had other thoughts, 'Or we can just sit still and let things be. If Lahore is hit, Pakistan will take time to recover. Enough time, I hope, for us to focus on a few terror camps still operating in PoK and close them. Strike when the enemy is down…do not give any respite. Plus, we will not have trouble establishing the fact that the missile was fired without our consent.'

He was countered by the home secretary, 'Yeah, as if Pakistan will not strike back, huh. It most certainly will, seeing this as a direct attack. Then we will be in an even greater soup.'

'As if they will not strike back even if we do tell them about the missile's target. I would have. Wouldn't you?' replied the admiral.

'Maybe, but that will not be enough to turn me into a barbarian with the blood of innocents on my hands,' clarified the air chief, offended by the naval chief's reply.

'Gentlemen, we are losing focus here. The fact remains— even if we tell them, the missile will hit Pakistan. They lack the technology to stop the incoming missile. Moreover, nobody is going to believe us. They will attack in return. They have to. It is a matter of their policy!' Sapra was busy trying to drive his point home.

'So what do you recommend we do?' asked Malhotra.

Another three-star general spoke up, his interest piqued by the naval admiral's argument. He calmly said, 'I, too, favour a pre-emptive strike. We augment the missile attack and destroy Pakistan's offensive capabilities. We know that Pakistan under even an iota of threat will not wait for our offensive, but rather launch one of its own aiming to occupy our territories near the border. Since corps-level mobilization will take about forty-eight hours, both armies will be evenly matched in the first twenty-four hours simply because the Pakistanis have to travel a shorter distance to their forward positions.

'We, on the other hand, will not be able to reach our maximum strength near the border for another forty-eight hours, as we need to travel greater distance to our own forward defensive-offensive positions. This unpreparedness on our part may give Pakistan parity or even numerical superiority against us, unless we attack first or make a move to mass-mobilize formations at the border. Why give a numerically inferior enemy chance to have partial parity, even temporary? I say, we attack!'

The room rang with plenty of reactions: 'What!', 'Impossible!', 'Maybe', and 'What a preposterous idea!'

Sapra lent his voice to the lieutenant general's argument, 'Why not? Why bolt the stable door when the horses have bolted? Let them run and win a race for us. That is the most logical way to proceed.'

'Yes, but certainly not the most ethical. Our war doctrine is based on self-preservation but no first-use or no first aggressive step. It is the hallmark of our Panchsheel policy,' replied the defence secretary.

'But Panchsheel cost us the 1962 War! What now? Ethics versus realpolitik. We are back to ancient Greece, are we not?

What will we discuss next? Chicken came first or the egg? Or whom to attack after Pakistan? China? Or how to let terrorists dictate our foreign policy?' said the air chief.

'Enough of this!' General Malhotra had been observing the proceedings with much distaste. He looked at the cabinet secretary who merely shook his head and looked down.

Malhotra continued, 'Gentlemen, thanks for your inputs. Tell Pakistan they are about to be hit by a rogue missile of ours, and that we are sorry and will extend any cooperation to undo the damage. Do not forget to sign off with our deepest regrets and sympathies.'

The voices subsided. Order and sanity were finally restored, two things that had fled the room in the past couple of minutes.

The naval chief shrugged, accepting the wisdom of the decision. The way ahead was clear. The debate had ended. The first among equals had spoken.

Lahore, Pakistan

Local time: 0430 hours
Date: 25 April 2014

Abdul Hassan carefully scrubbed his body with cold water from a rickety tap, and then dried himself with a towel. Done with his ablutions, the muezzin glanced at his watch and hurried towards the microphone. It was time for the Fajr azaan. 'Hurry up you clumsy oaf,' he scolded himself, 'Fajr time will pass.' Hassan increased his pace and reached the room. He entered and closed the door behind him to prevent any intrusions. He cleared his throat, adjusted the volume on the loud speaker and sung into the mike to call the faithful for the morning jamaat.

People were already stirring, but as his voice rang through the locality, more and more people started to get up. The cantonment was up too. The Pakistani army's 10th and 11th Divisions were stationed in Lahore. In addition, Lahore was the headquarters of Pakistani IV Corps. Jawans were returning from their daily morning run. Wives woke up grumbling officers to teach the kids.

Suddenly, the city heard a whoosh. A few joggers noticed an object streak past them in the sky. Some thought it was a new military aircraft; others thought it to be a comet. It slowly started getting bigger and more ferocious. The noise increased.

More and more people started to pay attention to the comet. It kept coming closer.

Glass started to rattle in homes and children jumped out of their bed thinking it to be an earthquake.

The noise was deafening by now. Those who were able to see it started to scream, afraid of its metallic, cold ferocity.

Seconds later, Pralay split into a thousand pieces in a high airburst mode that was meant to neutralize soft civilian targets on the ground—houses, shops, and markets. Metal seemed to ram into the earth, glowing red with temperature. The ground shook and a deafening explosion tore through the city; a blinding flash of light followed...then an ear-shattering boom.

A ball of fire seemed to emerge from the point of impact and engulfed the skies and the earth. The buildings at the epicentre were wiped off the face of earth. There was nothing left standing within a radius of one mile. Glasses broke tens of kilometres away. Its after-effects were deadly too.

All of a sudden, the entire area was engulfed in a deathly silence. Not a single voice was to be heard. Dust swirled and concrete rained. Finally, as things settled down, somewhere in the background, human shouts were beginning to be heard—pathetic, insignificant, and chilling.

Good morning, Lahore.

Aiwan-e-Sadr,* Pakistan

Local time: 0545 hours
Date: 25 April 2014

An officer rushed into the main conference room with disbelief written all over his face and reported, 'Sir, we have been hit.'

The civilian and military support staff, in addition to the top brass of Pakistani military, looked aghast as Shahid Abbasi, President of the Democratic Republic of Pakistan**, stared at the paper prepared to brief him on the situation and then back at the bearer of the grave news. A collective groan emanated from the group, as the president looked disbelievingly at the report. They knew what was coming, but hoped they would not hear the worst, that the missile would fall harmlessly into a forest or splutter high in the sky. The realization that they had actually been hit was even more frustrating.

Pakistan attacked! After 1971, this was the first time a major city was targeted by the enemy, he thought. Did our constitutional reforms make us appear weak in the eyes of the world?

---

*The presidential palace-cum-secretariat in Pakistan.
**As a reaction to being labelled a failed state, that too bitten by the bug of global terror, Pakistan's Constitution was re-amended in 2014 expunging the words 'Islamic' from its title.

'Where?' he asked.

'Lahore. Just as the Indians told us. Bank Square Market was the epicentre.'

'Damage?'

'Moderate damage to buildings and infrastructure. About fifty deaths reported yet...200 injured. Instead of a contact burst or a surface burst the missile opted for a high airburst meant to cause significant damage to civilian centres over a large area, even with a conventional warhead.' The reply was surgically cold. Almost chilling.

'My God!' People in the room did not know what to do. A horrible piece of information was fighting its way to sink in the collective psyche of the people present in the room. The PM sat with his head resting on his hands. Mourning. Yet some saw the silver lining in it.

'The figures could have been much higher...thank God we started the evacuations.'

'And that the warhead was conventional.' The lieutenant general shuddered to think otherwise.

'I do not know what would have happened if we had not started the evacuation, or if the missile had hit where the population density is greater than a posh, upper-class market that was closed at the time the missile struck.'

'Do you have imagery?' asked the acting PM, the actual one having been hospitalized owing to age and failing health.

'Yes, both satellite and imagery taken from the ground.'

A projector came to life at the far end of the room. The ground in Lahore was splattered with disorganized concrete. Buildings stood like ancient ruins. There was no sign of life, human, animal or plant. It looked like a ghost town.

The command staff were horrified to see the once bustling market razed to the ground.

'What is the status of the cantonment?' asked the interior minister.

'The cantonment is shaken but ready for mobilization,' pat came a reply.

'No significant damage to it?'

'No, sir.'

'Strange how the enemy avoided a strategic military target and opted for a civilian target.'

'What can you expect of the Indians?' spat out the director general of ISI. 'They want our country razed from the global map, by hook or by crook. Our transition into this sham of a secular, democratic state has eaten us from within. We are meant to be an Islamic state. Any deviation from it is not only unacceptable, but foolish as well. I was stupid to support you and go against the wishes of our founding fathers. Look what you have dragged us into! We should strike back at the enemy. It is time for the final battle. A nuclear response to this unprovoked attack is the only solution!'

'Let us not rush things. The Indians did warn us of the incoming missile,' Lieutenant General Chowdhury interjected. Heads turned immediately at this comment. They would not have been as surprised if Hitler had talked of universal goodwill right after the taking of France! Chowdhury was as jingoistic and shrewd a military commander as one could ever be. To have him defending the Indians was something...new. People looked at him, wondering. He was a known hawk. Why was he defending the enemy?

'A very clever ploy. The Indians know we would have nuked them straightaway had they attacked us openly. So they orchestrate this cock-and-bull story of terrorists taking over their missile base and firing at us instead of them,' the air chief said. He was about to add, 'That too terrorists! Ha! They will never attack on their motherland!' but thought better of it and kept his mouth shut. Times were changing in Pakistan, and he did not intend to be on the wrong side when past ledgers were opened.

'And then they say our nuclear weapons and defence bases are unsafe,' someone snorted.

'You do not believe them?' the president asked.

'Would you be naïve enough to?' General Akram had made up his mind. He thundered, 'Where is the proof that the missile base was actually taken over? Yes, the Indians did warn us, but did they tell us where exactly the missile will hit? What will be its precise flight path? Its control frequency? They knew with that information we could have had a chance to thwart the missile. Why give the enemy key to the door that jails him forever?'

'I am not so sure about it.' The civilian leadership was still not fully convinced.

'Moreover, if the missile had been actually launched, why did not they destroy it mid-air when they recaptured the facility?' Some other officers joined in.

'They say they had been locked out of their own system. Moreover, that the missile's on-board computer has been tampered with to result in this arbitrary flight path. They say they had no access at all to the missile.'

General Akram continued, 'And you believe them?'

'We had no reason not to,' said the acting PM and the president in unison. Clearly, both of them agreed on this.

'What?' It was Akram's turn to gape at the PM and the president.

'Yes, the missile did hit us. Things have changed now. With so many Pakistani lives almost instantly extinguished, I am not sure what to think of it now. Not giving a befitting response right now might create an extremely dangerous precedent,' the PM said. 'We have to hit back. Pakistan is a threatened state. We cannot let India get away with such impunity this time, or we will never be able to show our faces to anyone. Is this why we spend so much on our defence? That anyone can come hit us, apologise, and leave, as our men lie dying?'

The decision was unanimous and instantaneous.

'Get me the prime minister of India,' the president commanded.

The room suddenly fell silent. They realized it was time to change history.

7 Race Course Road, Prime Minister's Residence,
New Delhi

Local time: 0730 hours
Date: 25 April 2014

An orderly rushed in carrying a ringing phone, which was surprising as all telephone lines and communication devices had been jammed at 7 RCR. To rub salt on the wound, Bipolab Roy, the former PM, had been kept in solitary confinement since the coup.

He saw the phone beep. How can it work when all the other phones had been cut off? He took a closer look. It was not any ordinary phone; it was a direct satellite hotline to the office of the president of the Republic of Pakistan, installed after the last peace talks at Bangalore. It worked on a different frequency and with different technology. And, it was ringing.

Why were the Pakistanis calling him? To express their empathy, Roy thought dryly, they being old hands at the trick that had just made him vanish into thin air from India's political landscape. PM Roy pressed the hands-free button on the phone and it sprang to life.

'This is Bipolab Roy. Good morning. To what do I owe this pleasure?'

He was cut in the middle by a brusque, indicting voice. Shahid Abbasi? The president of Pakistan? PM Roy had known his voice for a long time. Both had been roommates at Stanford; they were first bitter enemies as hot-blooded youths (over a girl) and then bosom pals (over the same girl—she had rejected them both).

'Will India please explain?' The voice was sarcastic and angry. Very angry. Roy wondered what had happened. Last time they both had talked, they had ended on a cordial note. In addition, he was talking to a friend.

'Shahid, is this you? What happened? Why are you so angry? And explain what?'

'What happened? Are you kidding me, Roy?' The Pakistani president could not believe his ears. What gall!

'Look, this is irritating.' Roy, an incarcerated Roy at that, was easily irritable.

'It is indeed.'

'What do you want me to explain?' Roy asked, his judgment getting the better of his anger.

'India's recent attack on Pakistan. Unprovoked. Unmerited,' Shahid asked.

'What?' PM Roy jumped out of his chair. It cannot be true, can it? Malhotra cannot...no! He put aside the thought. It just was not possible. 'Are you sure?' he asked.

'Don't you watch the news, Mr Prime Minister? India has attacked us. Lahore is in ruins. About 100 deaths have been reported—all the result of an Indian missile that landed in a civilian area of Lahore. Civilian! It seems you really do not watch news.' Shahid's sarcasm was unmistakable.

Roy felt his anger rising. He was ousted from power, his country had attacked another, and he was being blamed for everything. Terrific, just what I need, he thought. He kept quiet for some time, processing the information, and then the bhadralok in him asked, 'Don't you watch news, Mr President?'

Silence at the other end. 'Why, what happened?' Now it was Shahid's turn to act surprised.

'Don't you know there has been a coup d'etat in my country? I have been deposed. Thanks to our neighbour, whose checkered history, I am sure, provided productive ideas to our forces on how to murder democracy.'

'What? When did this happen?' Shahid realized, in a flash, that he was not the only one having a bad day.

'Very recently. Perhaps you were too entangled in the Balochistan crisis to note that your democratically-elected neighbouring leader has been deposed by the military.' The tone was not sarcastic, Roy was merely stating facts.

Shahid felt the need to inquire further. The pain of an ousted power holder made him soft for a second. 'Why did it happen? I mean, why did the military rise up against you? I heard you were pretty popular.'

'Did you ever ask the same question to your Ayubs and Yahyas?' Roy retorted, a smile playing on his lips now that the absurdity of his situation was dawning on him.

'Hmmm...' came the monosyllabic reply.

'And about the missile? I have been under house arrest. No cable TV or Internet. Total isolation. I am really sorry about what happened. But I assure you we did not do it.'

'We? You mean the civilian government?' Shahid was on his guard.

'No, I mean India. We would never attack you in this manner—especially a civilian centre, that too without any formal declaration of war. We are a nation that firmly believes in the due process of law. We certainly would not attack you when track II diplomacy was succeeding in bridging the gap created by decades of mutual hatred.'

'Ha!' Shahid snorted, 'You expect me to believe renegade terrorists hijack a missile from your closely guarded base and then fire it at Lahore? You seriously expect me to believe that! What do you take me for?'

'Is that what our military leaders tell you? In case they do, then it must be true. General Malhotra might have deposed me, but he is an honourable man. He would never do something as outrageous as this! And that too without taking the government into consideration.' Roy was not sure why he was defending Malhotra. Maybe he sensed that the outcome of his call was going to decide India's foreign policy for the next decade. South Asia's future hung in the balance. This was no time to score brownie points.

'If he really toppled you, then he is the government, Bipolab da.' It was not a taunt by Shahid.

'Listen, there has been a terrible misunderstanding. I recommend we meet at once.'

'The time for meeting is past. Pakistan will not allow India to play with the lives of Pakistani citizens with such impunity and belligerence. I just called to inform you that Pakistan is declaring war on India. I thought I would tell you in person. I owe you this much. Plus, these days we too are a democratic nation governed by the due process of law.' The tone was alternately smug and angry. An interesting combination, Roy thought, but he had bigger matters to ponder over.

PM Roy could not believe what he had just heard. He was planning to visit Islamabad on his way back from Washington after having furthered the Indo-US nuclear deal. He also planned to visit Moscow and Paris. A decisive Ashvamedha

Yagna for him. He had ended India's nuclear isolation and was about to prove to the world that India was a safe country indeed — peaceful, progressive and democratic. Everything had been going so well. But what did India have on its hands now? A coup and a war!

'Don't do that! Please think of the lives that will be lost needlessly. Just imagine the bloodshed. We are both on the path to prove to the world that we are responsible nuclear states. With people-to-people initiatives like *Aman ki Asha*, things are beginning to look better for both our countries,' Roy implored him.

'You should have thought of that before you or your military hatched plans to attack us in this cowardly way, when we were busy dealing with our internal problems. In fact, the Maoists in your country are a nuisance for you too. You are as bogged down by them as we are in NWFP and FATA by Islamists. I do not know which genius in your army came up with a plan to attack us at such a time. Now we both will be fighting on two fronts! And fight we will, to our last breath, I assure you.'

Roy was shell-shocked. 'You do know that if you attack, we will be forced to respond in kind? And that we are stronger than you? That you will be, pardon me for using this word, totally screwed?'

'I do. Nevertheless, that will not make us sit as you torch our house and then deny doing it. Such games will not work.'

Roy was clutching at the last straws. Just when India was almost about to be recognized as a superpower, a responsible, democratic nuclear state, this had happened. 'Is there any hope that we...'

'No.' Shahid's answer was firm, his tone unwavering, 'And I guess we have nothing more left to discuss. Good day, Mr Roy.' The Pakistani president hung up.

After almost a full decade, a man named Shahid Abbasi had hung up on the Indian prime minister, and it still left a bitter taste in Roy's mouth.

**The Oval Office, White House, Washington DC,
The United States of America**

Local time: 1000 hours
Date: 25 April 2014

'What? You cannot be serious!' thundered President AC Wilson and stared at his advisors as they shrunk back, conscious of the lapse in protocol, the big faux pas they had unwillingly committed by not bringing news of a major event months before it actually happened. It was a fatal mistake for careers at the White House.

'Yes, sir. India has launched a missile at Pakistan — a stealth ICBM they were working on.'

'A secret ICBM? Is it the same missile that the Combined Intelligence Corps assured me was decades from being operationalized?'

Someone shifted uncomfortably and muttered, 'Yes, sir. India says its missile base was taken over by terrorists who then launched the missile at Pakistan.'

'Seems rather a nice coincidence that the terrorists fired the missile the very day the military seized power in India.'

'In retaliation, Pakistan has declared war on India.'

The president continued, 'Damn! CIC failed this time! However, why launch at Pakistan? Why not attack India itself if the terrorists were against the Indian state?' asked the president.

'That is the million dollar question.'

'Global reactions?'

'China condemns the act but will not be involved militarily with Pakistan to squeeze India, thanks to the Panchsheel-II treaty signed by Sino-Indian foreign ministers in the Russia-India-China meet held in Beijing last year. Since then, India has accepted Chinese suzerainty over Tibet, and China has reciprocated by withdrawing claims on Arunachal Pradesh. Both the economic powerhouses have opened their borders for trade. The relationship seems to have thawed. However, it is a cosy relationship which some in the Chinese military have not taken kindly to. As for the UNSC, it is non-committal too.'

'I thought we were the Security Council. Anyway, carry on,' said the president, smiling.

'The Indian diplomats have done a good job of proving to the world that the missile was rogue. The erstwhile allies of Pakistan—Iran, North Korea and Saudi Arabia—are still miffed at the treatment meted out to them by the new Pakistani quasi-secular regime and may not support Pakistan because of its recent shift in policy to persecute the mujahideen, thanks to us.'

'Russia?

'As for Russia, the traditional Indian ally, it has a nuclear and gas deal with the new government of Pakistan in response to our own deal with the Indians. They will not support either side. Call it the global balance.'

'We too have a nuclear deal with those guys! We brought India into the Nuclear Suppliers Group and the Vienna Group.

They seemed to be a stable lot. Why this hara-kiri?' The president shook his head and said, 'Get me the Indian ambassador. I will talk to him directly, protocol be damned.'

Twenty-five minutes later, President Wilson finished his conversation with the Indian ambassador to Washington, Dr Puneet Sharma. The soft-spoken Dr Sharma had sounded even more confused than Wilson himself, but was sure that India had not intentionally launched any attack against Pakistan. On this, the erudite diplomat had sounded very convincing.

President Wilson made another call, this one to the director general of Combined Intelligence Corps (CIC), and talked to him for a full hour.

CIC was not one to fail. Something was not right. Though Wilson had been arm-twisted by certain American industrial lobbies to appoint Jason Cartman as the director general of CIC, he had grown to respect the man as a patriot and a brilliant leader.

In his weekly International Ballistics Technology briefing a few days ago, Cartman had ensured President Wilson that the Indian missile was not a threat to anyone for at least a decade, maybe even more, and that the CIC had positive HUMINT corroborating it. Sanctions or even talks with the Indian government were simply not needed at this stage.

Well, it seemed he was wrong. Cartman had been behaving strangely since the past few months. Cartman's son, a defence contractor, was killed in Afghanistan a year ago. He was no longer the same man he had always been.

The president finally hung up and looked around the room, trying to ascertain what had gone wrong. He sighed, cleared his throat and said, 'Well, this is confusing indeed. We just cannot antagonize our nuclear partner so easily. We have deals with their energy and infrastructural companies worth multi-million dollars. So, until we have more information, we too sit on the fence.'

He returned to his files, not knowing what to do for perhaps the first time in his life.

7 Race Course Road, Prime Minister's Residence, New Delhi

Local time: 1100 hours
Date: 25 April 2014

The PM (or the former PM) Bipolab Roy sat on a cane chair, sipping tea and reading a Feluda story. Through his window, he saw the gates to the inner compound open and General Malhotra rush towards his room. Roy put the book down as he studied the lanky man walking towards him, though his mind was working furiously to extricate his country from the mess it had just landed itself into. Shall I try international pressure? UN? The US? OPEC? Roy thought, and hoped that Pakistan did not become an Israel when it came to brushing aside international pressure.

Roy's chain of thought was broken as Malhotra entered the room. He looked at the PM uncertainly, the swagger was now gone. He sat down, staring intently at the opposite wall. No one spoke for some time.

Roy finally broke the silence, 'Did you do it?'

'Of course not,' Malhotra muttered, hurt evident in his voice.

'Are you sure? What guarantee do I have that your men did not launch the missile when you took over? You knew that would lead to war. What could strengthen your position more?' Roy plunged the knife deeper.

Malhotra felt slighted. 'Do you think I can risk thousands of innocent lives for the sake of my personal ambition? I have a daughter; like me, she is in the military. Do you think I want to see her suffer the pangs of war?'

PM Roy nodded, 'Calm down.' He felt better as he came to know that he was not the only one baffled by the recent unfolding of events. 'I was just…confirming that you did not do it.'

'I did not do it.'

'Then might I be bold enough to ask why you are here?'

'Pakistan has declared war on us,' Malhotra said, his shoulders drooping. The last thing he wanted to give his country was a war, especially one that was bound to go nuclear.

'I know. I just spoke with the Pakistani president.'

Malhotra felt a chill run down his spine. Who else has he spoken to? Was not he supposed to be incommunicado? He decided to talk to the captain in charge of the PM's confinement later; for now, there were more pressing matters.

'Since we are under attack, I feel it is no longer about the internal polity of the country. The time for internal restructuring is lost. We face an even greater challenge — external aggression. Other concerns need to be put on hold for the moment.' Malhotra sagged into a chair and closed his eyes, tired of the events.

Roy spoke up, this time his tone understanding, 'What do you want from me?'

'I have decided to reinstate you,' Malhotra said, and his shoulders drooped even more.

'What?' Roy was not sure whether to be happy or offended.

'I mean, the military has decided to relinquish power and transfer it back to the civil government.' This time Malhotra chose the words with greater care.

'As your puppet? No thanks. I will stay exactly where I am now and let the people of this country decide my fate. If the people can vote the iron lady herself out of power, they sure as hell can vote me back. Moreover, thanks to what you did, I am now a celebrated icon of democracy,' Roy taunted the general.

Malhotra sat down next to Roy, looked him straight in the eyes for the first time since he had entered that room and said, 'OK, I speak bluntly here. At least, I will try to. I took over this country because there was no other option left. That was not the time for political dictatorship.'

Roy coughed.

Malhotra paused and then continued 'But now, it has proved to be bad timing. Plain bad luck. For me, at least. Some people hijacked our own missile and attacked our sworn enemy. Now it wants blood in return.'

'Whose blood? Yours or mine?' PM Roy said.

Malhotra shrugged helplessly, 'It is no longer about you or me, democracy or martial rule. It is about the survival of India. I can fight this war without civilian support, at least political, but the armed forces do not want to.'

Malhotra looked away and continued, 'After all, we represent, just like you, the will of the people. In light of the current exigencies, we submit to the democratic structure of this country. We will discuss and resolve this matter after the war. First let us tackle the external enemy and then we will handle the internal mess. I am sure you too will put India before your political ambitions.'

'This is just what Hitler had said. Fight for Germany now, we will sort out the domestic spats later. I want something more,' Roy said, no more willing to sweet-talk the man who had insulted him in front of the entire world.

Malhotra knew what was coming. He replied, 'I understand. I assure you I will resign and face disciplinary action when the war is over.'

'Will you give that to the people of this country in writing?' Roy insisted.

'In writing.' Malhotra nodded.

The prime minister thought for a few moments, 'It is done then. You are a good man, Malhotra.'

'Thank you, sir.' The relationship was back to square one.

'Well, with that behind us, let's rush to the president, shall we? I will ask the Cabinet to assemble there. Only the president can declare war or conclude peace, and now that we are back to being a democracy, I suggest we proceed as per the Constitution.'

'Yes, sir.' Malhotra suddenly felt a lot better.

'Brief me on the situation,' Roy asked, knowing that he would be required to take major tactical and strategic decisions on diplomacy and war very soon.

Malhotra said, 'Sir, the Pakistani strategy has been to attack us in case of any threat to it. They want to throw us off-balance. They know that if they attack us first and capture our territory, not only will they prevent us from launching an offensive into the Pakistani territory, as we will be tied up defending ourselves, but will also inflict collateral damage on our side of the border.

'Moreover, if they capture our territory, they will use it as a bargaining chip in the aftermath of a ceasefire brought about by international pressure and the fear of nuclear escalation. Which will happen soon, judging by our international positions.'

'Hmm…and what counter-steps are we talking about?'

'We have mobilized our forward divisions, both holding and strike, and readied them to a state of full alert. Depending on your decision to either defend ourselves or counter-attack, we can deploy the respective formations. We hope you will be able to give us a better direction.'

'We will see to it. As for facilitating your war effort, will a national emergency under Article 352 provide you with enough space to operate efficiently?' PM Roy asked his chief of army staff as they both walked towards the general's convoy.

Malhotra was pleasantly surprised, 'It will indeed, sir. Moreover, I hope after your visit to the Rashtrapati Bhawan, you can join us in the war room at the integrated defence headquarters. If we are going to fight, it should not be amongst ourselves. Let us face the enemy as we always have—united.'

The duo climbed into a car. The ground realities had not changed, but it seemed that the problem was no longer irresolvable.

Air Force Base Mushaf, Sargodha, Pakistan

Local time: 1000 hours
Date: 25 April 2014

Wing Commander Nadeem Ilyas adjusted his flight suit and led the way, trying his best to keep his inner turmoil from spilling out. His boys ran out with him from the Operational Readiness Platform (ORP) to their respective F-16/A fighters of the No. 9 Squadron Graffs.

The F-16, initially produced by General Dynamics, was a multirole jet fighter aircraft with a frameless bubble canopy (for better visibility), side-mounted control stick, reclined seat (to reduce the effect of g-forces) and the first use of a fly-by-wire flight control system, making it a highly capable dogfighter.

The aircrafts were lined up like ducklings behind their mother, except that they were fuelled, armed and ready for combat. So were the men. They had already been briefed about their mission. No. 9 was to launch, pretend to patrol the India-Pakistan border, suddenly rush into the Indian airspace, attack and move out before the Indians had a chance to react. The Graffs would hit and run, whereas a couple of Chengdu J-20 fighters of No. 11 Squadron Night Arrows—recently 'borrowed' from China—were to travel with the Graffs in close-knit battle formation (to reduce their radar signature) until they reached the border, and then were to move to attack a different location. The target of the Graffs was clear.

That was why Wing Commander Ilyas was worried. The target was too familiar to him. Amritsar, his grandfather's pind. Not a day passed when his family did not recall, nostalgically, the old times spent on the streets of Amritsar. Bombing his old home, which also happened to be a purely civilian target, was not an easy task for an air warrior.

The command believed that only Amritsar would be a befitting reply to the attack on Lahore by the Indians. Pakistan had to show it was serious. If it were cowed down now, Pakistan would always be looked upon as a spineless nation that failed to utilize its might when it was needed the most. Still, the twin hearts of Punjab were about to be crushed, mutilated and thrown to the dogs of war.

He tried to divert his mind. He was a soldier, under direct orders to achieve a task and he expected to do just that. Ilyas realized that his morality or individual past was irrelevant when his country was confronted with the larger national realities.

National? Ilyas thought. Cannot Amritsar be as close to my heart as Lahore? Lahore nourished me, made me what I am. Amritsar, on the other hand, fed my family for generations. It made *them* what they are. Without them, I could have been nothing. Will the sixty years of bitter hostility negate all our past and decide what is ours and what is theirs? But then, someone had to pay.

Oh, his loyalties were not conflicting, he thought. He was a Pakistani foremost and proud of it. In addition, he was a brilliant officer. Ilyas had graduated with top honours at the Combat Commanders School and was rewarded with the command of the Graffs. Not that he was not ready for it. He had practised — all his life — to strike at key enemy targets when his nation was under threat. Their airbases, cantonments, forward posts, defence factories, supply installations, and the like. Never a populated city. It was disgraceful. Who attacks Harmandir Sahib, he thought? What drives people to such desperation? A thought flashed in his head: the same people who almost flattened Nankana Sahib.

He gritted his teeth. Making up his mind, he reached his bird and climbed in. After strapping himself up, he requested permission to take off — this was granted immediately. There was no time to taxi.

As the aircraft gained speed, Ilyas pulled the joystick back and he was airborne in a minute. He reached the cruising altitude and was directed to an initial vector by his controller. A formation from the Night Arrows joined his group at the rendezvous. He coordinated with the flight commander of the Night Arrows and ensured that they were flying low, skimming treetops, that too in a tight formation to confuse the enemy about their numbers. From a distance, it looked like one large airborne mass.

The birds of prey were out to hunt.

Uri, Jammu and Kashmir, India

Local time: 1200 hours
Date: 25 April 2014

The eight-year-old Sophia sat in a low ceilinged, two-storeyed makeshift bunker, which passed as the village school's classroom. The thick mud splattered walls did little to stop the steady tat-tat of a not-so-distant firing; nor the shouts of playing children coming from the school's playground outside. Sophia shook her head, trying to clear the disturbing noise from her mind.

It was then that she heard it.

A groan, a wail that soon became ear-splitting. She ran to the window to see silver birds streaking past and dropping black eggs on them. As they touched the ground, there was a loud bang and the earth started to shake. The Night Arrows had unleashed their lethal bombs.

Sophia screamed. She felt dizzy. She tried to steady herself by getting hold of the small desk in front of her and gave the teacher a quizzical look. The teacher was standing dumbstruck in the middle of the classroom, with a look of utter amazement on her face. The walls of the classroom started shaking on their own accord, as if occupied by evil djinns. There was a sudden roar in the distance, louder than even the artillery shells that sometimes used to bombard her village. The teacher shouted at everyone to get outside.

Sophia did not need to be told twice. She stood up and proceeded towards the door. Unfortunately, it was becoming difficult to walk with the ground shaking so vehemently and the door seemed farther with each passing second. She looked up to see her teacher who was urging Sophia to hurry. Sophia nodded to reply in affirmative, panic starting to clutch at her heart. She was still nodding when, with a crash, she saw something fall on the exact spot where her teacher stood.

A second later, there was a blood-splattered arm sticking out from under the rubble. Sophia suddenly stopped, shell-shocked. She again heard a noise overhead. She looked up to see something right on top of her head, approaching her with great speed. Then, everything went black.

Meanwhile, the predatory birds of the Pakistan air force kept pounding the earth until the Indian air force scrambled the newly acquired Dassault Rafale multirole fighters from Srinagar Air Force Station that intercepted the F-16s, forcing them to retreat. PAF had found and exploited a window in the Indian air defences.

Angered at the intrusion, the Rafale pilots swore that the Pakistanis would pay for their aggression, and followed them over into the Pakistani airspace laden with deadly GBU-12 Paveway-II laser-guided bombs.

◆

A moan escaped the lips of the stirring figure. Sophia saw black spots dancing in front of her still closed eyes—she was gaining consciousness. She forced her eyes open, only to realize a nano second later the fatal folly she had committed.

Her head felt as if being split with a sledge hammer. She gasped but lay still, as she did not have enough energy to move even a finger. She closed her eyes and did what she would always do in situations she could not comprehend — she prayed. In between praying and crying, she lost track of time. Finally, when the pain in her body had slowly receded to a dull throbbing in her right leg, was she actually able to think.

Her heart almost stopped beating as she heard loud bangs and screams in the distance as the earth shook further. Loud sounds usually meant gunfire and terrorists. Moreover, it meant that her father, as the head of the Village Defence Committee, would have to go and investigate. And that in turn implied that he was not coming to look for her.

◆

Bent by old age and fate, the old man wandered aimlessly for now he had no reason left to live, waiting for nature's coup de grâce. The Pakistani bombing raid had killed his granddaughter. Mohammad Shabbir need not bury her, she already was buried. He scanned the horizon. The once beautiful landscape was now dotted with the tale of terror, havoc and destruction.

Shabbir was too immersed in his own thoughts to notice that he had wandered near the school building. Or rather, the bunker which had been the school building, for now it was a junkyard of building material and human remains. He heard noises. Shabbir bent down and put his ear to the rubble. There it was: a voice loud and clear. The old man forgot his woes, and with a trembling, withered hand, started working the rubble away, reaching towards the source of the voice. He had already lost his granddaughter, and he did not want any other grandfather to lose his, too.

Shabbir kept digging, seldom stopping, and trying to mouth words of hope to the poor soul trapped in the abyss of despair below. It was after four hours that some soldiers from the 8th Sikh Battalion stationed nearby noticed the old man, with bloody hands and a sweaty face, trying to clear the rubble at a distance. They approached him, having long abandoned hope of finding anyone alive inside, but were astounded to hear a slight whisper emanating from the rubble. The soldiers immediately swung into action.

◆

Sophia felt fresh air and light. Before she knew what was happening, she was lifted out of her small burial hole by two feeble hands. Shabbir was moved to tears to see the tiny girl in his arms crying her heart out. He recognized her, for she was the daughter of one of his friends, who had perished along with his entire family in the earthquake. Now, the poor child was without a father. He knew only one thing that he could do now. He would adopt her and raise her as his own.

Panting with physical exertion and a myriad of emotions, Shabbir fell to the ground, but not before having carefully handed the child over to an army doctor. Yes, he thought, he would raise her. He would be, at last, happy again. Lost in his own world, he never felt the sharp pain of an exertion induced cardiac arrest. Tears had dominated his life, but at least he had died smiling.

Somewhere Over Punjab

Local time: 1300 hours
Date: 25 April 2014

The entire world seemed to be coming apart.

The Graffs patrolling the international border were clearly in a soup. Not the delicious creamy soup you get in a five-star hotel! The Graffs had reached the border and were scanning the area hoping to find any blind spots in the round-the-clock Combat Air Patrols launched by the Indian air force. Ilyas's formation hoped that the Indians regarded their posture as defensive and went after the other aircrafts of Graffs and Night Arrows when they split and headed towards India, thus leaving the border undefended for a crucial ninety seconds, giving them time to execute their penetration.

At a short command from Ilyas over R/T, most of the Graffs and Night Arrows veered up north to attack a different target, a target less defended as per intelligence, and burst into the Indian airspace. Only three Graffs were left to take care of their target, hardly a minute of flying distance away from their current location that was well within the Pakistani border.

Hardly a minute. Provided they went unchallenged. There was no use dogfighting over Indian territory if the target escaped bombing.

The Indian fighters raced away to intercept the incoming Pakistani horde as Ilyas listened intently to Pakistani air force's

Saab 2000 Erieye AEW&C (Airborne Early Warning and Control) craft for information on any openings in the Indian air defence.

None was forthcoming.

As planned, his boys got behind each other in a stream, pulled up in a steep climb to attain a height of about 5000 metres, and adopted a defensive patrolling posture. So far, their attempts to confuse the Indians had failed. The Indians did not take the bait and follow the majority group. Rather, they were still on the three Graffs' tails.

The radio silence was broken by rushing voices belonging to the group that had gone into India. 'Target ETA 03 [...] we have incoming bogeys [...] multiple contacts [...] flankers [...] engaging [...] more bogeys [...] bombs away [...] heavy fire [...] damage [...] two at six [...] under fire [...] mayday.'

It continued, 'Damn...'

It seemed an entire Indian squadron was waiting for such an attack to commence. The Indians knew what the target of the Pakistani aircrafts would be, thanks to their superior AEW&C capability. IAF waited for PAF to come close enough to the target, close enough to even partially bomb it, but the gamble paid off. The Pakistani F-16s that were deep in the Indian territory, were outflanked by MiG-27 fighters from Evepore, cutting their egress, and were then massacred as a MiG-29 squadron from Srinagar swooped on them. Of the eleven Pakistani F-16 aircrafts from the Graffs and Night Arrows, only one made it back to its base in Sargodha.

Meanwhile, Ilyas stared at the Indians patrolling on the other side of the border. This is what happens when one fights an enemy who has such numerical superiority, he thought. The Indians need not chase our second group. Another Mig-29 squadron can take off from Evepore and handle the matter. Whereas we are left to deal with them!

'How many did you say?' Ilyas asked.

'Six bogies, shadowing us on the other side of the border.'

'It was expected that the Indians would have increased patrolling, but...'

'Classification?'

'Fulcrums. Mig-29s.'

Ilyas swore under his breath, 'Couldn't they have sent Mig-21s instead?', knowing fully well that the last Mig-21 was phased out of IAF about an year ago.

Someone else snorted, 'Yeah, why not hope for Gnats then?'

'Our plan has failed, sir. Not only was the initial attack party intercepted, we failed to create an opening to rush in their...' Fareed was not able to complete his sentence. His on-board computer started screaming of a lock. 'Shit,' he cursed. He was so busy in cracking jokes he just might have bid his life goodbye. The enemy had fired upon him. He had just kissed the Beyond-Visual-Range (BVR) zone of the Mig-29 and it had taken its chance.

As he would have.

The air-to-air missile streaked towards Fareed's F-16 with a speed of over Mach 5 and carried a high explosive fragmentation warhead. Meteor BVR, newly acquired by India, was integrated with the Russian MiG-29, as Fareed was about to find out.

'Furry, climb to 20 klicks...climb, climb,' Ilyas screamed. He tried to dodge it, used chaff and flares, and swerved at the precise moment, but it was of no use. The missile hit. Fareed managed to eject and glided towards the ground as his plane crashed in a burning ball of molten steel and fire.

Ilyas did not react for a minute. This was the first loss under his command. He felt responsible, frustrated and…angry.

'Ok boy, listen up,' Ilyas said to the last remaining Graff, anger seeping into his voice, 'the Night Arrows have left us for bombing sector Khmer. We are outnumbered but we will do what we have to do.'

'Yes, sir!' his eager wingman echoed.

'Get Arrington!' Ilyas confirmed.

He and his wingman jumped into the fire.

◆

Meanwhile, an IAF Beriev A-50EI Mainstay AEW&C aircraft was flying far away, directing the MiG-29 archers of the Number 47 squadron to incoming threats or potential targets. The AEW&C aircraft was divided into sections, with every cubicle having a radar console and was manned by the technical personnel of IAF, who were monitoring the international border in excruciating detail for any intrusions.

The eyes in the sky had started scanning again for any other hostile crafts that came within the kill range of the MiG-29 archers. The chirps and beeps on-board faded into the background as someone swore loudly. It was Flying Officer Shameem Aftab. Before his CO could admonish him, he continued, almost hurriedly, as if to explain his behaviour, 'Contact, sir […] two unknowns […]'

'Specify,' asked Squadron Leader AS Raina, commanding the Beriev A-50EI flying somewhere over Haryana.

'Sir [...] two F-16s penetrating Indian airspace in 02 minutes [...] Amrit 1 sector [...]' gushed Aftab, his eyes gleaming with the thrill of kill.

Squadron leader Raina, rubbing his hands in glee, immediately switched to the predetermined frequency. He sent a 'Murder Murder Murder' command to the MiG-29s with the location and direction of the incoming Pakistani F-16s.

The IAF fighters moved to intercept and Raina realized that it was time to have a scotch on-board to celebrate the occasion.

Aiwan-e-Sadr, Pakistan

Local time: 1600 hours
Date: 25 April 2014

'Sir, the news is mixed,' General Akram, the chief of Pakistan army, reported to the president.

'What happened?'

'We did not manage to strike Amritsar. Only some outlying areas were bombed. The Indian air force intercepted us and we lost on count of both sheer numbers and technology. In Rajasthan too, we were stopped by enemy aircrafts. We have had massive casualties. Twenty-four aircrafts have been lost. Expected enemy aircraft kills: seven. On the other hand, we have been able to successfully bomb the Line of Control in Kashmir.

'We succeeded in Kashmir only because the enemy did not expect us to bomb it. It concentrated all its might in the Rajasthan and the Punjab sector. We are heavily outnumbered. The enemy aircrafts just don't stop coming!'

President Shahid exhaled; it seemed it was time to take the tough decision. 'This is why we created the last resort. Why do you think we created the bomb? Not because we wanted to use it, but because we were so outnumbered that we needed to gain at least some parity. They may have more aircrafts and guns than us, but for every nuke they have, we have two.'

'Sir, do you intend…' asked General Akram, cautiously.

'No, of course not. At least not yet,' replied the president, 'Ask your men to hold their ground. Reinforce them and launch fresh offensives. Pull out your forces from all operations in the North West Frontier and prepare assaults deep into the Indian territory. Focus on Rajasthan. Ask the air force to provide you what you want, but we need to go on the offensive. Now!'

Heads turned abruptly as Shahid Abbasi continued, 'And yes, I want a meeting of the National Command Authority.* ASAP.'

Voices in the room flickered like a dying candle on a windy night.

---

*NCA is the Pakistani organization responsible for policy formulation and the exercise of employment and development control over all strategic nuclear forces and strategic organizations.

Thar Sector One, Rajasthan, India

Local time: 1900 hours
Date: 25 April 2014

Serving in the cavalry always had benefits of its own. Sipping bitter, lukewarm coffee inside a stuffy T-90 Bhishma, enjoying gusts of dust-laden winds on a hot Jaisalmer day, and waiting for an enemy attack were some of them, thought Captain Gurwinder Singh Ahluwalia of the 262nd Cavalry, and shook his head in mock disgust.

IMINT* had picked up massive mobilization by the Pakistani army across the Rajasthan border. The Pakistanis, as per RAW reports, had shed away the stand-and-fight approach of 1965 and 1971. They had realized that it would lead to the destruction of their forces by the numerically superior Indian forces. Therefore, the Pakistani intent was clear: go on an offensive. A thrust across the Indian mainland by the Army Reserve South of Pakistan was on the cards. As Kashmir, Line of Control and northern Punjab were heavily fortified by both sides and thus ill-suited for large mechanized offensives, it was assumed that Pakistan might launch its offensive in the semi-desert sectors in southern Punjab and the Sindh Province.

---

*Imagery Intelligence collects information via satellite and aerial photography.

The Pakistani strategy was clear. Try to rage a six-day war on India, in a shock and awe Blitzkrieg. Trample across the Indian mainland, cut supply routes, hold territory, terrorize the Indians, wait for an internationally-brokered cease-fire and then bargain using the conquered ground. Make India surrender in the first twenty-four hours of intense battle. The Pakistani II Corps had been tasked with the invasion of this particular sub sector that Singh was supposed to protect.

Surrender my unwashed-in-four-days-socks, thought Singh. He had studied mechanical engineering at Punjab Engineering College, Chandigarh, and had been involved in many a college brawl to realize that there was either total victory, or eternal shame.

Moreover, defence is always easier than offence, especially when the defender gets the time to prepare. By now, they had mined the entire border of Rajasthan with Sindh, thereby creating another 38th parallel. The Pakistanis had no chance to penetrate that. He put the radio to his ears and awaited further news.

Singh eagerly heard the chatter. The radio was abuzz with updates. II corps was striking. But where? It was when he saw a Jaguar fly over his tank. Where is he going, we can take care of the enemy, Singh thought and snorted. 'Oye yaar,' the burly captain shook his fists and shouted at the plane passing overhead in mock anger, 'you are supposed to come at the end!'

His tank loader smiled; the gunner, on the other hand, looked unsure of whether to feel reassured by Singh's bravado or be worried about going into battle under this Don Quixotic commander. However, Singh knew how important it was to keep one's spirits up in battle. Wars are won on spirits, he thought, and paternally patted the Old Monk in his pocket.

A minute later, he was glad he had fighter protection. Six enemy aircrafts streaked above him, each one of them in a bombing dive to decimate him. PAF was attacking, paving way for the II Corps. Good thinking by the command, we needed the air support, he thought.

He cursed and dove into the tank, clamping the hatch shut with a metallic twang. His platoon did the same as Singh prayed that Bhishma's three-tier shield system comprising of the composite armour, the Kontakt-5 ERA (Explosive Reactive Armour) and the newly installed Shtora-1 countermeasures suit, gave his tanks not only adequate conventional, but also nuclear, biological, and chemical protection.

Singh strained to see anything via the optical periscope, listened intently for any updates, and waited for the bombs to fall. They never came.

Unknown to Singh, an IAF Rafale patrol flying from AFS Suratgarh and led by Flight Lieutenant De Kosta of the No. 23 squadron, Pouncing Panthers, had been on combat air patrol over Rajasthan when the JF-17 Thunder multirole combat aircrafts of PAF had decided to attack. An Indian UAV drone had picked up the intrusion; the Rafales were ordered to intercept the attacking Pakistani aircrafts of No. 26 Squadron Red Spiders.

The Pouncing Panthers had moved to engage the Red Spiders and the bloody dogfight ensured that the unguided CBU-100/Mk-20 Rockeye anti-armour cluster bombs carried by the JF-17s hit mostly radar and signal installations nearby rather than Singh's T-90 tanks.

The PAF fighter bombers were soon beaten back. An excited Singh was about to come out when an explosion, amplified by the radio, almost deafened him. A PAF fighter had managed to drop its bombs near him before being shot down.

Singh waited for the all-clear, and opened the hatch to climb out. It was extremely dusty outside and smoke billowed in all directions. The dust storm and the smoke had reduced visibility to almost zero. Only the bright flame of a burning tank, hit by the lone aircraft's bomb, was visible. The men were safe and had taken shelter in another tank. They waved their helmet at him to indicate all was well. They would live to fight another day.

Meanwhile, the dust storm started growing bigger in the distance. Visibility was rapidly falling. No use of eyes now, Singh thought, and clamped the tank hatch shut again and switched on the infrared. It was then that he saw them: the Pakistani tanks. Scores of them. Multiple contacts stretched all over the horizon. They were responsible for kicking such a dust storm. He saw armoured columns advance towards him. A tank stepped upon a mine and blew up.

Their mines were working. Good, Singh thought. The tanks kept coming. Another couple of tanks exploded. The mines were working very well indeed, thought Singh as yet another tank blew up. Many of them hit the mines and blew up, but others kept coming.

More explosions. More wrecks. Yet others kept taking their positions. They seemed to have innumerable tanks. Is the entire Pakistani army trying to break through this sector, Singh wondered.

There were further explosions as the tanks advanced without pausing to reconsider. This puzzled Singh. Should they not be trying to evaluate what was taking such a heavy toll? Why were they not sweeping the mines first? Was it bad leadership or were they just too charged-up to think rationally? No man deserves to die like this. Not even the enemy.

Singh was not able to look at them in the storm; he could only see their signature over the infrared. However, he wanted to confirm what he was seeing. He opened the hatch, climbed out of his T-90 and scanned the area with his binoculars. The tanks looked…weird.

For the invasion, Singh expected Pakistan to send forth its crème de la crème—Al Khalid Main Battle Tanks (MBTs). However, this was not how the Al Khalid MBT-2000 looked like, Singh realized. Based on the Chinese Type 90-II MBT and Soviet technology that laid emphasis on decreasing the size of the tank, Al-Khalid was operated by a crew of three and was armed with an automatically-reloadable 125 mm smooth-bore tank gun. However, the 'tanks' approaching Singh's location were rather tiny. They were too small to be Al-Khalids.

It was then that it struck him. He peered even more carefully at the tanks through his binoculars. Singh almost screamed. They were not tanks, he realized. They were old jeeps, driven by lone drivers or by jammed accelerators, modified with cardboards and made to look like tanks to fool the enemy. The mines are hitting the jeeps and damaging them, Singh deduced. They just want us to feel that we are doing damage.

Nevertheless, where are their tanks? Singh's brain was whirring. He looked all around. He took a 180-degree turn in the direction of Jaisalmer and saw white umbrellas all over the sky.

'What are they doing?' he muttered. And then he grasped the Pakistani tactic.

God! They send their air force. We send ours. We think it is there to pave way for their attack. We beat them back into Pakistan and relax. Radars on Indian side are targeted by the Pakistani air force. Not by chance, but purposefully.

We mine the border. They wait.

We prepare. They wait.

When a dust storm arrives, they send jeeps made to look like tanks, at least from a distance and lure us into a false sense of security as we see their 'tanks' unable to penetrate our defences. We lighten up. Just what they want.

A dust storm. Approaching twilight. Zero visibility. Sensor ghosts. Malfunctioning radars. An over-confident enemy. Just what they want.

And then, Singh thought bitterly, as satisfied Indians rub their bellies and congratulate each other, Pakistani armour and airborne troops para-drop behind the 262nd Cavalry and surround it. We are hit even before we realize it. Pakistani paratroopers commandeer Indian tanks, and drive them into India—with the Pakistanis acting as Prisoners of War. We wave them through with arrogance. They strike when they are within the range of a major city.

What bastards! Who was their strategist? Rommel?

Singh rushed towards the radio to warn others. He barely had time to climb into his tank and seal it shut when every speck of desert sand around him started to explode. The enemy tanks had started firing. It would take time for the tanks and turrets to move 180 degrees, until then, with precise attacks, tanks of the Pakistani II corps could decimate a lot of our own, thought Singh.

'I will see you in hell,' screamed Singh, and ordered his tank to fire at the nearest Pakistani tank in range.

He shouted on the radio to regroup and counter-attack. All he heard was static. The Pakistanis were jamming their communication frequencies. The battle was on.

Aiwan-e-Sadr, Pakistan

Local time: 2015 hours
Date: 25 April 2014

The room was not only tense but also beginning to get decisively gloomy, as the events of the day weighed down heavily on the shoulders of everyone present. The Chairman Joint Chiefs of Staff Committee (JSHQ), Chaklala, stood in front of a map and mournfully addressed the combined meeting of the president, the Cabinet and the military staff.

'We are holding the line in Kashmir,' he began. 'The battle for Rajasthan is equally poised too. Both sides have rushed reinforcements for respective forces, but since we have already thrust whatever we had in the initial few hours and the Indians did not, a long line of unending Indian reinforcements are breaking the troop's morale. The fight is quite bloody. There are heavy casualties on both sides. We have to pay in blood for moving every single centimetre deeper into India.'

'And now the bad news,' he continued, 'India has penetrated our border defences in Punjab. Our offensive was met with a counteroffensive that outmanned and outgunned us.'

There were collective groans of anger mixed with shock. Punjab invaded! The president looked around helplessly until someone else spoke up.

The air chief reported, 'As regarding the air, it is only a matter of time before IAF bursts through the defensive installations at the perimeter. PAF cannot hold them out much longer. We will lose air superiority and dominance over our airspace soon. About 100 of our aircrafts have been destroyed. About thirty per cent of our runways are no longer operational because of Indian attacks on our bases. PAF bases in Samungli and Chaklala are no longer combat-worthy. The Indians can cope up with what we throw at them, but we cannot.'

'Same for the seas, sir. All my ships are engaged in defensive positions as the Indian navy tries to break through our defensive cordon and come in shelling distance of Karachi and Gwadar,' the Pakistani navy chief joined in, too.

'At least on the land we have some fighting chance, but in the air and water we are completely routed...unless...' murmured the interior minister.

'No they won't.' President Abbasi shook his head sadly, getting the drift. 'I have already talked to the Chinese premier. He has made it very clear that China is not willing to open a second front against India. Of course the Indian markets cater to them better than our own.'

'But then we...' the voice of the defence minister trailed off.

'Yes. Like all drills, we may have to fall back on our last resort. Can't we do without it?'' said the president, not realizing what he was saying.

'You know as much as us. We need it. Now!' said the commander, Army Strategic Forces Command, Rawalpindi.

'So be it! Let us meet again in half an hour with detailed plans and specifications on how to utilize the bomb most effectively without causing any long term, permanent damage to us.'

'Are you sure we need this?'

'Do you have a better idea?'

'Er...but we...'

'Gentlemen, you have your orders,' said the president with finality.

Integrated Defence Command Headquarters, New Delhi

Local time: 2030 hours
Date: 25 April 2014

The prime minister sounded concerned, 'We seem to be winning the conventional war but...'

'Yes, sir. Everything seems to be under control,' replied an officer.

'Hmm...yes.'

'But what if they...?' mouthed someone, quavering at the prospect.

'They can't! It is too dangerous! The international community will sanction them forever,' someone said half-heartedly, trying to reassure himself more than the others.

A voice was almost taunting, desperately hoping to be proven wrong, 'Are you sure they won't?'

'Well yes. They cannot deploy it...it is MAD.'

'You are wrong, my friend. They just did.'

The illusion was finally shattered.

'The crazy bastards! Are you sure?' The defence minister could not believe his ears.

'Yes, sir, positive. The Pakistani leadership has just called an emergency meeting of the Nuclear Command Authority.

They may want to exercise the nuclear option.' General Malhotra's face was grim. Very grim.

'So now that they are losing in conventional warfare, they want to nuke us!' said Admiral Sapra giving everyone an I-told-you-so look.

'My God! How did it come to this?'

'That is irrelevant. The question is what do we do now?' Malhotra tried to talk business.

'We will defend ourselves. We need to safeguard civilian population and strategic food, fuel, military and economic assets,' Bipolab Roy gave the orders in a firm voice though his mind was whirring, thinking of the possible solutions to avert this impending catastrophe. If they resorted to nuclear warfare, he had to ensure India was able to rise out of its ashes.

'But will we go nuclear?' asked the defence minister.

'Of course we will retaliate...*if* we are struck first,' said PM Roy.

'But we will not strike first?' Malhotra asked cautiously.

'No. It is a matter of our official policy. We will not strike with nuclear weapons first. Ever,' Roy faltered. Others saw his hesitation. They realized that Roy understood the futility of such policy but was trying his best to find reasons to support it.

'No pre-emptive strikes?' Malhotra asked again.

'None,' PM Roy said.

'Can't the policy be changed?' Malhotra continued, 'I find it self-defeating. Nuclear weapons are a credible deterrent, but if war is inevitable, it is logical to wipe out the enemy's capability to wage war or it will wipe out ours. What is the use retaliating if millions of lives have already been lost in the first strike directed against us. Can we let our morality hold ourselves back from defending the millions of our people who could be killed in the first strike by the enemy?'

'I guess it is the Rangers Course speaking in you…'

General Malhotra continued to drive his point home, 'Do you know we are the only nuclear power in the world with an officially declared no first-use policy? Even China says it will not attack first with nuclear weapons *only* if its enemy at that time is not a nuclear power. Please, I beg you to reconsider, millions of lives are at stake.'

Prime Minister Roy responded, 'Millions of *our* lives at the expense of millions of *their* lives. I am still not convinced. However, since you are so insistent, let us come to Level 1 of nuclear alert, to be on the safe side. Let there be the highest state of preparedness to execute strike plans. We will decide upon the targets and any nuclear belligerence on the part of Pakistan would result in launch. But we will not use nuclear weapons first.'

Roy shook his head and rushed out of the room, the enormity of the situation pressing upon his shoulders with sharp, biting claws.

Aiwan-e-Sadr, Pakistan

Local time: 2045 hours
Date: 25 April 2014

The final details of deploying the tactical nuclear device had been worked out and special units were on stand-by to initiate the mechanism. The time for relaying the final commands had come. President Abbasi looked at his men and was about to reach for the telephone for conveying the final sequence of codes to that effect when the door was flung open by an orderly.

A shocked General Akram paraded in a red-faced Lieutenant General Asif Chowdhury, the military secretary.

'Arre, General sahib. I was wondering where you were. I thought you were busy with some tactical matters so I did not even ask for you,' said the president.

'The matters were very vital indeed,' Akram said and turned to stare at Chowdhury, who looked away.

The president nodded in understanding, not realizing what was going on, and was about to dismiss the meeting when General Akram spoke up again, 'Sir, before this meeting breaks up, I want you to hear what our military secretary has to say. I was coming to this meeting when Chowdhury told me something truly incredible. I want you all to hear it.'

'Of course. Any new, radical battle plans, eh, Chowdhury?' His reputation preceded him.

Chowdhury merely hung his head. Had the people not known him better, they would have thought he was ashamed. Ashamed? Of what? Chowdhury came to the centre of the U-shaped table. His eyes downcast, his manners mild, and his voice soft. Very unlike the haughty man that he was.

'India did not attack us,' he whispered.

A chorus played, 'What?'

'Are you kidding? Go to Lahore and see for yourself,' someone muttered.

'Has the pressure gone to your head?' Another officer was furious.

'I mean, yes of course the missile was fired at us, but it was not done by India. They were as clueless about it as we...er... you were.'

'What do you mean?'

'I knew about the missile,' Chowdhury managed to say.

'What? Why didn't you tell us?' President Abbasi said, hair at the back of his neck starting to stand up at this revelation.

'I knew about the missile and I still did not tell you about the strike because...I ordered it,' Chowdhury said stoically.

'What?' Someone almost screamed. The room was slowly coming to life again.

'Chowdhury!'

'How dare you!'

'Lahore was not my target. How could I kill my own people?'

'Then what are you talking about? Have you gone mad?'

'Please let me explain. Some months ago, I met an old friend from SSG. Someone you all know. He was court-martialled for disobeying orders. He refused to fight fellow Pakistanis.'

'Basheer? Yasser Basheer?' the president asked.

'Yes.'

'He came to my house in Rawalpindi. We had a long talk that day. I too was not happy with the army killing our own people in FATA and NWFP and the way we were handling things. He knew it.'

'Yes, we know. So?'

'He tempted me. He said that if I helped him, not only will the Pakistani army stop its operation against its own people as there will be no need for it, but also that we will be able to show India down, malign her reputation, and regain our lost glory. All done while preventing a civil war.'

'What help did he want?'

'He wanted supplies, primarily. And he wanted someone who could have taught novices a few tricks in ballistics and missile technology.'

'You provided him that?'

'Yes, with a little assistance from some rogue elements in PLA who were not happy about the recent bonhomie between India and China. All off the record, of course. Also, a major whose brother was killed by our army in NWFP volunteered to be the team leader.'

'What did he intend to do with the men and material?'

'He said he wanted to take over an Indian military base and launch a missile at India'.

'Why did you comply?'

'It achieved many of our objectives. One, it channelized the jihadi forces attacking our bases towards India. The attack on Mehran was still fresh in my mind. I wanted such people to go out and attack the actual enemy, not us. Two, such an act would have caused friction with India and consolidated our domestic position — we as a nation can only unite when we are under threat from India. That is the truth, though politically incorrect it may sound, and we needed such a wake-up call. Three, it would prove to the entire world that Indian weapons too could find their way into the hands of terrorists. Four, it destroyed the stability and security in the hearts of Indians.'

'Launch a missile at India itself. Its own missile fired against India...no one to blame except her own self. It was a tempting offer. That sounds too good to be true!' interjected the director general of ISI. 'I can see why you agreed. What more could we have wanted? India fighting itself. Not to mention our forces here getting some breathing space.'

'Are you both enemies of Pakistan or what?' shot back Abbasi, and turned to Chowdhury, 'Why didn't you have him arrested on the spot?'

'He was a brother officer.'

'Then why the hell did the missile hit Lahore?'

'This is what stupefies me as well. I gave him the supplies, provided some men for training and assured him of all the support I could muster. His men were tasked to fire a missile at Delhi, with a conventional, low-yield warhead. Just to make them shake in their boots. They fired the missile. After that, Yasser Basheer went out of touch.'

'But where did he get men do to such a thing?'

'From the Taliban, where else would you find a bunch of such loonies? He hinted that he had support from some Indian anti-state groups too.'

'So according to the plan the missile was to strike at Delhi, but it deviated and hit Lahore? And India had nothing to do with it?' the president said in bafflement. The men in the room were not able to believe what they had just heard. All this bloodshed caused not by their mortal enemy but by their own defender.

'Yes, sir.' Chowdhury sighed and closed his eyes.

The chief of air staff shook his head and muttered, 'You fool! Do you know what you have done?'

'I know, sir. I am prepared to face the charges. My ADC was also involved. I speak for him as well. I tell you this in good faith. I acted for the betterment of my nation.'

'Do you know how many innocent lives you have cost us? He used you! You still do not realize what Basheer is doing, do you?' Shahid Abbasi, with a PhD in Mathematics, leaned back and thought for a full minute and then said, 'By God, that man has the brain of a seasoned politician. Here, let me explain...'

He stood up as shocked faces started to turn curious, the facts of the matter sinking in. Just then Abbasi realized he needed to take an important decision and said, 'But I must do something first. Ask our forces to stand down. Now! And call the director general of Military Operations in India. Tell him, Pakistan wants an unconditional ceasefire and that I will speak with the Indian premier very soon.'

'But, sir...'

'Do as I say.'

An officer hung his head and exited the room to make the call.

With steps taken to ensure the end of war, Shahid Abbasi turned to others and said, 'I believe I owe you all an explanation,' his sharp mind formulating a theory to pin the pieces of the jigsaw puzzle together. 'Imagine this: two countries. Bitter enemies. However, populated by more or less the same people. Currently, both on the path of reconciliation. Both these countries have internal problems. We have the

Talibanis, the Baloch separatists and other insurgents. India too has similar problems. Separatism, Naxalism, etc.

'We are both plagued by terrorism, extremism, poverty and violence. However, since we are sworn enemies, two things happen. First, we ignore terrorism in our own country, for we believe that the greater enemy is out there, on the other side of the border. Secondly, we fund terrorist activities on the soil of the other country. For example, our policy to make India bleed from a thousand cuts.

'With a recent spate of normalization of relationship and strengthening of ties, the two things above cease to exist. We stop trying to destabilize the other country and start looking at our internal problems like fundamentalism, poverty, regionalism and communalism, unemployment, to mention a few.'

The men looked at the president, wondering what he was up to.

He continued, 'Who is at the receiving end of this sudden self-introspection by the two nations?'

'The war-mongers,' Shahid Abbasi answered his own question, 'the criminals. The hawks. The anti-state actors who want to seize power. The mens rea who wanted the state's attention to be focused outside the country so that their own dirty games could go on unhindered. This is what Yasser Basheer did. His Islamic radicals were on a run. Our army was suppressing them successfully to create a new Pakistan. But how can Yasser have fought us with a handful of men and outdated weapons? So he loaned men with similar plans to destabilize India irrespective of their ideology, merged them with his own followers, took material from you and started on his bloody megalomaniacal conquest. His aim was simple — peace is bad for terror. Start a war. Think Soviets and Mujahideen, gentlemen. Foe of my foe is my friend. That is why we were with the US. Moreover, the decision to strike at Lahore was strategic. You know why?'

'Why?' someone asked, even though the question was almost rhetorical.

'Let me give you some hypothetical scenarios. Tell me what you think will happen,' said Shahid in the tone of a schoolteacher.

Others merely nodded, too confused or shocked to say anything.

'Case I: Pakistan attacks India,' Shahid said, 'what will happen?'

Akram instantly replied, 'India will attack Pakistan in return.'

'Yes, it has to. Every state is bound to defend its sovereignty. But is Yasser Basheer powerful enough to dictate our foreign policy?'

'No...at least, not yet,' replied Akram.

'Thankfully! Therefore, he cannot spark war. Case cancelled. Case II: India attacks Pakistan,' spoke Shahid. 'What will be the outcome?'

'Pakistan will retaliate,' came the reply.

'Correct, but as Yasser Basheer is not the Indian president, there is little he can do. He can only try to goad India to attack us by pervading it with low-intensity conflicts, something that India has been able to absorb far more than our predictions. Case cancelled.'

'Now to the next case,' the president went on. 'Here I will use the much famed term: non-state actors. Case III: Suppose the Pakistani non-state actors attack India employing the conventional modus operandi—bombings, assassinations, shoot-outs, what will happen then?'

'It already has...' someone quipped.

Shahid nodded, 'Yes, the 26/11 Mumbai attacks. India did not respond. Why? To be candid, simply because we are not that big a threat to them and they know they can absorb such blows. We cannot. No war still.

'Case IV: the Indian non-state actors attack Pakistan using the same devices as in Case III. Then?'

'Ideally, we would have responded, but not in the light of 26/11. They did not retaliate when our men were found attacking India. We are morally bound not to. If we do, we will be the hypocrites of the international community,' said the prime minister.

'Absolutely. What will happen? A joint investigation between the two countries. Cooperation. Not exactly something that the anti-state elements across the borders want. For it is our jingoism that keeps them safe from a state clamp-down. No war still!'

Shahid continued as others heard him in rapt attention. 'Case V: Indian non-state actors attack India. I mean, for example, the Maoists attacking a train in Jharkhand. What will happen then?'

'Nothing!' said a naval commander, realization dawning on him, 'It is internal disturbance. No war, at least no war against any external political entity.'

'Precisely,' confirmed President Shahid Abbasi and continued, 'Case VI: Pakistani non-state actors attack Pakistan. What will happen then?'

'The same result as in Case V. It will be internal disturbance again and we will clamp down, like we have on the fundamentalists. So, gentlemen, we have discussed six scenarios till now and apart from two of them, none leads to war. And the cases that can lead to war are out of the reach of our anti-state actors. This leads me to my last and final scenario, the only case that can be influenced by non-state actors like Yasser Basheer. And trust me, with this, war is definitely possible,' Shahid said solemnly.

'Case VII: non-state actors from either of the two countries attack Pakistan or India using the respective state machinery. Suppose a rogue Pakistani civilian shoots innocents in India, it might not go to war. However, what if a rogue Pakistani battalion enters India? In such a case, there is an extremely high probability that India might respond in kind, which will create a vicious circle and Pakistan will have to respond with even greater force. Simply because tangible state apparatus is being used that can be traced back to the source, and the fact that for the operationalization of such apparatuses, explicit assent of the state is required. The attacks and counter-attacks will start a war. And sustain it.

'However, in such a case, it is also possible that India might think twice before declaring war. It will not invade us until we do something really extreme or it feels really threatened from us. Or if we convince her that the element was truly rogue. So there still is some glimmer of peace. The only fool-proof plan of action to incite war is exactly the one Yasser Basheer utilized. If non-state actors, from either India or Pakistan, were to attack Pakistan, the weaker and thus the more paranoid state of the two, that too using lethal apparatus from the Indian state, in this case, a missile, Pakistan would have to declare war on India. It has to open hostilities. It has to retaliate. Or its very raison d'etre is threatened. Because it is the weaker state of the two, it has to…bite in the face of an existential threat. This is what Basheer did. He fermented unrest, very intelligently, and tried to barbeque his own ambitions over the fires of war.'

Shahid, his monologue over, looked in the direction of the military secretary. Chowdhury was a broken man. He sat, unmoving, his gaze fixed to the floor. He shuddered as a tear ran down his cheek, 'What have I done?' He broke down completely.

No one in the room could decide whether to console him or be mad at him.

NWFP, Pakistan

Local time: 2100 hours
Date: 25 April 2014

The Thuraya SO-2510 satellite phone was active, as evident from the softly blinking red light in the left corner.

'Yes...Agyaat? Basheer speaking. How are you...? Yes, India and Pakistan are at war...ha ha! Do not thank me. Thank the agents at the Eleventh Bureau of the Chinese Ministry of State Security (MSS). They may have been rogue officers, but they helped train our men. You feel better, eh? Indian army's operations against Naxalites have stopped? They are moving away to the front? Very good. That gives you some breathing space. You can get your men across the border in the meanwhile. Things are better here too. The Pakistani army has stopped attacking us...they face a bigger threat right now.' Soon Yasser Basheer hung up.

A contented smile of victory had lit up his face. His men had stopped being attacked or followed, and the intelligence operatives had been taken off their tails. He was no longer the focus of the establishment. A much-needed break, by the grace of God. His men needed to recuperate, recruit and re-arm so that they could continue their fight against the puppets of the West. After all, tehzeeb had to be preserved. Basheer knew that the ideals of the West had corrupted young boys and girls who were fast losing their roots, their culture and were increasingly adopting a godless, decadent, atheistic lifestyle that solely focused on Epicureanism and self-gratification. Someone had to stand up to reinforce the fear of Almighty in such blackened hearts, even if that required the use of force. He knew this was a shared feeling between him and his saffron counterparts on the other side of the border. He respected this thing about them. At least they knew what was right, no pun intended, he realized and chuckled.

His chain of thought was broken when his aide spoke up. A young Sindhi who had joined him when he realized that multinationals would be the end of the world after he was fired from a high-profile investment banking job.

'Sahib,' he began, 'things are looking better. We are off the radar. Even the CID sleuths stationed around our party headquarters have vanished. They have other things to do, it seems. To top it all, the war is going bad for Pakistan. I would not be surprised if they ask us for help.'

Basheer chuckled loudly and said, 'They will have to. Everything is going according to the plan. They ask for our help, we help them in defending Pakistan. Our valiant fight puts the enemy on the backfoot. People start sympathizing with us even more. Finally, despite all our efforts, Pakistan loses. India wins. The Pakistanis will feel humiliated.'

The aide was all ears. 'But why should we aim to be defeated?'

Basheer looked at him patronizingly. There is so much this boy needs to learn, he thought. But then, that was why he was with him.

He continued, 'The Pakistanis will blame their democratic government for the failure. That is where we come in. We provide the Pakistani people an alternative and fight against the Indians. After a long struggle, we manage to drive the Indians out. People hail us as heroes from the bottom of their hearts. We become liberators and are catapulted to the seat of power in a glorious Islamic revolution. What more can we want?'

The aide looked at him with wonder. Basheer was certainly a master strategist. However, there was one thing he did not understand. He wanted to ask his master who had already anticipated his question, and started speaking: 'I talked to Chowdhury, an old friend, and told him I needed supplies so that my men could attack India. He obliged, the poor fool. Even that fox decided it was best not to mistrust me. However, what would have happened had we attacked India? Another inquiry, international censure, snapping of diplomatic ties, what else! This would have forced Pakistan to hunt us with even more zeal. We wanted the state off our backs, not hunting us down!'

'But how did the missile lose its way to our own territory?' The aide was curious.

Basheer looked offended for a moment, and then recovered to explain, 'I asked my man to change the target from Delhi to Lahore. We would have been in serious trouble had the missile hit Delhi. Pakistan would have cooperated with India to find the perpetrators. Even Major Rana, who was leading the mission, did not know that the target will be changed to Lahore.'

'But what purpose will it serve? Killing our own people?' The aide was confused. He needed foresight to see through this foggy discussion.

'Our own people! Bah! They who hunt us down! They who sing and dance to the tunes of Bollywood. They who have distorted Islam to be a religion of passive peaceniks and idealist dreamers! They who are a repository of evil and things haraam. They who have forgotten how to lead their lives according to the Sharia. They are not our people. Even then, we used a low-yield warhead. A conventional one. For God is merciful. Moreover, as a great man once remarked, the needs of the many outweigh the needs of the few. If by sacrificing a thousand people we can save the soul of this country from Western hegemony, so be it.'

'What did you do then, sahib?'

'Simple, I had a sub-programme installed in the navigational array that gave me control over the flight path of the missile. Pralay already had a variable trajectory planner so no one suspected the crazy turns to be extraordinary. I counted on Chowdhury to keep his mouth shut due to the ignominy that would have followed any revelations. Moreover, attacking Lahore gave us multiple advantages.'

The aide thought for some time and said, 'It turns Pakistanis against Indians. So they can then support our policies readily. The war would have ensured that Pakistan's attention would be diverted from us! And India's from her own internal troubles. No wonder, some far-seeing anti-state actors in India helped us with men.'

Basheer patted his shoulder zealously. The boy was on the path of learning.

Aiwan-e-Sadr, Pakistan

Local time: 2230 hours
Date: 25 April 2014

'Yes, thank you. And we will meet soon. I will call you with more details... Goodbye.' President Shahid Abbasi came off the phone call with the Indian prime minister.

A ceasefire had been declared. The war was over. All the forces were to withdraw to their respective pre-war positions. Shahid Abbasi had told the Indian prime minister exactly what had happened. PM Roy was more than willing for a ceasefire and discussing damage control. If the non-state actors from both sides could have cooperated to achieve this, then it was not impossible for the two states to sit together for mutually beneficial talks.

Abbasi had correctly analyzed what had happened vis-à-vis Yasser Basheer, and his vanity was puffed by what he thought was the correct explanation of the anomalous phenomena. However, he was also scarred by the loss of life. Over a thousand casualties, 150 aircrafts lost, 260 tanks destroyed, thousands of prisoners of war and immeasurable damage to infrastructure and economy.

How could Chowdhury have been so stupid? The perpetrators were our own. Cunning bastards.

He hoped that tomorrow would be a better day.

Integrated Defence Command Headquarters, New Delhi

Local time: 0015 hours
Date: 26 April 2014

'It is still hard for me to digest this. They could be lying?'
General Malhotra looked at PM Roy sceptically. He needed
time to study the developments. Was the enemy playing a
new game?

'I do not think so. Their version seems extremely likely.'
Roy shook his head. For him, a nightmare was about to end.
He did not want to be the leader under whom India launched
a nuclear weapon. He just wanted to rest now.

'Anyway, only a fool would not take the opportunity to
stop a war,' Air Chief Marshal Sharma said.

'I agree, even though we were winning,' nodded Admiral
Sapra .

'But we were winning!' The defence minister, a young Turk,
could not believe he was about to miss on a glorious opportunity
to win votes. A war won always gets the government another
term, and the defence minister another run in the office. After
all, it implied that he was a masterful and strategic player.

'Winning? How do you define winning?' Malhotra
snapped at his shortsightedness.

'I mean, we were almost about to overrun their defences,'
the defence minister defended himself unsuccessfully.

'Yes, and then what would we have done?' Roy asked him, his expression patronizing.

'Er…what do you mean?' The defence minister knew he had committed a faux pas, but was biding time to figure out a way to defend himself.

'What would you have done when you had thoroughly overrun their defences?' Prime Minister Roy continued, 'This is not the medieval age. The boundaries of nations have now been so deeply embedded in the minds of our populace that any attempt at military conquest would fail. There would be massive insurgency. Do you want to be a modern-day British Crown ruling Pakistan?'

'No, of course not.' He was slowly beginning to see the point.

'Imperialism is against our policy. Moreover, I can assure you that Pakistan would have used the nuclear option if they had realized there was no hope left. Being attacked by a nuke is not what I call a victory. Are you sure that you are ready for that responsibility?' Roy was almost shouting, frustrated at the defence minister's implicit suggestion to carry on the war.

'No,' the defence minister managed to murmur.

The phone rang and PM Roy picked up the hotline.

'Yes? I was just doing that […] are you sure? Naxalites from our side and Taliban from yours? Are you positive? […] OK […] they […] what? […] But […] yes, we too want a piece of action. Of course! Thank you! Merge units […] I will let you know. Bye.'

Roy was visibly shocked as the call ended.

He began, 'Pakistanis have corroborated our own findings. Rogue SSG-ISI elements joined hands with the Naxalites for this operation. They also told me about the mastermind.

Yasser Basheer, leader of a jihadi outfit, collaborated with our own Comrade Agyaat. Pakistanis think that they have located Basheer in a town in NWFP and are planning an operation to nab him,' Roy declared.

'Good,' muttered General Malhotra, 'This will show us how sincere they are. I just hope he is not a scapegoat for their own treacherous deeds.'

'And the Pakistanis also said that we are most welcome to join in the hunt.' Roy dropped the bombshell.

'What?' The naval chief was shocked. 'What! This is insane! We working with the Pakistanis! Barely after we've disengaged ourselves from a war with them!' Sapra said furiously.

The cabinet secretary, Ajay Mishra, countered him, 'There are no permanent friends or foes, just national interests. We should cooperate.'

'Is there a catch?' asked Malhotra cautiously.

'Yes. They want us to allow Pakistani soldiers to join the operation in India to hunt Agyaat,' remarked Roy.

'Hang on. Let me get this straight: Indian and Pakistani soldiers working together to catch Yasser Basheer in Pakistan and Agyaat in India?' Malhotra could not believe his ears.

'Yes.' Roy's expression was unreadable.

'This is utterly ridiculous. They are the enemy!'

'But it seems a symbolic enough gesture. *Gadhe ko baap*...' said the air chief.

'Do you agree?' asked the PM.

'Hmm... Now that I think of it, no sane man can refuse this offer. Revenge is a dish best served cold. Whoever caused these many deaths deserves to be punished, even if I have to work with my greatest foe for that,' said the general.

'Foes and friends are epistemological constructs, General, not ontological entities,' Mishra spoke up again. Malhotra gave him a dirty look and he looked away, smiling.

An orderly rushed in and addressed PM Roy, 'Sir, there is another call for you. It is the American president.'

Heads turned towards the PM. Roy got up and took the phone. The US president urgently whispered something in the phone that made Roy's face twitch. He eyed the gathering uncertainly, pressed the phone tightly to his ear and swept out of the room.

Topi, NWFP, Pakistan

Local time: 1345 hours
Date: 26 April 2014

Captain Habib of the 7th Zarrar Battalion of the Special
Service Group waited patiently as an Antonov-32 transport of
IAF completed its final approach to a covert military airstrip.
The PAF F-16s that had been escorting the Antonov streaked
away to their own base in Kohat, their task complete the
moment the plane was safely on the ground.

The Antonov-32 gracefully landed on the Pakistani soil. It
taxied on the runway and stopped as per the directions given by
ATC. From now on, its safety was Habib's concern, alongside
his duty to ensure that the Indians were upto no espionage.

The door flew open and the passengers started to disembark.
Habib walked to the first man who was down, knowing that he
would be the ranking officer, and who was, by the stars on his
shoulder, a captain. Habib saluted the moment Shyam Singh
Rathore of the Indian National Security Guard was within
range. The two captains, having exchanged pleasantries,
looked at each other with an expression that was a peculiar mix
of surprise, distrust, and yet a desire to cooperate.

Unbelievable, thought Rathore, next to impossible.

The two captains started walking towards a truck parked
nearby as the NSG men trooped down the ramp with their

luggage. They saw Rathore's gesture and understood. They were to follow, at a discreet distance.

'Welcome to Pakistan, Captain Rathore. I am Habib, your liaison. Follow me please. We hope your stay in Pakistan will be fruitful.'

Captain Rathore started and gave Habib an intense look. Is he serious? Or am I stuck with a Pakistani Special Forces psycho with whom I will be going into combat soon, Rathore wondered.

Habib remarked hastily, 'Er...have I said something wrong? What I said was taken straight out of PIA's handbook. Thought it would make you feel comfortable. I apologize if I caused any offense.'

'No, no!' protested Rathore, 'It was just that I was not expecting someone, least of all a military officer, to welcome me into Pakistan, you know.'

Habib smiled, 'Ha ha! Yes, our history is quite loaded for that. However, things change. Before the war, you were half as much of a threat to us than the insurgency on our North West Frontier. 'The war...' Habib was suddenly reminded of the civilian deaths on his side of the border.

There was an awkward silence for a while. Even the Pakistani JCO talking with his Indian counterpart seemed to sense that something was wrong. The following groups stopped talking. Only the regular rhythm of boots pounding asphalt remained.

Rathore seemed to have felt his counterpart's discomfort. 'War was bitter, as always—but thankfully short.'

'I lost friends,' lamented Habib.

'So did I,' said Rathore as gory images of dead pals flooded his mind. He checked himself. He was here to carry out a mission. And for that he needed full support of the people who he would be fighting with. Rathore tried to cover up for this painful digression, 'You were telling me about the insurgency...'

'Oh, yes. Pardon me,' Habib came back to the moment, 'they are slowly and steadily gaining a foothold – if they continue, the going could get really tough for us.'

Rathore did not react, unsure of how he was expected to react.

Habib sensed his thoughts and remarked, 'Oh! If you think we are bad right now, wait until you see them! They will not even let you play football! Exposing shins is a sin for them, you know!'

Rathore's interest was suddenly piqued by the reference. 'Football? You play football?' he asked in sudden excitement.

'Yeah, I do. In fact, I...' was all Habib managed to say before he was cut by Rathore.

'So do I, a passion from my school days...EPL?' He hoped the other captain was not the La Liga type.

'Of course!' Habib exploded with enthusiasm and a new-found respect for Rathore.

'Team?' Rathore wanted to know.

'Man U, of course. The Red Devils all the way!'

'Huh! I thought you were a good man.' Rathore suddenly felt another wave of anger sweeping him. This really was the enemy. He turned his head away to hide his scowl.

'What happened?'

'Nothing. Just your club choice. Stupid, if I may add. Any intelligent and sane man would support Liverpool! It is *the* team. Reds all the way!'

Habib merely shook his head and repeated, 'Man U', this time in a much louder voice.

'Liverpool!' Rathore shouted back at him, frothing.

'Man U!!!' Habib screamed at the top of his lungs, his face red.

'Liverpool!' repeated Rathore, shaking with anger.

The men had been watching their officers curiously. They saw them about to come to blows. The Indians caressed their guns and started choosing targets. The Pakistanis did the same. Commandos are the same world over. Shoot first, talk later. Even better, don't talk at all.

Then, suddenly, the situation got defused, as both the captains burst out laughing and put an arm around each other. Rathore was the first one to speak out, 'It does not matter which team we support, at least we both love football!'

They reached the truck. The men loaded their gear in the truck as Habib led Rathore to his jeep stationed ahead of the truck. They would be travelling in it.

'Your unit will be joining mine for the raid, as you must know by now. I will take you to your quarters. After you have rested, we will assemble together for the mission briefing, Captain.'

'Please, my name is Rathore, but my friends call me SS.'

'And my friends call me Haba.' Rathore's eyebrows shot up. Habib saw the look and asked, 'You don't happen to understand Bangla by any chance, do you?'

The jeep started moving. They pulled out of the military air base and started to move towards the cantonment. Rathore noticed another truck follow the one carrying his men. This one full of Pakistani soldiers. Is it meant to keep us in, or others out, he wondered. His gaze returned to Habib urging him to answer his question.

'Bangla? As a matter of fact, I do. Although I belong to Rajasthan, I spent my formative years in Kolkata. My father, who was in the army too, was posted in the Eastern Command.'

'Oh...'

'What happened?' asked Rathore.

Habib sighed and accepted what was about to come, 'Then you know.'

'About what? Your name?'

'Yes.'

'Might I be bold enough to enquire what got into you? Or was it merely linguistic ignorance?' Rathore said.

'I am a Baloch, but my father, like yours, was in the army. I had a Bangladeshi godfather, my dad's colleague who had to leave West Pakistan in 1971 but he always kept in touch with us. He saved my father's life when he was posted in Dhaka. My father decided he would be the one who would name me when I was born. He named me Habib. Habib Rehman. My *bhalo naam*. And following the glorious tradition of Bengal, I got a *dak naam* too...this one not so glorious. Haba.'

'Haba...the fool?'

Habib nodded serenely, and then pressed on the gas, 'Precisely. It is not fair. You get the name of a cool, dreaded organization while I get to be the fool.'

'So you watch Second World War flicks too, despite the ban by Islamists! As for the name, do not worry about names — you are an inch taller than me.'

'That only makes me a bigger haba than you!' Habib retorted.

Rathore went silent for a moment, and then said, 'Guess what, back home I would not have realized that Pakistanis had such a sense of humour.'

'What!' Habib replied grinning, 'You are telling that to a nation whose comedians adorn your TV shows? Why we even bother firing at you, I do not know. We could just tell you jokes and tickle you to death! However, to be fair, your Bollywood rules our hearts and minds. I will let you in on a state secret. If we ever nuke India, we will have to leave Mumbai untouched. Otherwise, how will we enjoy your movies? That is our national pastime!'

Rathore started to guffaw with Habib. Things suddenly looked upbeat. Both of them were captains, second-generation army officers on deputation to Special Forces, and football fans; they kept talking until they reached their destination.

The NSG men were allowed to rest and were then called for a joint briefing. The plan was all set. Get in, get Yasser Basheer, get out. Simple enough, wasn't it?

◆

Hours flew by. The briefing, insertion and the raid—everything had happened so quickly. Captain Habib, his eyes wide with horror, tried to shout for a medic over the din of the chattering Heckler & Koch MP5s and AK-47s. His hands, with a wad of bandages and cotton in them, were placed on the profusely bleeding chest of Captain Rathore.

He had taken a direct hit to his chest as a hidden assailant fired at him just when he was about to finish off another attacker. It was an ambush. The house where Yasser Basheer was reported to have been seen last time was booby-trapped, planted with mines, and left to be guarded by zealous fanatics of TNSM who were now firing indiscriminately at anyone in range, whether the military or civilians. The joint commando team of SSG-NSG had taken positions at the perimeter and had tried to smoke the well-equipped terrorists out, who in turn began shooting civilians from the windows.

Damn! He should have known. These terrorists were at the receiving end of the American forces in Afghanistan and had made a note of counterterrorism tactics. And guess who trained the Pakistanis in such operations? The terrorists knew of what would come and from where.

The team had realized this and the two captains had a talk. They had to do this some other way. The local police had cordoned off the area though civilian centres were still within the reach of the holed-up terrorists. Rathore had come up with a tactic to infiltrate the building. Create a diversion, and then attack simultaneously from the roof and the doors without waiting for supporting fire to catch the terrorist off-guard. Brave, almost foolhardy, but bound to succeed.

The commandos were in. There were just two downsides. One, that Yasser Basheer had escaped long ago. Two, Rathore was lying in a pool of blood, severely injured.

The last words Rathore heard before blacking out were Habib's screaming on his radio for an emergency medical airlift.

Chabahar, Iran

Local time: 2100 hours
Date: 26 April 2014

Yasser Basheer made his way across the harbour, unseen and all alone.

Those who trusted him were busy defending his lair in Pakistan. Those he trusted were waiting for him to come to them — to safety across the seas, ending his long mission. His final mission. Almost complete, he told himself, and smiled in self-satisfaction.

His young Sindhi aide had driven him to the Iran-Pakistan Border, from where his Balochi comrades had taken over. After sneaking him past a Basij Pasdaran border post, they had travelled to the port of Chabahar by car. Basheer was left a kilometre away from his rendezvous point where he was supposed to meet his contact.

It had started to drizzle. He wrapped his cloak around him and kept walking, following the directions he was made to memorize. Basheer did not care where he went as long as he was able to escape. He reached a deserted pier. A small boat was waiting for him. A man saw Basheer and gestured him to stay where he was. He walked upto Basheer and frisked him for weapons.

None were found, as the message he received a day ago

was very clear: 'If you want to live, come to Chabahar, alone and unarmed.' Upon finding Basheer clean, he motioned with his head, asking Basheer to climb into the boat.

Am I expected to escape in this, Basheer thought? Damn. I should never have accepted this ridiculous escape plan. Then, another part of him thought, what he was about to do was necessary. He had to take this chance, or all would be in vain. He stepped in the boat nimbly. His contact merely smiled and thrust the speed lever all the way to maximum the moment they were both on-board. The boat sped forward. Basheer knew better than to strike conversation with his transporter. They seldom talked. The tugging and the gentle swaying motion made him dizzy. Water lashed his face. Basheer kept awake for an hour, and then, as the seas calmed, sleep took over.

After what seemed like an hour, a light tap on the shoulder awoke him. He felt something sticky on his fingers and realized he had been finger-printed to confirm his identity. What will they compare my prints with, he thought? Basheer groggily got up. The man stood over him, grinning. Basheer looked around. It was nightfall. The constellations looked down on him. The sea was calm, almost surreal in the moonlight. Then suddenly, the sea began to move. Basheer started, a rare profanity escaping his lips.

He thought he saw a whale. A huge whale, just off the boat's port bow. It made him suppress a scream. Combat in water was never his forte. Basheer looked at his contact who seemed unperturbed. How can the other man be so calm? They were about to die!

Basheer looked at him again. The man was gesticulating. He cocked his head to one side to understand, and then it struck him like a bolt. The man was motioning Basheer to jump in the water and swim towards the whale, which was now slowly coming near them.

He must be mad! I am not jumping off this boat. And swim towards that monster? To hell with you! It was then that he heard the noise. A steady whirring, gradually coming closer. Basheer squinted at the whale. God, he muttered under his breath. The whale stopped near him and its...turret flew open. Basheer looked closer and saw a yellow sphere emblazoned on a black flag at the whale's fin. He finally understood it was the al-Qaeda flag, and was filled with wonder.

The man pushed him into the sea and Basheer landed with a loud splash, the cold currents rudely jolting him to reality. In an eye blink, the man started his boat and vanished, as if afraid of what lurked inside that ship. Alone, Basheer had no choice but to swim towards the monster. Someone on top of the whale threw him a line. He held it and was hoisted upwards. He heard his contact's boat fade away in the distance. Basheer touched the whale. There was no soft cartilage. Its skin was hard. Steel hard, he realized.

He climbed to the top and was met by a tall, thin man with a beaked nose. He extended his hand to him. 'Welcome, Mr Basheer. I command this boat. Now, please follow me. The master wants to see you.'

They went down and sealed the hatch. Basheer looked around, thunderstruck at the enormity of what was about to happen, closed his eyes and muttered a prayer of thanks. A diving alarm assaulted his ears as the submarine sank into the seas.

Basheer's hard work, it seemed, had paid off.

On-board INS Vismaya, Arabian Sea

Local time: 0700 hours
Date: 27 April 2014

'Men, we have received vital inputs,' Commodore M. Mansoor from the Indian Directorate of Naval Intelligence (IDNI) addressed the select gathering of officers in the ship's conference room, 'SIGINT* from the Intelligence Bureau has given us extremely valuable leads. We have been ordered by the Flag Officer Commanding, Western Fleet, to follow the exact course charted for us without *any* deviations.'

They were on-board INS Vismaya, a Type 1145 Kiev-II class aircraft carrier, that was leading, at the behest of urgent orders from New Delhi and Islamabad, a hastily assembled task force comprising of INS Dharti, INS Ranthambore and PNS Shamsheer.

'We have concrete evidence that Yasser Basheer was seen at Chabahar in Iran very recently and that he left the port in a speedboat with limited range.'

Mansoor continued, 'Our agents immediately swung into action and followed him. No surface vessels were encountered

---

*Signals Intelligence is intelligence-gathering by interception of signals, whether between people (COMINT), or involving electronic signals not directly used in communication (ELINT), or a combination of the two.

en route. He just vanished. We should have been more careful in shadowing him.'

'So he just vanished, sir? But how?' asked Lieutenant SP Dadwal, a communications officer.

'That leaves us with only one possibility. It seems he was rescued by a submarine since no surface ships were seen in that area by the Pakistani and Iranian Coast Guard that moved to intercept,' said the commodore.

Dadwal said, 'And since we have had no news of that rescue, we can only infer that this submarine was commanded by someone friendly with Yasser Basheer.'

'Which nation will be friendly with him? Could it be a rogue sub?' asked Lieutenant Commander Sudhir Jain.

'Rogue? Is not a submarine going rogue big news? It would have been in the headlines all over the globe,' replied Dadwal.

'*If* it was leaked,' countered Jain.

'But this is big news. We should have known about it.'

'Money can do wonderful things, my friend. Almost any country could have sold that submarine to whoever currently commanded it. Or it could have changed hands till it reached its current owners, who, it seems, are hand in glove with Basheer,' the wizened old sailor Mansoor spoke.

The captain, who had been silent until now, spoke up, 'We will find them, sir. INS Chakra too is actively pinging all possible routes the sub may have taken.'

'The submarine will try to get as far as possible. The moment we find it, we move to intercept, but remember, weapons have not been authorized till now. Await specs from IDNI.'

'Yes, and we have orders to operate in this sector only. Strict orders from the admiral himself. I do not know why,' confessed Mansoor, 'but this is precisely what we are going to do. Let's go!'

The meeting dispersed and the officers headed to their respective stations to complete the task assigned.

On-board Ghazi, Arabian Sea

Local time: 0800 hours
Date: 27 April 2014

Yasser Basheer was given a set of clean clothes after he had had a much-needed wash. He dressed and ate in the small space allotted to him, his privacy maintained by greasy curtains, space being a premium in submarines.

Basheer was just finishing the last morsel when the curtain parted and a man poked his head in. He looked at Basheer and barked, 'Come. The sheikh will see you now.' He stalked off without waiting to hear Basheer's answer.

It was not a request. The message was clear. Basheer was on this boat for a purpose, and he better fulfill it. He followed the agile man past the narrow corridors of the submarine. Basheer tried to avoid hitting his head in the cramped spaces. Soon, he reached an unmarked area and his guide ushered him in.

Basheer entered and looked around the small room. It was tiny but clean. He saw something move. A man stood up, smiling warmly. Basheer saw his face, and something registered. Something important. Basheer started so hard that his head hit the wall. Pain blinded him for a second. Pain. Surprise. Shock.

Fear.

He moaned. The man paternally took Basheer's arm and seated him. When Basheer regained his senses, he fell grovelling at the person's feet.

'Janaab...! Sheikh! You! How can it be! They say you were killed in Abbotabad. They say the ISI betrayed you to the Americans ...' The man had been the US' most wanted fugitive, and if recent reports were to be believed, he had been killed by the US forces at his hide-out in a posh town in Pakistan. However, doubts were expressed about the credibility of those reports since nobody, other than those who claimed to kill him, had seen the body of the deceased man.

The eyes of Basheer's interlocutor twinkled as he said, 'They say a lot of things. Do you believe them all?'

'Er...no, sheikh, no.' Basheer felt like a schoolboy being chastised by his idol.

It was then that realization hit him. The man who was killed by SEALs in May 2011 was only a lookalike. Basheer's boss had told him that although he suspected the sheikh was not really dead, he needed proof before going public. The world needed to know the truth. And all of Basheer's efforts were directed to ferret out that truth. It was now or never.

'Believe only in what Allah says. Everything else is irrelevant. We came in this world not only with the purpose to make it a better place as per the will of Allah but also to prepare others for after-life. All this,' the sheikh pointed at the walls of the submarines 'is temporary. Only jannat and dozakh are permanent.'

Basheer nodded and asked, 'Why am I here, sheikh?'

'Why? Do you want to be someplace else?' the sheikh enquired teasingly, his tone alternating between the mocking and the scary.

Basheer was almost horrified by the soft tone and the slight touch of insanity in the man. He fumbled for the right words.

'I heard that you were looking for a place to hide as India and Pakistan were after you,' the sheikh went on.

Basheer merely nodded. He opened his mouth to explain but was cut short, 'I know you were the one responsible for changing the target of the missile and direct it at Lahore. How many innocent Pakistanis died that day because of you!' The eyes were no longer merry.

All of a sudden, Basheer felt scared. Sweat appeared on his brows. He heard the man continue, 'Basheer, I know who you are. I know where your loyalties lie. You need not pretend any longer.'

Basheer gulped, did he *really* know? However, before he could say anything, the man continued, 'I know killing your compatriots would have been hard for you. Nevertheless, what you did was in our best interests. Casualties did ensue, but they were infidels who died. They were the ones who supported the army's operations against us and treated us as pariahs. Let us not waste our tears on them. Basheer, my brother, you have done well to merit a place amongst my choicest followers. You caused India and Pakistan to gnaw at each other's throats so that the lives of our brethren could be saved and our movement could continue. Well done!' He patted Basheer on his back and said, 'I appreciate your bravery. '

'You know of that, sheikh?' Basheer felt exhilarated, and at once, immensely relieved. All was not lost. He could not believe that here he was, being praised by the most wanted man in the world.

'Word travels fast,' was all that the sheikh said.

Basheer was almost crying with joy. 'What do you want me to do, sheikh?' he asked. Even if the man asked him to swim naked with sharks in the Indian Ocean, he would have done it.

The sheikh realized it was time to make his offer. Any earlier or later would not have had the same impact. The timing of when to ask people to follow decided to what extent people were willing to go for a leader.

He said, 'Basheer, join my closest group of followers in spreading the true message, and in fighting the vile powers of Western hegemony. I need men like you—dedicated, fierce, loyal and intelligent.

'But you have so many like me,' Basheer tried to be humble.

'I do not want mindless suicide bombers. I have many of them. I want someone who can think on a macro-scale,' the man confessed, 'someone who can look at the larger picture and help me to make plans and plenty of contacts so that we can utilize all the resources at our disposal.'

Basheer was ecstatic. 'I would be honoured to help you, sheikh.'

'Good, Basheer! From this moment, you have become an integral part of Al-Qaeda.' Basheer felt so elated that he hugged the man. 'Come, now we must go to the bridge', the man said. 'We have some unfinished business to attend to.'

Basheer followed him with a spring in his step.

◆

The Chinese-built, Belarus-modified, Type 09 SSN was purchased covertly and symbolized the legacy of the puissant Soviet war-machine. Having been renamed Ghazi by the man himself, it currently lay dormant on the seabed as an Indo-Pakistani Task Force searched the oceans. Ghazi was intentionally dead in water, perched on a reef. Shoals of deep sea fishes swam by, unaware of the powerful monster that lay just metres away from them. There was just one difference. This dormant beast knew where its enemy was. The enemy, on the other hand, was blissfully ignorant of Ghazi's presence.

'Are you sure we do not have a sonar signature?' the sheikh asked his bridge crew.

'Absolutely sure,' the captain replied, 'I have fully integrated the submarine with the reef and based on the positions of the task group, their sonar scans cannot reach us.'

'You are an experienced man. I trust you, Captain,' replied the sheikh as the captain reddened at the praise.

A machine beeped. The captain went towards it, checked the console for a moment, and reported, 'Two ships of the task force are in torpedo range. A Pakistani Sword-class frigate and an Indian Kiev-class carrier. They will be out of range in seven minutes if they maintain their present bearing and speed.'

'Hmmm...Kiev class, did you say? An aircraft carrier?' the sheikh asked. It seemed like a long time ago that he had to memorize designs of Soviet war crafts, aerial and naval, to be able to find flaws in them for successful counter-attacks. His memory still served him well.

'Yes,' the captain said, realizing what his master was thinking.

'I preferred to remain hidden but this seems like a worthy target,' the sheikh said.

'I would advise against it. The torpedoes could be traced back to us,' the captain spoke up apprehensively. His primary duty was defence, not offense.

'Well, I would have to admit that the aircraft carrier is pretty tempting, especially in light of recent events,' the man glanced meaningfully at Basheer and continued, his tone changing to brittle lava, steel creeping into his voice, and a strange glow in his eyes, 'for too long we have remained hidden. Too long have we been on the defensive. Now with a new strategist in our team, I say we take our fight to the infidels.'

The man turned to his latest protégé, 'What do you say, Basheer?'

Basheer was a little surprised by the sudden change in the man from a paternal figure to a commander of retribution. But then he knew what he had to do. He had to match his ferocity and dedication with his own. Basheer's lips curved and he hoarsely whispered, 'Kill them, sheikh. It will be a great triumph for us. It would strike terror in their cowardly hearts. Attack them! They need to know our leader is still alive!'

The captain was watching the two men with subtle disdain. He did not like the idea of giving away their position, but he had sworn to follow the man in his company. 'Orders, sheikh?' he asked.

The man laughed, his eyes twinkled, but there was no warmth behind them, 'So be it. Attack them, Captain. Hit them hard. It must be the end of this aircraft carrier.'

'Might I be bold enough to add another thing?' ventured Basheer. At an encouraging nod from the man, he continued, 'After we hit them, let us immediately run in the opposite direction, at full speed.'

The sheikh looked at Basheer and then made a quick gesture to the captain, who understood that the order was to be implemented at once. The captain barked orders and the sub started coming to life.

On-board INS Doon, Arabian Sea

Local time: 0830 hours
Date: 27 April 2014

The destroyer was about to be destroyed. Damn the unknown sonar signature, cursed Ranjan Pandey, the Officer of the Watch (OOW), and realized his day was going to get a hell lot worse. The fact that his ship, Delta Zero Seven, was most likely going to suffer a fate worse than his did not make him feel any better.

Pandey saw something streaking towards the ship, something that he immediately recognized from hours of training demonstrations. Identification of such streaks was the primary goal of such classes. Always be observant. Raise an alarm on time. Live.

Pandey tried to scream but no sound came out of his parched mouth. He may have passed the course, but now when it was time to act, it seemed he was headed for failure. He might even have noticed it had the captain, for inexplicable reasons, not asked him to look for hostiles in the opposite direction. So busy was he scanning the horizon that he forgot to check near the ship.

The sonar operator jumped off his seat, threw earphones away and called the bridge of INS Doon, a Kashin-class destroyer, with a shaking voice. About ten second later, the klaxons started screaming, beckoning the officers and men to their action stations. Sailors wore life jackets and ran to secure their sections.

Captain Rajesh Sahgal reached for the Push-to-Talk Motorola and his voice boomed over the ship's intercom, 'Action stations…action stations.'

'Damn the lousy ASWO (Anti-submarine Warfare Officer),' Sahgal muttered under his breath, 'I am going to give him so many "NEGAT Bravo Zulus" that he will never be able to step on a ship again.'

The bridge was thick with tension and status reports. The XO glumly reported, 'Torpedo in water, sir. Bearing 077. Estimated time of impact ninety seconds.'

'Hard at starboard…full speed ahead. Deploy the ANT (Anti-torpedo Net),' Sahgal roared as the engines were switched to maximum power.

'Engines at full. Turning starboard fifteen. ANT is online,' the bridge crew repeated as every order was deftly executed.

'All hands, this is the captain speaking. Brace for impact… thirty seconds,' Sahgal ordered over the intercom again.

There was a flurry of activity at the bridge. 'All decks check-in, sir. They are ready for impact.'

'Inform the flag,' the captain spoke. Having taken immediate counter-measures to defend his ship, the lead ship had to be warned of the danger to the battle group in case it had not yet picked up the threat.

Sahgal took out his binoculars and scanned the area as lines with dead weight attached to the hull, especially along the keel and around the rudder and propellers, were lowered from the ship's deck. This was the newly acquired ANT. The net was supposed to trap the torpedo, reduce its speed, and veer it off course.

He saw two streaks of white foam making their way towards his ship. It was frustrating for the captain of any ship to see impending doom arriving so majestically, yet not be able to do anything about it. The sheer size of the ships made them slow in movement. It was the first law of Newtonian motion. But the massive ship had started turning. Slowly and surely, it was moving away from the torpedoes.

It was when the sonar operator screamed again, 'Another torpedo in water!'

Before Sahgal could ask for particulars, he was thrown to the portside plexiglas. The torpedo had sliced right through the net and hit its target. With a deafening bang, INS Doon caught fire, a section of its hull cracked open by the impact of the torpedo. Sea water rushed into the compartments. Some sailors who were not careful were thrown off-board.

Captain Sahgal knew it was a mortal wound. Still, he contacted the Emergency Response Room (ERR) and asked for a damage report, knowing what he would hear.

He heard coughing induced by smoke before the Lieutenant handling ERR finally spoke up, 'Decks 4-9 flooded, sir...fires in three sections...ASP is out of action. Engine room is hit. We have lost hull integrity... Sinking is imminent.'

'Send ERR teams to the affected areas. Secure bulkheads and try keeping her afloat as long as possible,' the captain ordered, his eyes getting moist.

'Roger,' was what the lieutenant managed to say before the captain cut him off.

Sahgal looked around his ship. Only a captain knew how one felt for the ship one commanded. It was a feeling that was simultaneously paternal, filial, and romantic. The ship was one's baby, one's paramour, and one's comrade—all rolled into one. The bond was too deep to be broken. No wonder men preferred to go down with their boats.

He saw boats being launched from INS Dharti and INS Ranthambore for rescue. Only one ship did not send its boats towards Doon. INS Vismaya. Its deck was on fire. From a distance it looked like the entire deck would explode. Wait... wasn't there something kept on the deck? Something that no ship would carry?

However, the captain had no time to spare for Vismaya. His own ship was in mortal peril. He took the Motorola in his hands, pressed the PTT button and gave the decisive command, 'All hands, this is the captain speaking. Abandon ship. Repeat, abandon ship.'

The crew of approximately thirty officers and 350 sailors looked longingly at the ship for one last time, and then jumped off their sinking home.

Life, they knew, would no longer be the same.

On-board INS Koyna, Arabian Sea

Local time: 0900 hours
Date: 27 April 2014

'Captain, we have contact with a Type 09 SSN. Unknown signature...running at half speed...heavily damaged. Should surface soon,' reported Commander Kunal Menon on-board a ship with a second battle group in the Arabian Sea.

Captain TB Rao merely nodded and turned to the sensors to confirm it himself. The ship gently rocked and stabilized. Belonging to Shivalik class, the indigenously-built Koyna incorporated features to minimize radar cross-section, infrared and acoustic emissions, thereby rendering it almost invisible to conventional sensors. Moreover, the presence of ISD (Integrated Services Digitalization) enhanced its battlefield capability by enabling electronic information from the ship's systems and sensors to be integrated with external sources like UAVs and AWACS. It was a ship that was a lethal, invisible predator.

And they were out fishing.

Captain Rao checked the Combat Information System (CIS) that provided him with decision support in selecting the optimum weapons system for the threat detected, and smiled at his number one, 'Just what the command told us to expect.'

'I do not get it, Captain,' asked a puzzled Menon.

'Well, we just had a flash, didn't we, number one?' the captain said.

'Yes, but what is all this about, sir?'

'Hmm...I guess I can tell you. We have some time to kill before the sub surfaces.'

'As you know,' he began, 'we were on the trail of Yasser Basheer, the man who ignited the Indo-Pak war. With Agyaat already dealt with, the two governments, thanks to American egging, agreed to a joint operation to flush Yasser Basheer out from his hide-out in NWFP. The raid took place as planned. However, Basheer managed to escape.

'The cat and mouse game began. ISI traced him near the Pakistan-Iran border. They were about to apprehend Basheer when another development happened. RAW reported that Basheer was going to Iran to meet...he-who-must-not-be-named.'

'But he was killed! His body was buried at sea! He's no longer a threat!'

'I personally believe he's dead, but ironically someone high up in the American intelligence does not agree with that assessment. It does not matter to me. I merely follow my orders. Anyway, it is a matter of conjecture. Think he is dead, and our purpose here is to catch only Yasser Basheer. Think he is alive, and we are here to take them both.'

Menon fell silent for a few moments. The captain resumed, 'It was said by the Americans that OBL was desirous of meeting the man who almost had Pakistan nuke India.'

'Wow.' Menon whistled in excitement. However, he also hated it when the captain made it sound like a James Bond flick. It made him realize how Commander Menon had done nothing in his life when compared to Commander Bond — especially in terms of wine and women. 'Go on, sir.'

Captain Rao continued, 'A high level chiefs-of-staff meeting was called, and it was decided that Basheer should be allowed to escape and meet the maybe-dead, maybe-alive primus inter pares of global terrorism,' he chuckled, 'and then we were to attack and bust the gang red-handed.'

'But that's an awful risk. How was the command so sure we would have caught him again, sir?' Menon was sceptical.

'That is the catch, Commander. I myself have sketchy details of it. For now, hear the rest,' said the captain, 'Basheer was seen exfiltrating the port of Chabahar and was reportedly picked up by a sub. The command may have had let him go, but it also wanted him badly. And since we cannot have combed the seven oceans, the command hoped to formulate a plan where rather than we searching for the needle in this haystack, the needle came to us instead!'

'Were not they running away from us? Why would they come to us?' asked a curious Menon.

'The lure of victory. Of causing maximum damage to their foes. That is why the command dispatched two battle groups: one with INS Vismaya in command and the second was ours — a flotilla of stealth ships that were not easy to pick amongst the clutter of the ocean.'

'Why two? So that we cover more area?' Menon asked.

'No. It is more than that. Soon after the hunt began, we took pictures from RISAT and calculated the probable locations of the rogue sub. Then we sent a carrier group with our flagship, INS Vismaya, as bait and assigned it a course that took it near all the probable locations of the sub. Their orders: happily sail by these locations. Take no action. Just wade around.'

'Oh. So we hoped that the submarine will be tempted by the plush targets and fire upon them.' Menon was beginning to realize the beauty of the plan. 'But why did we send our best ship? Why risk it?'

'Had we not sent our best ship, the submarine may have laid dormant till we went away. This would have been terrible, as we would have lost both our targets. All our plans would have backfired. We just hoped and prayed that this target will be too much for them to resist. As you know, it did tempt them.' Rao never thought he could almost feel happy to see a ship of his colours be fired upon.

'So they fired at the battle group.' Menon suddenly became serious. One of his batchmates was the XO on that ship.

The captain said, 'Yes, the deck of Vismaya was purposefully loaded with inflammable material that exploded and fizzled out harmlessly. Vismaya is safe. Sadly, Doon is not. But it was a worthy sacrifice to make the attacking submarine over-confident. And that, Menon, is dangerous for piloting.'

Menon gave a start. 'Very dangerous indeed! But, sir, a ship lost to capture a man…the command works in mysterious ways.'

'I agree. So what do you think would have been their next step now? What would you have done if you were the submarine's commander?' the captain asked Menon.

'Er…hit and then run in the opposite direction, at full speed,' he answered.

'Exactly. The rogue submarine took the bait and attacked the group. We, out of its sensor range, tracked the torpedoes back to it and triangulated the submarine's position, keeping the torpedo range of that class in mind.'

'Once that was done,' the captain continued delineating the plan, 'we predicted its future course vis-à-vis the group that it attacked [...] in the opposite direction [...] a full 180 degrees.'

'Oh. So that is why we mined the Arabian Sea with the American anti-submarine mines!' Things were finally falling into a coherent sequence for the commander.

'Yes. The fleeing sub was caught in the magnetic mines and wounded, but not mortally. Now the sub is limping towards us, and will surface soon. No pain, all gain.'

'But what about the loss of life aboard the ships it sunk, sir?' Menon interjected.

'Relax, the command knew of it. A volunteer skeleton crew that bailed out at the first sign of trouble operated the ships in the task force. We lost a ship, but no lives. The command believes no more lives are to be jeopardized presently, only infrastructure, that too only this one time. Cannot say I disagree with it. We already have lost bright young men and women in the war. Better a piece of machinery go down to the bottom of the ocean than human bodies.'

'But why did we not attack the moment we had its location?' Menon, as always, was a bundle of questions. The good part was that his captain encouraged questions.

'We need these men alive. The information they can provide would be crucial to vanquish the sectarian movements in both India and Pakistan. Think of it as decimating the entire command and coordination centre of global terrorism at one go. In addition, it was a policy decision. Straight from PMO.' The captain pointed up at the sky.

'But how can we get them alive? They will fight to their deaths! You know that, sir,' Menon asked.

'Relax.' Captain Rao was pretty chilled out.

'Look, Captain, the sub is surfacing. Beware, they can fire at us,' Menon was frantic. He was about to ask the captain's permission for targeting the submarine with the ship's Otobreda 76-mm guns but something in the captain's manner made him stop. Yes, the captain remained calm in the most fiery of all battle situations but right now, he was plainly indifferent.

Soon the captain explained the reasons behind his behaviour, 'Blacked-out men cannot fire. Why do you think we used these special US mines? They served a dual purpose. One, they made microscopic incisions in the sub's hull. Tiny enough to allow water in, but at a very slow rate that meant the sub would not have lost integrity over an extended period. There were chemicals present in those mines that penetrated the sub and made its air-supply run short by clogging its pumps while simultaneously emptying its tanks, thus forcing the sub to surface. Two, the chemicals infused a neurotoxin in the air supply that acted as a slow sleeping pill. These men would have fallen unconscious the moment their sub had made contact with air on the surface. Chemical warfare, yes, but these bastards deserved it.'

Menon could not believe his luck. Take Yasser Basheer without firing a single shot! Still, he ordered the ship to be on battle alert. It was no use taking chances.

The sub surfaced with waters frothing all around it. The ships closed in on it. Menon took out his binoculars and focused on the submarine. The morning sun shone brightly on it, making it look like a floating, burnt hot-dog. Menon patted his stomach. Either you are too hungry or you have gone mad, he thought, or maybe both, a voice at the back of his head whispered. He grinned.

At a command from Captain Rao, he made his way towards the flight deck. A company of Marcos, specially assigned to Koyna for this mission, was ready to storm the sub. Lieutenant Acintya K, or AK as he was better known, looked at Menon and saluted.

Menon simply patted his back and said, 'Take care, lad.'

AK nodded and rounded up his men. They first lowered a speedboat in the water, and followed it with a surprising agility despite their bulk. An engineering team from the ship also joined them. An engine revved. The boat shot towards Ghazi. The Marcos had been briefed on what to do and what to expect. A dozen guns were firmly trained on the submarine.

They reached the sub and climbed up. And then the Marcos cut through the hatch and entered its belly. The Marco group split into teams and headed towards the various areas they were assigned to sanitize. They undertook a quick tour of the sub and reported back to AK, who in turn briefed his Koyna-based controller.

No resistance had been met but the submarine was in a sorry state. Smoke billowed from the engine room. The pumps were clogged. The sub was operating on battery power. The lights were out. The propeller was damaged. Water was gushing in from the cracks. Some bulkheads had collapsed, but the sub was still intact.

Ah, the triumph of technology, thought Menon as he heard AK report in.

Water was beginning to flood a few compartments and its level was rising. The Marcos hurried. The teams returned to the bridge with their precious cargo—the occupants. At an all-clear sign from AK, the engineering team that had tagged along immediately started on the repairs. They had to seal the leaks first to ensure the sub did not sink. Then they started cleaning the filters of the air pumps.

The bridge was soon full of bodies, except that they were breathing, though unconscious. They ignored the bodies first and stripped the sub of any information that might be useful later. Then, as per orders, the Marcos started to take the unconscious crew of the submarine into custody. One by one, they rolled over the slumped crew and transferred them to the speedboat. From there the men were taken to the Indian ship that was patiently waiting for them.

The speedboat swayed as it carried them back. The sea spray hit their faces and some stirred, only to be overtaken by an unnatural drowsiness again. Finally, they reached the ship, which was by now hosting a carnival as evident from the multitude of ebullient faces thronging the deck, irrespective of rank and unit. The crew of Ghazi were pulled up to the deck from the speedboat. A doctor was already waiting for them. The crew of the submarine was given medical attention and then identified by naval intelligence.

Those high up in the command ladder who had been lucky enough to see Basheer's picture, started to hunt for him in the mass of piling bodies in the makeshift sickbay on the deck. One by one, they turned bodies over, peered, and elbowed each other.

A lieutenant commander cursed. He had found him. Yasser Basheer lay semi-conscious, chewing a tablet. Damn! What was he eating, the lieutenant commander thought. He immediately shouted for the doctor who came running. 'No, not cyanide,' he assured the others after a brief check-up. This man had to live to face the consequences of his doings.

The men saw Yasser Basheer alive and congratulated each other. Then they saw another of the crew member lying on his stomach in the speedboat wearing a camouflage jacket. Only a fool would wear this at sea instead of a life jacket, they thought, amused at the stupidity of the man. They decided to turn him over to identify him when the captain's voice rang out over the loudspeakers.

'Clear the deck, NOW!'

The festive atmosphere shattered like a glass hit by a speeding bullet. The men gasped and rushed to comply and discipline units swung into action. They heard a beating noise in the distance. A bird was coming nearer. It was Commodore Mansoor—he arrived in a Westland WS-61 Sea King helicopter and intentionally landed squarely in the middle of the gathering, thereby dispersing the officers and men observing the entire operation.

Mansoor took the man with the camouflage jacket into custody, along with Yasser Basheer. Both their unconscious bodies were put in a naval helicopter and were flown away immediately. It was suspiciously hush-hush. The helicopter disappeared in the horizon in a matter of minutes. However, sailors were able to have one glance at the man in the camouflage jacket. They tried racking their brains over who he resembled.

They were in for a shock.

Epilogue

Directorate General of Combined Intelligence Corps, Washington DC, USA

Local time: 1200 hrs
Date: 27 April 2014

Jason E. Cartman, director general of CIC, had a splitting headache — and for a good reason too. The Symmetrists, who were against providing his organization with federal funding, were getting stronger in the Congress with each passing day. Economy was being destabilized by a sudden spurt in Chinese imports, a popular majority in the Middle East had elected the Islamic Brotherhood to power and some meddling public litigators were insisting on reopening the JFK files.

A reappointment for Cartman looked unlikely, unless the conglomerate backed him up again. Moreover, the conglomerate had made it amply clear that it would support him only if he dug out the truth about the man America had wanted for so long. The conglomerate's objective was clear — the current president had to go. His quasi-socialist goals were too radical for their interests, not to mention quite unprofitable. Cartman was tasked with finding skeletons in the presidential closet. To top it all, he had to work in total secrecy. Operating independently of the White House was not an option but also a prerequisite for one simple reason. The conglomerate had reason to believe that the White House itself had duped the American public by killing a lookalike of the country's most wanted man, and toted it to strengthen a sagging presidency.

That man had to be found. Not that the conglomerate meant any harm. It just wanted to apprise the president of its knowledge of certain facts and then reason with him to soften his policies pertaining to the industry. Being pro-people was fine for a president as long as he was not anti-industry. It did not work. Not in America. Not anywhere else.

Cartman opened a drawer to reach for a painkiller. He groped for an aspirin but to no avail. It seemed he was running out of them, too. He cursed, rubbed his temples and stared at the sunlight streaming in the spacious room through the open windows, illuminating the swirling microscopic particles. Suddenly the door was flung open.

'Sir…!' A deputy burst in, panting and said, 'We got him, sir! The real one! Congratulations!' Forgetting the protocol, he extended a hand towards Cartman, his eyes gleaming with excitement.

Cartman looked up at him in astonishment. He involuntarily jumped out of his chair.

'What! We have? Really?' Cartman too, it seemed, was in no mood to stick to formalities. The aide nodded at him zealously as Cartman continued, 'This is splendid news indeed.'

The aide kept nodding all the while, trying to stop himself from giving Cartman a high five, 'I cannot believe it, sir! We got him!' The young deputy was jumping all around the room.

Cartman was thunderstruck too. 'What's the status of the entire operation?' he asked.

'Check, sir. The plan was a roaring success,' the deputy remarked, 'Operation Ragnarök* has successfully achieved all its objectives.'

'Elucidate.' Cartman wanted to hear all about it. Genuine success stories orchestrated wholly by CIC have become rare indeed.

'One,' the deputy began, 'we have captured the man we have been hunting for so long. There is DNA proof that he is the real one. The Indians are interrogating him but should part with him soon. As for our agent, he was handed over to our military attaché in New Delhi some time ago and is now here.'

'Good. Dangle the Shadley-Anders carrot in front of the Indians regarding our target. It should not be difficult considering all this became possible only because of *our* assistance.'

'Yes, sir. Secondly, because of their war,' the aide spoke up, 'both India and Pakistan, with their fractured economies, are looking at us for guidance and aid. All caps on foreign direct investments and FIIs have been removed.'

'Hmm... Seems they require rapid infrastructure reconstruction to make up for the damage caused by the war. Let us be good Samaritans, shall we?' Cartman winked.

'Thirdly, the Naxalite-Maoist combine has been ousted from India. The Indians clamped down on them very heavily,

---

*In Norse mythology, Ragnarök is a series of future events to result in the submersion of the world in water. Afterwards, the world will resurface anew, the surviving gods will meet, and two humans will repopulate the world.

thanks to the no-nonsense attitude and dedicated synergy of the military and bureaucratic top brass. The Red Corridor is no longer red, or green for that matter.' The aide patted the desk and continued, 'With China too opening up, it seems Communism will no longer be a potent threat to any part of the globe.'

'Great! No more of this people's revolution hogwash. It always used to freak me out.' Cartman heaved a sigh of relief and said, 'there is nothing more empowering than a democracy.'

Cartman reached out to drink a glass of water, decided against popping an aspirin into his mouth, and returned to his aide. His headache seemed better all of a sudden.

'Fourthly, the Islamic fundamentalists are on the verge of either surrendering to the Pakistani government, or are mending their ways. NWFP and Pakistan are returning to normalcy. The companies owned by the conglomerate and mining for Lithium in Afghanistan have reported lesser and lesser attacks with each passing day. The Jihadi morale is on an all-time low except in Xinjiang and Chechnya where, surprisingly, it is not only resurfacing but gaining momentum as well.' The aide smiled slyly.

'This gets even better!' So does the splitting head, Cartman thought and suppressed a smile, 'And?'

'Fifthly, India and Pakistan have finally begun to cooperate economically and politically. India and Pakistan have conferred the MFN status on each other and are trying to create a free trade area that comprises of all the SAARC countries. The countries in the East Asia Summit have already exhibited interest to form an FTA with the SAARC countries. Grapevine posits the possibility of the formation of an Asian Union on the lines of the European Union. I can safely say that South Asia is going to be a slightly more stable region now onwards.'

'Good. Dealing with one unified trading bloc, especially one that espouses free markets, is better than dealing with many.'

'Sixthly,' the aide kept checking points on a data pad he was holding and said, 'both India and Pakistan are wary of China because of its suspicious role in the entire affair. The intelligence reports of ISI and RAW indict rogue elements of the Chinese People's Liberation Army for fomenting unrest and mutual discord amongst the two countries, not to mention PLA's air force's loaning of couple of J-20s to PAF during the Indo-Pak war raising hackles on all sides. Moreover, investigators will soon find out that the party that attacked the base was trained by China.'

'With this, India and Pakistan both are definitely out of the Chinese sphere of influence,' Cartman said.

'This sure looks like it, sir. Pakistan has already thrown China out of the Gwadar project and is looking for new partners. We have already applied, of course. It is India now that controls the ports of Chittagong and Hambantota. It seems that the Chinese string of pearls has started to rot and fall off.'

'Ha! Today, it seems, is my lucky day!' Cartman was rubbing his hands in glee by now. 'Where is our man?'

The aide smiled and replied, 'Waiting outside your office, sir. He is the *Times* person of the day, I tell you!'

'Only if they find out,' Cartman muttered softly. The aide nodded, the order understood in a split second.

Cartman continued, 'But yeah, the fact remains that it is only because of him that our strategy succeeded. Rescuing him unintentionally from the Mujahideen camp was one of the best things that happened to us. And tell the psychologists at CIC that they did a good job. His actions have merited him a place in history as one of the greatest patriots. Call him in.'

'Yes, sir.' The deputy moved to a desk and whispered something into the intercom.

The door opened and a man slowly walked in. Voices in his head egged him to absorb every detail, every contour of the room, his mind sizing up potential threats and evolving escape strategies at the same time. An old habit.

He sniffed. Another old habit. Sniffing always told him what to expect. He could smell danger very well from years of experience. There is a time to run and there is a time to walk, the voices said. There is a time to eat snakes in the jungle and there is a time to have a fifteen-course meal in a seven-star hotel.

Life was all about dialectics, the voices in his head whispered, and how the larger picture in life invariably played out as the deciding factor.

Cartman got up and shook hands with him, then offered him a drink. A bearer rushed in with two steamy cups of tea.

As they sipped, Cartman began the well-deserved vote of thanks, 'Colonel, not only the Combined Intelligence Corps, this entire nation, nay, the fraternity of all free nations will be grateful to you forever. It is only because of the exemplary services rendered by you that we can stand today and imagine a future with peace and justice.'

Cartman took a breath and continued, 'It is because of your great sacrifice that dogmas and fundamentalism find themselves overshadowed by hope, liberty and freedom. It is only because of you that this nation could have had justice... when all our efforts failed, you have succeeded.'

The man was still shaking his head nonchalantly, a faint smile playing on his lips, as Cartman added, 'You stayed away from your family and friends for so long. You devoted your life to catch this man at any cost. And succeed you did!'

Yasser Basheer merely shrugged and looked away. His lips finally curled up in a broad, genuine smile. He smelt flowers.

Basheer kept smiling to himself as the eulogy continued. Cartman kept portraying him as a hero. For Basheer, he was only contributing his bit to make the world a safer place. Minutes passed as Cartman sung praises for Basheer.

The men finished their tea and bid each other goodbye. Basheer stood up to shake hands with Cartman again. Then, he turned around and walked out without looking back. He had earned the courage to be indifferent to one of the most powerful men in the world.

Three suited men greeted Basheer as he emerged from Cartman's office. They walked him through the hallways as deferential heads turned to appreciate the honour guard. The men escorted him to a GMT900 Chevrolet Tahoe, its engine already purring. One of them held a door open for Basheer. He climbed in and made himself comfortable as the door shut with an inaudible click. The partition separating the rear seat from the driver's was already up. Basheer knew that privacy was a sign of power.

The car started to move. In the blink of an eye, it had crossed the compound walls. The three men stood watching the receding car until it was a distant speck in the horizon.

Yasser Basheer was never seen again.

Author's Note

The first draft of this novel was written in May 2010. For the past two years, with everyday's newspaper comes a sickening realization. Something written somewhere in this novel comes true. When that happens, a part of me is freaked out (I was writing fiction, not the future), but a major part of me is extremely annoyed (with the newspapers stealing a part of my plot). It does not occur to me that it could be the other way round: that it is me who is subconsciously borrowing from the contemporary reality, and not vice-versa. Anyway, deranged brains tell good tales, so I hope you put up with that.

This novel is pure fiction. It does not seek to malign any nation, group or community, and indicts none but the scourge of terrorism and the deleterious effects of machtpolitik on the contemporary world order. I have tried to be non-partisan in my approach, but in a thriller, some black and white portrayals are imposed by the genre itself, and someone has to take the fall. This should be regarded as a flight of fancy that is not intended to cause any offense or hurt. The end message of this novel, if any, is an appeal for mutual respect, tolerance and peaceful co-existence. The *only* purpose of this book is to tell a story that people enjoy reading—for I loved writing it. Lastly, all the information regarding social, military and political structures contained in this book is freely available on the Internet.

Acknowledgements are due to many people. The foremost names that crop up when I think of people without whom this book would not have been possible are of my parents, Barkat Zaman Khan and Shaheen Anjum. Dad, you taught me how to write, and Mom, you gave me the conviction to keep at it. My younger brother, Salman, who lent me his newly acquired laptop for days at a stretch, even when his engineering exams were about to begin, and Aamir chacha, who let me use his PC. My grandmother Zeenat Begum at Sardhana (Meerut), UP, and the entire Khan *khandaan*.

I would also like to thank my teachers and my school — Bal Bharati Public School, Pitampura, New Delhi, where AHM Lewis made us realize that 'the sovereign must not always be obeyed'. I will be ever grateful to the departments of English at Rajdhani College and Hindu College, University of Delhi and Jawaharlal Nehru University, where I met great philosophers and guides: Dilip K. Basu, AL Khanna, Ashok Celly, Rao, Vijay Laxmi Pandit, and SS Abbas Jafri from Rajdhani College; Late Lalita Subbu, Sunil Dua, Tapan Basu, and Brinda Bose from the Hindu College; Kapil Kapoor, SK Sareen, Makarand Paranjape, Navneet Sethi, Dhananjay Singh, Padmini Mongia and Tulsiram from JNU; and Philip Lutgendorf from the University of Iowa.

My eternal debt remains to professors GJV Prasad and Saugata Bhaduri — the coolest guides ever possible — for providing me with the time and encouragement to finish this project. Prof. Prasad's comments on an earlier draft helped a lot. He's our Indiana Jones, just as Bhaduri sir is our Feluda!

Ajay Prakash and Archana Sinha, for the constant support, ideas and encouragement. All my other friends who had faith in me: Akash, Vivek, Shaival, Sharad, Sunny, and many more, including my MA-MPhil classmates at JNU—you guys rock!

Obaid Niazi, who read the first draft and suggested vital changes, and Safdar H. Khan, for all the support.

My fauji bhai-log—Santosh, Satyajeet, Adityakiran, Koustubh, Vikram, Abhijat, Suresh, Vikas, Colonel PK Dutta, and not to forget NCC 1 (Air) Squadron (Delhi)—this one is for you!

Kapish Mehra and Rupa Publications, for having faith in me, and my editor, Shikha Dimri. Last but not the least, this book would not have been possible without the Internet. Websites like Bharat-Rakshak, Wikipedia, and IDSA, etc, gave me the raw material for the plot, and Flipkart ensured that any book I needed for research was at my doorstep in just two days. I hope those names that I may have inadvertently missed out do accept my heartfelt apologies.